Escape

WARNING, REACTOR SHIELDING DAMAGED, flashed Sturm's readouts. His clever plan had trapped him in the valley. The *Uller* was covering his means of escape. Sturm watched the enemy 'Mech as it raised its arms to fire again. He was certain this attack would be the one to finish him.

Cursing, he slammed down the ejection switch. A moment later he felt a blast of cold air as he was launched out and away from the dying BattleMech. The last thing Sturm saw was the *Uller*'s lasers and autocannon clobbering the *Thorn*. The 'Mech fell backward and crashed into the ground, a miniature sun blossoming in its chest as the fusion reactor went critical.

Then the black face of the cliff rushed at him, and Sturm's world was swallowed up in darkness. . . .

MECHWARRIOR

GHOST OF WINTER

Stephen Kenson

A ROC BOOK

ROC
Published by the Penguin Group
Penguin Putnam Inc., 375 Hudson Street,
New York, New York 10014, U.S.A.
Penguin Books Ltd, 27 Wrights Lane, London W8 5TZ, England
Penguin Books Australia Ltd, Ringwood, Victoria, Australia
Penguin Books Canada Ltd, 10 Alcorn Avenue,
Toronto, Ontario, Canada M4V 3B2
Penguin Books (N.Z.) Ltd, 182–190 Wairau Road,
Auckland 10, New Zealand

Penguin Books Ltd, Registered Offices:
Harmondsworth, Middlesex, England

First published by Roc, an imprint of Dutton NAL, a member of Penguin
Putnam Inc.

First Printing, October 1999
10 9 8 7 6 5 4 3 2 1

This book would not be possible without the help of a great many people. The author would like to thank Bryan Nystul, for his expertise and guidance in all things BattleTech; Randall Bills, for his eye for detail; Mike Mulvihill, for suggesting that BattleTech would be fun; Donna Ippolito, for her skillful editing under pressure; and all the many authors and artists who have brought the world of the 31st century to life and made it such a fun place to be.

*To my parents, George and Lynn,
for always believing in me.*

1

Kore
The Periphery
11 April 3060

The sensors screamed a warning as the missiles arced in. Sturm Kintaro pulled hard on the control stick, spinning his 'Mech as quickly as possible into an evasive turn while trying to maintain top speed across Kore's icy terrain. The fifty-ton *Centurion*'s servos whined as its internal gyroscope fought to keep it upright through the maneuver. The missiles roared past, missing by barely a meter, impacting on the ground nearby and sending up a cloud of dirt, snow, and pulverized rock. Sturm fought against the shock wave of the near miss and managed to keep the 'Mech upright, spinning toward the new attacker.

He used the dust and dirt kicked up by the missile attack as cover and quickly took stock of the newcomer. It was a Clan 'Mech, of course, one the Inner Sphere had dubbed the *Uller*, after the Norse god of archery, though *Kit Fox* was the Clan name for it. This particular *Uller* looked like an alternate configuration, equipped with long-range missile packs. The enemy 'Mech was hunched and crablike compared to the sleek humanoid form of the *Centurion*.

At thirty tons, the *Uller* was smaller than Sturm's *Centurion*, but it was faster and more maneuverable. Its missile packs also gave it the advantage at longer range. The *Centurion* was armed with an autocannon and a single LRM 10-pack. If Sturm kept his distance from the *Uller*, he would probably get pounded into scrap by missile fire while the faster 'Mech evaded his attacks. He decided to close the distance and put his 'Mech's superior size and close-range firepower to work.

All this happened in an instant of recognition. Battle-trained reflexes took over and, a split-second after the *Uller* glowed to life on his display, Sturm was slamming the control stick forward. The *Centurion* accelerated toward the enemy 'Mech at near top speed, almost sixty kilometers per hour across the frozen tundra.

Sturm thumbed the firing stud for the *Centurion*'s own LRMs as he closed in, sending a wave of missiles trailing white smoke screaming out from his 'Mech's chest toward the *Uller*. As he expected, the *Uller*'s pilot was quick enough to get his 'Mech out of the way of the incoming missiles: Inner Sphere missile systems were often unguided, and relied far more on skill and luck than electronics to hit their target.

Sturm took advantage of the frozen ground, covered in a white blanket of snow that was rapidly being churned into gray-brown muck by the pounding tread of the metal giants. There was a danger of slipping and losing traction on the icy ground, but this time, Sturm was counting on just that. Fighting to keep control of the joystick and relying on his 'Mech's gyroscopic stabilizers, he slid the remaining distance between the *Centurion* and the *Uller* like a ball player sliding into home plate. It was a maneuver intended to catch the *Uller* pilot off-guard, and it worked.

The *Centurion*'s legs collided with the *Uller*'s left leg with a shriek of protesting metal and the crash of armor. Flashing red lights on the damage schematic indicated some minor harm to the *Centurion*'s leg armor, but no significant damage to its internal systems. The steel-titanium alloy skeleton of the giant war machine was stable. The *Uller*, on the other hand, flailed its arms in a very human, almost comical, gesture before falling over with a thunderous crash, muffled by the sound systems inside the *Centurion*'s cockpit.

Sturm didn't waste any time enjoying the sight of the *Uller* lying on its back like a turtle flipped over by a mischievous child. He gripped the controls tightly and maneuvered the *Centurion* into a firing position as quickly as possible, bringing the humanoid 'Mech back up on one knee so he could bring its weapons to bear. The *Uller* pilot fought to do the same, but non-humanoid 'Mechs often had trouble righting themselves from a prone position.

The *Uller* pilot brought up his 'Mech's right arm, trying to bring its LRMs to bear on the *Centurion*. Sturm grinned savagely. LRMs were notoriously inaccurate at such close range, and the enemy warrior would be lucky to hit the broad side of a planet.

The LRMs roared and streaked toward the *Centurion* on trails of fire. Several slammed into its left arm and torso. Warning indicators screamed of damage to the *Centurion*'s own missile system. The firing mechanism was badly damaged and off-line. Damn!

Sturm growled a curse and raised his 'Mech's right arm, bringing the heavy Luxor-series autocannon to bear on the *Uller*'s underside. With his other hand he trained the floating cross hairs of the *Centurion*'s medium laser over the center of the enemy 'Mech. He punched down hard on the firing buttons.

A dull roaring filled the cockpit as the autocannon spat fire and a stream of heavy 80mm shells that shredded and tore the composite armor of the *Uller*. At the same time, a lance of emerald light blazed from the medium laser, vaporizing armor in clouds of superheated smoke, cutting into the *Uller*'s vital internal systems.

A bright light blossomed in the depths of the *Uller* as Sturm's laser found the other 'Mech's fusion reactor. Sturm pulled the *Centurion* to its feet and backed away as quickly as possible as the *Uller*'s damaged reactor began to go super-critical. There was a dull *wumph* from the damaged 'Mech as the pilot attempted to bail out. Sturm couldn't tell from his position whether the enemy pilot was able to eject from the crippled 'Mech or not. The *Uller* flared up like a miniature sun and its reactor melted its internal systems, leaving only a blackened hole and molten slag as it began to dim and fade.

But Sturm didn't get a chance to enjoy his victory. Just as he checked the *Centurion*'s damage again and began to sweep the battlefield for signs of other enemy 'Mechs, he got one. The sensors barely had time to shriek a warning before a flight of missiles slammed into the *Centurion*. The wireframe schematic lit up to show armor blown away by the impact along the 'Mech's right side. The missile warheads were followed by twin crimson lances as lasers seared and melted armor off the *Centurion*'s torso and arm. Sturm spun toward his new adversary, bringing all his available weapons to bear, and froze.

It was a *Mad Cat*, one of the deadliest Clan 'Mechs in existence. At seventy-five tons of state-of-the-art weapons and armor, it outweighed the medium *Centurion* by fifty percent. It had a hunched-over design similar to the *Uller*'s but looked far more ominous. The *Mad Cat* packed heavy and medium lasers in each of its clublike arms, a long-range missile rack on each shoulder, and a row of heavy machine guns and lasers under its long, pointed "chin." Its wide, splay-footed legs pawed at the frozen ground, almost like a predatory bird.

Sturm hesitated only an instant before letting loose at the *Mad Cat* with everything he had. The *Centurion*'s autocannon roared and its medium laser lanced out. Autocannon shells smashed against heavy ferro-fibrous composite armor, and the laser left a blackened scar along the *Mad Cat*'s right leg, but the heavier 'Mech kept on coming, firing its own weapons as it lumbered forward. The *Centurion* tried to move, but too late.

Damn it! Sturm thought, *not only is that thing bigger than me, it's faster, too.* The *Mad Cat*'s ruby lasers slashed across the *Centurion* like red-hot blades, slicing away chunks of armor and laying bare myomer muscle and delicate internal structures. Another wall of missiles screamed in and slammed into the 'Mech's leg, sending red indicators flaring to proclaim the loss of vital armor in that area. The damage wasn't critical . . . yet, but there was no doubt that the *Centurion* couldn't take much more of that kind of pounding.

The cockpit of the *Centurion* was stifling and Sturm's body—clad only in boots, shorts, and a coolant vest—was drenched in sweat, making the controls slick under his hands. He pressed his head forward slightly against the inside of his neurohelmet and quickly considered his options.

Thing is, he thought, *if I turn my back on this guy, I'm definitely a dead man.* The *Centurion* was one of the few 'Mechs that mounted rear-firing weapons, but Sturm seriously doubted that a single medium laser would do any significant damage to the *Mad Cat*. In the meantime, the Clan 'Mech's weapons could cut through his light back armor in an instant and make hash of its internal systems, much like Sturm did to the *Uller* just moments before. He also couldn't back away from the *Mad Cat*, not on such treacherous ground and with the *Mad Cat* moving as quickly as it was. He immediately decided that his only chance was to try and outflank the bigger 'Mech; do an end run around it and run like hell before the *Mad Cat* could recoup enough to wipe him out.

Sturm dodged his 'Mech to the left as another storm of missile fire came in, missing him narrowly. He gritted his teeth and slammed the control stick forward, pushing the *Centurion* up to top speed as he ran almost directly toward the *Mad Cat* on a zigzag path intended to give him the most chance of avoiding any incoming attacks. The *Mad Cat* pilot never even wavered at the sight of the fifty-ton *Centurion* rushing at him, continuing forward in the same almost casual gait.

Sturm triggered the *Centurion*'s autocannon, stitching a line of fire along the *Mad Cat*'s left leg and torso as he charged forward, evading the incoming missiles and laser fire. A medium laser cut across his already damaged left torso, and the wireframe schematic lit up with some internal structural damage.

"C'mon, baby, hang together," Sturm muttered under his breath as the *Mad Cat* swelled in his viewscreen and the distance indicator on his heads-up display dwindled. Damn, but it was big. Only a few more meters. . . .

As the *Centurion* neared the massive Clan war machine, Sturm shifted the control stick hard to the left and changed direction. Almost like a bullfighter waving his cape, the *Mad Cat* swiveled its torso and swung one of its massive arms like a club. Sturm saw it move, but he couldn't react fast enough to do anything about it. The giant metal arm filled his entire viewscreen as it rushed toward him.

There was a deafening "CLANG!" that shook the cockpit as the impact sent the *Centurion* tumbling out of control. Sturm fought the controls to keep it upright, but gravity held the fifty tons of BattleMech in its relentless grip, and the *Centurion* toppled over onto the ground like a punch-drunk prize fighter. Sturm got the wind knocked out of him as the cockpit rattled, its shock-absorption systems strained to their utmost.

Still, Sturm wasn't about to give up. Almost by reflex he threw the *Centurion* into a roll to the side, trying to avoid the strike he knew was coming next. Instead of swinging its other arm, however, the *Mad Cat* kicked with its clawed foot instead. The impact boomed through the cockpit as the kick smashed armor and internal systems, lighting up flashing red indicators on the damage display. As Sturm tried to bring his autocannon to bear on his enemy, he looked up at the viewscreen and saw the *Mad Cat* point its massive arms downward at his 'Mech. As he grabbed for the controls, a hellish red light filled the screen, the heat in the cabin skyrocketed, and then everything went dark.

2

Kore Lancers Training Center
Niffelheim, Kore
The Periphery
11 April 3060

The door of the pod opened with a hiss, and cool air wafted inside as Sturm released his seat harness and reached up to remove his neurohelmet and let the air begin to dry the sweat dripping from his face and soaking his skin. He set the helmet aside, careful not to get tangled in the cables, and climbed out of the hatch to face the music. He ran one hand through his damp, dark hair, trimmed close on the sides to facilitate contact with the helmet's neural pads, worn longer on the top, a style common to MechWarriors.

He gave the man waiting outside the training pod a jaunty grin, but it was clear from the other man's expression that Master Sergeant Aaron Krenner was in no mood for humor.

The master sergeant of the Kore Lancers stood more than two meters tall, his entire body a mass of bulging muscle, kept steel-hard with grueling daily workouts at ungodly hours of the morning. The fluorescent lighting of the training bay glistened off his ebony-dark skin and the bald pate of his head. Krenner shaved his hair, with the exception of a nearly trimmed goatee that some thought gave him a vaguely sinister look (probably why he kept it, Sturm thought).

He was dressed in the standard duty-fatigues of the Lancers: a gray and white cammo pattern suited to urban or arctic environments, which were the only terrains to be found on Kore. His massive arms were folded across his chest and he wore an expression of strained patience on his grim face. Sturm knew right away that he was in for a lecture.

"Sergeant—" he began, but Krenner, as if he'd been waiting for the young MechWarrior to finally speak, broke in with his deep baritone.

"That was a poor showing, Kintaro."

"But, Sarge, I—"

"Don't 'but Sarge' me, MechWarrior! My job is to train you. You may not be an apprentice anymore, but you've got a hell of a lot to learn if you expect to see any real action. That kind of performance would have gotten you killed in a real battle!"

Sturm almost shook his head. Like he was going to see any real action out here, on a mining colony at the farthest reaches of known space, light years away from all the action in the Inner Sphere.

"It was just a training session," he protested weakly. Krenner was right, he hadn't handled it very well, but there was a reason. "Besides," he continued, "it wasn't fair. I mean, a *Centurion* up against a *Mad Cat*?"

"Fair?" Krenner exploded. Sturm cringed, knowing he'd said exactly the wrong thing. "We're talking about war here, Kintaro! This isn't some game. Out there in the real world you're going to be sitting inside a real 'Mech and there are going to be real people trying to kill you. And some of them are going to have bigger 'Mechs than you, understand? If you screw up against them, there's no 'reset' switch. If that *Mad Cat* had been for real, you'd be dead right now. That's the whole point of training you—teaching you how to stay alive."

Sturm opened his mouth to say something else, then thought better of it. He looked down, then back up at Sergeant Krenner. The Sarge was right, after all. He usually was.

"I'm sorry, Kren," Sturm said. "I'll do better next time." For a moment, the grim look on Krenner's face softened. For all his bluster, he considered Sturm almost a foster son. Krenner had taken it upon himself to look after Jenna Kintaro's boy after she died ten years ago, and he'd be damned if he'd let Sturm get himself killed the first time he saw action on a battlefield.

"Sorry doesn't make any different, Sturm," Krenner said firmly. "Doing better does. That's why you've got to practice, and that's why you've got to learn, if you're going to be a MechWarrior and survive the experience."

Sturm nodded. He understood.

Krenner now moved over to the console next to the pod and punched up the training logs of

Sturm's session. He ran them through to a point, then froze the image.

"All right, then. Let's start with how you handled the *Uller*."

"What was wrong with that?" Sturm protested. "I thought I handled it fine. I took it down, didn't I?"

"Yeah, you did, but you were sloppy. The charge maneuver was pretty well executed, and it would have worked perfectly against an Inner Sphere 'Mech. But you forgot that Clan LRMs don't suffer the same close-range limitations that ours do. By closing with the *Uller*, you didn't give yourself as much of an advantage as you thought. The *Uller* pilot took advantage of it and destroyed your missile launcher in the process. You got lucky, but you might not next time. Know your enemy, MechWarrior."

Sturm nodded. Damn, he'd forgotten about that property of Clan missile launchers. He'd been surprised when the *Uller* managed to get a hit in at such close range.

"As for the *Mad Cat*, trying to make an end-run around it was damn foolish."

"What should I have done?" Sturm asked. "Just let it pound me into the dirt?"

"No. You should have turned your tail and run, right there and then, the moment you saw it."

Sturm's face must have hardened, because Krenner seemed to know exactly what he was thinking.

"That's right, you heard me. I said *run*. There's no shame in that, Sturm. Only an idiot stays and fights when he knows he can't win. You said yourself that a *Mad Cat* versus a *Centurion* isn't all that fair, so you know what I'm talking about. That Clan 'Mech outweighed you by more than twenty tons. It had more armor, more weapons, and it was faster than you. There was no way you could win. The second you saw it, your first thought should have been how to get the hell out of there in close to one piece."

"I didn't think a MechWarrior was supposed to bail when things got tough," Sturm said.

"You're not. A MechWarrior is expected to lay his life on the line for his unit, *when and if* the situation calls for it. A MechWarrior is also expected to know when he can serve himself and his unit better by retreating. A warrior who knows when it's time to fight to the death and is willing to do so is courageous. A warrior who's unwilling to retreat is just stupid, and probably a dead man. You had the option to pull back in that situation. You should have taken it."

Sturm looked into Krenner's dark eyes for a moment, an unspoken question forming in his mind. He stood silent for a bit, then nodded.

"I understand, Sarge."

Krenner nodded back and turned to the display.

"All right then, let's look at some of the ways you could have pulled out of there and kept your 'Mech in one piece, maybe even turned the tables a little and done some damage on the way out." He pointed that out, using the downed *Uller* as cover from the *Mad Cat*'s weapons, and emphasized once again the importance of studying Clan tactics and way of thinking in order to know the enemy as well as you knew yourself.

Sturm listened to Krenner's advice and critiques, thinking about other ways he could have handled the situation. He also thought about what Krenner had said. *Sooner or later*, he thought, *a MechWarrior can't retreat anymore. Mom had found that out. Sometimes you've got to stand your ground, even if you know you're not going to get out alive.*

The debriefing was over fairly quickly, and Sturm had a bit of time before he was to be on duty for the arrival of the DropShip *Tammuz*. He hit the showers to get cleaned up and changed, replaying the analysis of the training exercise over and over again in his mind.

Krenner was right. Hell, the Master Sergeant was *always* right. Sturm may have completed his apprenticeship and become a full-fledged Mech-Warrior of the Kore Lancers, but he still had a lot to learn, and he was just starting to understand just how much.

Sturm had always wanted to be a MechWarrior, for as long as he could remember. At first, it was just a childish dream. Every kid in known space probably wanted to pilot a 'Mech and played with toy BattleMechs like Sturm did as a child. Later, it was the dream of a boy who idolized his mother. Jenna Kintaro, commander of the Kore Lancers. Dashing mercenary MechWarrior. Hardly the image most people associated with motherhood, but Jenna loved her son and always took good care of him.

Sturm had fond memories of his mother bringing him to the command base of the Lancers, showing him the awesome BattleMechs, towering ten and twelve meters tall, like silent meal giants standing among the repair gantries. Sturm recalled watching the combat exercises and maneuvers from afar, seeing the giant 'Mechs given life by the men and women piloting them, including his mother. From the moment he'd seen a 'Mech in action, Sturm wanted to pilot one himself. Jenna always encouraged his interest, bringing him games and 'Mech toys. For young Sturm, that's what BattleMechs were—giant toys to play with.

For centuries, the BattleMech was the ultimate war machine in all of human space. Across hundreds of worlds, BattleMechs fought for the supremacy of the various Successor States, the inheritors of the old Star League, which collapsed into endless war as one faction or another sought control of the whole of humanity, a vast sphere of stars hundreds of light years across. Although fortunes and borders shifted and battles were won and lost, the Succession Wars went on, and on, for centuries. MechWarriors were the new knights of the modern battlefield, riding their mechanized steeds. There was a certain romance to the image of the heroic MechWarrior, especially for a young boy living on the edge of known space, a boy who'd never witnessed the horrors of war firsthand. That is, not until the Clans came.

When the Star League fell and the various Inner Sphere leaders began to fight for dominion over the others, the Star League military had to choose sides. Human space was being carved up between the squabbling Successor States, and the powerful BattleMechs and military forces of the Star League would not be allowed to stand idle. Rather than choose a side to support, or be torn apart by conflicting loyalties, many of the Star League regulars chose a different option. Under the command of General Aleksandr Kerensky, the Star League Defense Forces formed a massive armada of JumpShips carrying their BattleMechs and military equipment. Then they jumped outward, toward uncharted space, beyond the Periphery of human-settled worlds.

Nothing was heard about them for hundreds of years. The Exodus became shrouded in myth and legend. People in the Inner Sphere talked about how General Kerensky and his Star League forces would return one day, when human civilization needed them most. They had no idea how that prophecy would actually turn out.

Ten years ago, mysterious BattleMechs suddenly appeared from beyond the Periphery. They struck without warning at worlds along the border, capturing them and moving quickly onward to the next. No one know who these attackers with their strange new 'Mech designs were, only that they were ruthless and efficient and that their BattleMechs were far superior to anything seen in the Inner Sphere since the days of the Star League. They were the children of Kerensky, the descendants of the military forces that had left the Inner Sphere centuries before. Forged in generations of war and conflict, shaped into the ultimate warrior culture that existed only to conquer. They had returned, like the stories promised, not to aid the Inner Sphere, but to conquer it and reclaim the heritage they'd left behind. They called themselves the Clans.

Kore, which lay some ten parsecs from the edge

of the Lyran Alliance, was on the outer fringes of the massive wedge Clan forces drove into the Inner Sphere. It was an isolated world, of little interest to any would-be conqueror, valuable only for its mineral resources and mining operations. Still, that was of no concern to the Clans. Their forces seized whatever territory they came upon and moved on to the next world. Clan BattleMechs came to Kore to take the world as their own, with only the Kore Lancers standing in their way.

Sturm didn't get to see much of the battle they fought out on the frozen tundra. He was only eleven years old at the time, hiding with his father in a shelter, packed in with dozens of other civilians as the sounds of battle roared outside. Sturm knew that his mother and the Lancers would stop the invaders. After all, there was nothing she couldn't do. He wasn't worried, although the sounds of battle frightened him. His father looked pale and sick the whole time. He told Sturm that everything would be all right, but Sturm knew his father was lying to him. That was when Sturm started to worry. He never saw his mother again.

He knew now that the battle was over before it began. The forces of the Lancers were no match for the superior Clan 'Mechs.

"A warrior who knows when it's time to fight to the death and is willing to do it is courageous. A warrior who's unwilling to retreat is just stupid," Krenner had said. What did that make mom? Sturm wondered, scrubbing the last of the sweat from his skin. Was Jenna Kintaro a brave woman who'd sacrificed herself defending her home and her family against overwhelming odds or was she just too damn stubborn to know she couldn't win? Maybe it was a little of both. Sturm stuck his head under the hot spray of the shower, allowing it to wash away his troubled thoughts. He preferred to think of his mother as courageous. It was her courage that had solidified his desire to become a MechWarrior.

The Clan 'Mechs didn't remain on Kore for long, only a few months. They were on a mission of conquest, and a single, isolated world in the Periphery was of little interest to them. After pacifying the local population and securing their position, the bulk of the Clan forces left Kore, continuing their march toward the heart of the Inner Sphere. They left behind only a token force of 'Mechs and warriors wearing powered armor, whom they called Elementals, to watch over the conquered populace of Kore.

Sturm remembered seeing the Clansmen in the streets of Niffelheim and hating them. The Elementals were particularly frightening. Genetically bred to handle the demands of piloting Clan power armor, they stood some 2.7 meters tall and were heavily muscled, like mythical ogres or giants. The Clan warriors were so aloof, so superior, looking down on the people they conquered, likes wolves among sheep.

Sturm hated their cold arrogance. How he'd wanted to just take a rock and smash in one of those leering faces. But his good sense prevailed. There was nothing to be gained by an eleven-year-old boy against a trained soldier and killer. Maybe that was my first lesson in the better part of valor,

Sturm thought as he turned off the shower. He padded across the cool tile floor, grabbed a towel from the rack and started drying off.

Eventually, the battle lines had shifted. Kore was owned by the Alfin Mining Corporation, not controlled by one of the ruling dynasties of the Inner Sphere. Ironically, while the powerful star nations were struggling, even with their vast military forces, to oppose the Clans, Alfin was able to call on the mercenaries in their employ to avenge the deaths of their comrades in the Lancers and to liberate Kore. The Storm Riders company had worked with the corporation for more than fifteen years by then, and they fully intended to make the Clans pay for what they had taken.

The Storm Riders attacked Kore in force. This time, it was the Clan Steel Viper forces who were outmatched, isolated from their front lines and faced with an overwhelming enemy force. The Clan warriors fought fiercely to the death to defend what they'd taken, but the Storm Riders prevailed. Kore was liberated, and a new group of Kore Lancers was installed to protect the plant. The 'Riders took some heavy losses from the capture and liberation of Kore and they were allowed by Alfin to recruit from the population of the Kore colony. Sturm Kintaro was one of those recruits, now a full-fledged MechWarrior and member of the Storm Riders company, of the Kore Lancers.

Tossing the towel aside, he picked up the thin leather cord that lay coiled on the countertop. From it hung a small piece of metal, burned around the edges and pierced with a hole for the cord. Reverently, he replaced the fragment of his mother's BattleMech around his neck. The new commander of the Lancers had presented it to Sturm after the liberation of Kore, and he'd kept it with him all through his training and whenever he was on duty. It was a reminder to him of what had brought him here.

He stood in the steam-filled room, holding the cool metal for a moment. Then he put on a clean uniform and ran a comb through his hair. There was just enough time for him to stop off at home before heading over to the command base. There would be time for wool-gathering later.

Duty calls, Sturm thought, and he headed for home.

3

Niffelheim, Kore
The Periphery
11 April 3060

Sturm took a Lancer jeep from the training center to the small house near the Alfin geosciences research center where his father worked. It was late in the afternoon, and the streets of Niffelheim were busy with people going about their business, moving briskly through the cold air in the brittle light of day. Kore's pale sun shed a watery light over the frozen planet. Even at its closest to the star, Kore's surface temperature only warmed into the teens. For the vast majority of its year, the planet was locked in perpetual winter. Sturm had heard stories about planets with seasons, and greenery. He hoped to see some of them someday. With luck, working with the Lancers would be his eventual ticket off Kore and into the Inner Sphere.

He hardly noticed the chill of the air through his company-issue jacket with the patches and rank insignia of a Lancer MechWarrior on the shoulders and collar. He was used to it. Cold didn't bother him. Like other native Korans, Sturm had "thick blood," even if he did lack the tall, blond Nordic features of most of the colonists.

Kore had been settled by people from worlds on the edges of the Lyran Alliance, which had only recently seceded from the larger Federated Commonwealth. Many Lyran worlds held people of Germano-European stock. Sturm's mother Jenna was one such: tall, blond-haired, and blue-eyed, with a strong, rugged build. Sturm's father, however, was nearly pure-blood Japanese. His family was from a world on the edge of Draconis Combine space, and Hidoshi Kintaro was quite proud of his heritage.

Sturm didn't quite share his father's pride. It was difficult growing up different on a colony world as small and isolated as Kore. Sturm was one of the few mixed-race or non-European kids, although they were becoming more common as the corporation settled additional colonists on the planet.

Sturm was taller than most Japanese, and some thought his Eurasian features made him look exotic among the pale, blond- and brown-haired populace of Kore. He had his father's dark hair, almost raven-black. Sturm often tied the longer hair at his crown into a topknot, similar to the style of the samurai of old.

His eyes were his mother's, however, pale, icy blue, like the depths of a frozen tarn in the heights of the Jotun Mountains. They had slight epicanthic folds and thin, slightly arched brows. His face was somewhat thin and pointed, with a sharp chin and a narrow mouth. Sturm glanced up at himself in the jeep's rear-view mirror and smiled. He liked the way he looked in his fatigues, and he still hadn't quite gotten used to seeing himself in them, especially with the thunderbolt emblem of the Storm Riders on his shoulder. He'd only been a full member of the company for a few months.

He was planning to move into the barracks on the command base shortly, now that there was room. As it was, Sturm practically lived at the base or the training center, often grabbing a spare bunk at the base to sleep between duty shifts and training sessions. He only visited home occasionally, to pick up some needed things or to grab a quick bite to eat, since the house lay between the base and some of his other haunts in Niffelheim. And he usually made sure to stop by during the day, like now.

He pulled the jeep into a spot in front of the collection of row-houses that was home to some of Alfin's researchers and senior staff. They were very functional; dull gray ferrocrete exterior with tall, thin windows intended to let in pale sunlight but trap in as much heat as possible. Sturm often thought they looked like military bunkers, which wasn't far from the truth. During the Clan invasion of Kore, most of the buildings of Niffelheim survived completely intact. They might not be pretty to look at, but they'd been built to last.

Besides, nobody spent much time outside, anyway, so there was little point in beautifying the exterior of buildings. That effort was generally saved for the interiors. Sturm knew homes in the colony that looked like frozen gray rocks on the outside, but were warm and homey inside. Of course, that didn't really describe his house.

The place was as cluttered as usual. Various print-outs and transparencies were scattered over the kitchen table and counters, weighed down with heavier objects, usually computer datachips and various electronic tools. They contained geological survey maps of the planet's surface, gathered by small satellites in orbit designed to ferret out the largest concentrations of valuable metals and minerals for mining. Kore had little to offer apart from its rich deposits. The whole planet was a mineralogical treasure trove, guaranteed to keep the Alfin Corporation supplied with saleable ores and materials for decades to come. Once the planet's resources were tapped out, it was entirely likely that the colony would have to be abandoned. Maybe by then Kore would have other industries. In another hundred years the colony could encompass most of the planet. It didn't matter much to Sturm. He wasn't planning to stick around and watch, anyway.

He went directly to the refrigerator and pulled out a bottle of water. Training exercises caused Sturm to sweat buckets, given the extreme heat inside a 'Mech cockpit during combat. He was always thirsty right after a training session. He would have preferred a beer, but he was going on duty and his father never drank beer himself, so there was none to be had.

Taking a long, deep swallow of the cold water directly from the bottle, Sturm closed the refrigerator door and nearly choked in surprise on the mouthful of water. He managed to lower the bottle without spilling it and wiped his mouth with the back of his hand.

"Sturm," the figure standing in the doorway of the kitchen said.

"Father!" Sturm replied. "I didn't expect you to be home. I thought you'd be working."

Hidoshi Kintaro was not a large man. Sturm stood at least seven centimeters taller than him, and he was small by the Nordic standards of Kore. Still, in Sturm's mind his father always seemed like a giant. Dr. Kintaro's face was strongly angular, with high cheekbones and black eyes beneath narrow, dark brows. Those eyes always seemed to be watching, analyzing, and judging. In Sturm's case, he felt that they rarely judged kindly or favorably. His father's salt-and-pepper hair and mustache were neatly trimmed, kept short so he didn't need to bother with them. Over his clothing, he wore his ever-present white lab coat, the pockets bulging with instruments, datachips, and similar items.

Dr. Kintaro was a man of science and learning. He had very little time for anything other than his work. For about the millionth time, Sturm wondered what had attracted his mother to the man in front of him. Jenna Kintaro seemed to have been the only person in the world able to penetrate the shell of formal behavior and cool politeness that surrounded her husband. However she did it, Sturm certainly didn't have the secret.

"I *am* working," the doctor said, his tone suggesting that he was deeply offended by the suggestion that he would ever shirk his duties. "I decided to go over some of these survey maps and results here at home, to take advantage of the peace and quiet."

While I'm not here, Sturm thought silently to himself. His father had opposed Sturm joining the Kore Lancers and moving out of the house, but he certainly seemed to be enjoying the situation now that it'd happened. Sturm suddenly felt like he was intruding.

"Well, I'm going on duty shortly," he said, setting the water bottle down on the table. "I just came by to grab a change of clothes and something to drink."

"Of course," Dr. Kintaro replied with a nod. He moved past Sturm into the room where the survey maps and readouts were spread out on the table. A chair scraped back as he settled down in front of them, setting the other small stack of printouts he carried on top of the others already piled on the table. Without a second glance at Sturm, he set to work, reading over the maps, searching for any information that might reveal a new mineral deposit or geological phenomenon that he could report to the powers-that-be back at the Alfin head office, a new opportunity for profit and progress.

"We got some interesting readings from the Jotun Mountains," the doctor said absently, not looking up from his work. "The heat vents and the high concentrations of metallic ores make it difficult to get accurate magnetic and infrared scans, but there are indications of a lot of natural lava vents and tunnels there. Some of them probably contain interesting metallo-crystalline formations that are worth examining.

"Can you tell Lieutenant Holt that I might require some assistance from his machines in performing a surface reconnaissance sometime in the next few days?" Hidoshi never referred to BattleMechs by their proper name, or even by the common diminutive of 'Mech. He always called them "those machines," or occasionally "those damned machines," like there was something vulgar about them. He didn't like having to deal with them at all, but the 'Mechs on Kore were still the most adaptable and toughest vehicles on the planet, which made them useful for carrying out some scientific surveys, particularly since there wasn't much else for MechWarriors to do on a world as isolated as Kore.

"Sure, I'll tell him," Sturm said. Holt would be less than thrilled. All of the Kore MechWarriors disliked performing scientific surveys. It was slow, onerous work, and Dr. Kintaro was an exacting taskmaster. It seemed like nobody's efforts were good enough for him.

His father made a "hmmm" to acknowledge Sturm's reply, then returned to the study of his data. Without another word, Sturm turned and headed down the hall to his room.

He closed the door behind him and stood for a moment, taking in the small chamber. *Why do I let him get to me*, Sturm wondered. The maddening part was that his father probably wasn't even trying to make Sturm angry, he just did what he did out of habit. Sturm knew he should stop expecting to see some spark of interest from his father about his career or other activities. It'd been this way ever since his mother died fighting the invaders of Clan Steel Viper. Hidoshi wrapped himself up in his work and didn't bother to come out for anything, including his son. Sturm knew it was his father's way of dealing with his grief, but it had been ten years! Ten years without so much as a single word of approval, without . . .

No, Sturm thought, running one hand through his hair and adjusting his topknot. *I'm not going to do this, not now. I'm tired of it.* He went over to the small bureau pushed up against the wall and rummaged through it for a few sets of clean clothes, then shoved them into his duffel bag. As he did, he slowly began to calm down.

It was just a matter of time before he moved into quarters on the Lancer command base, and then he wouldn't have to worry about it. He would only need to see his father on official occasions, when the scientific staff required the assistance of the Lancers to perform some survey scan or other similar task. Other than that, Sturm could stay out of his father's way and leave him to his beloved data and research materials. That seemed to be the way Hidoshi wanted it.

Eventually, if things went well, Sturm would get off this frozen, isolated rock and score an assignment on one of the other worlds the Storm Riders protected, maybe even see some action along the border of the Clan Occupation Zone. He sure as hell wasn't going to live the rest of his life wondering about might-have-beens. He wasn't going to be like his father, a lonely and bitter old man with nothing but his work. That was for certain.

He picked up his duffel bag and took another look around his room. A lot of it was still a kid's room, with toy models of BattleMechs sitting on a shelf above his bed and clothes and datachips scattered around. Sturm walked over and picked up a framed picture of his mother, wearing her uniform and standing on one foot of a giant BattleMech. It was one of the only pictures Sturm had of her.

How did you handle him, mom, he wondered. He looked at the picture for a long moment before putting it into his bag on top of the clothes and pulling the drawstring tight. He slung the bag over his shoulder and took a deep breath before heading back to the kitchen. His father was still bent over the table, just as he'd left him.

"I'm going," Sturm said, walking through the room.

"Ummm," Dr. Kintaro replied. "Don't forget to give my message to Lieutenant Holt."

"I won't." Sturm did his best not to slam the door on his way out.

As the door closed, Dr. Kintaro paused and looked up from his work. He stared at the door through which his son had just departed, his dark eyes softening a bit. The sound of an engine roared outside as the Lancer jeep pulled away from the row houses and turned toward the 'Mech base outside of the city.

"Sturm. . . ." the doctor said, his voice barely above a whisper. He shook his head sadly, then turned his mind back to the work that was ahead of him. His son was gone.

4

Kore Lancers Command Base
Outside Niffelheim, Kore
The Periphery
11 April 3060

The command base of the Kore Lancers was located just a few kilometers outside of the city of Niffelheim, across the flat, open tundra of Kore, gleaming with a layer of ice and snow that covered the permafrost that made up most of the planet's perpetually wintry terrain. A single road led from the city to the base, wide enough for ground vehicles, and kept clear for traffic by the near continuous efforts of Lancer personnel. Road-salting and -clearing duty was one unpleasant memory Sturm had of his time as a trainee, whenever Sergeant Krenner thought he was in need of some additional discipline, or time to think about his mistakes in training.

The command base itself was a gray ferrocrete structure, like most of the buildings of Kore. It consisted of a broad, skirted field, leveled off and layered with ferrocrete to form a landing area for the massive DropShips that visited the planet to deliver vital supplies and goods, while picking up shipments of processed ore. The base was the colony's main spaceport, since very little interstellar traffic ever came this far out into the Periphery. The only ships that visited Kore were those belonging to the Alfin Corporation or carrying relief personnel from the Storm Riders, who usually traveled on corporate ships.

The multi-level command building contained the instruments needed to handle space traffic control, coordinating landings with DropShips as they entered orbital distance of Kore. They also maintained communications with the interstellar JumpShips, which remained at one of the system's jump points, millions of kilometers above either of the star's poles, just outside of its gravity well. JumpShips didn't leave the jump points, but remained there to recharge their jump drives for another leap back toward the settled systems of the Inner Sphere.

Sturm glanced up into the pale blue sky, which held only a few white wisps of clouds. Somewhere up there now was a corporate DropShip, burning its way in toward Kore at 1G of thrust, bringing news and supplies from the distant Inner Sphere.

On the outskirts of the command building itself was the bay housing the unit's BattleMechs, four of them in all. The 'Mech bay was like a vast cave where the metal giants stood among gantries and other rigging to be serviced and maintained by crews of technicians. A BattleMech was a sophisticated piece of thirty-first century technology and, even though the 'Mechs of the Kore Lancers were already several decades old, they were still incredibly valuable and carefully maintained. The bay also held the Lance's various ground- and air-support vehicles, although they saw considerably more use on recon and mapping expeditions for Alfin's planetary survey division than they did in combat, much like the 'Mechs themselves.

A stiff wind blew white streamers of snow across the gray ferrocrete as Sturm pulled his jeep into the perimeter of the base. The perimeter guards needed only a glance at him before waving him through. Security on the base was fairly lax by Inner Sphere standards, but that was because Kore had few, if any, political problems to concern its defenders. Everyone on the planet was either a corporate employee or dependent, including the Lancers themselves, so there was virtually no concern about terrorists, political dissidents, or common criminals. There wasn't much to steal and who the hell would be interested in a world like Kore, anyway? Krenner sometimes grumbled about the planet being like R&R compared to some of the posts he'd seen, but even he knew there wasn't much point in insisting on the strictest discipline required of an Inner Sphere post. Things were allowed to slide, if only a little bit.

As Sturm pulled the jeep up near the 'Mech bay, several techs wearing parkas came out of the open bay doors. One of them waved when he saw Sturm climbing out of the jeep.

"There you are!" Junior Technician Tom Flannery yelled over to him. "You'd better get your butt in gear, Kintaro! C&C says the DropShip is going to be touching down pretty soon, and they're going to need you big, tough MechWarriors to do all the heavy lifting!"

Sturm flipped the tech off, and Flannery laughed while returning to his business. He was only joking, but it was the sad truth. Lieutenant Holt wanted all the MechWarriors of the lance on duty whenever a DropShip entered Kore airspace.

The ostensible reason was to provide security for the command base and the city. But Sturm had seen numerous DropShip landings, starting from when he was a kid, continuing into his trainee days and now as a MechWarrior. The corporate DropShips visited every few months like clockwork and everything always went off without a hitch. With the exception of the brief time when Kore was occupied by the Steel Vipers, DropShip runs had been going on for decades without a single problem. The massive ten-meter-tall BattleMechs usually ended up working as glorified humanoid cranes for moving heavy loads of material quickly and efficiently. It had become something of a joke to the Lancers, but Sturm still found himself reddening at Flannery's comment. Why bother to become a MechWarrior if all the action you're going to see is in the inside of a DropShip cargo bay?

Once again, Sturm reminded himself of the chance to eventually do well enough to earn a rotation off Kore and into the Inner Sphere where the other Storm Riders operated, maybe somewhere else in Lyran space where the Alfin Corporation had interests, or even serving one of the company's other clients, operating near the Clan Occupation Zones or along the Free Worlds

League border. Sturm thought about all the places in the vastness of the universe he would rather be as he headed into the 'Mech bay. He stopped near the door and looked up with pride at his 'Mech.

My 'Mech, Sturm thought proudly. *Mine.* Despite all of the grunt-work, Sturm still felt a thrill whenever he set eyes on the tall BattleMech and knew that it was his.

The *Thorn* wasn't a big 'Mech. Far from it, in fact. Weighing in at only twenty tons, it was classed as a light scout 'Mech, despite the fact that it outweighed many tanks and armored vehicles. Standing some nine meters tall, the *Thorn* was vaguely humanoid, with the exception of its right arm, which was replaced with a weapons pod mounting a Zeus-5 long-range missile launcher. The left arm featured a fully articulated and functional hand, along with a Hellion medium laser.

A second medium laser rested under the metal giant's "chin," just beneath the cockpit itself. Personally, Sturm wished the designers had put the secondary laser somewhere else, even further down in the torso, for example. As close to the cockpit as it was, the laser tended to really heat things up when fired.

The entire 'Mech was painted in a gray and white arctic cammo pattern standard for the Lancer 'Mechs, with the thunderbolt logo of the Storm Riders on its leg and shoulder plates. Sturm shouldered his duffel bag and walked across the bay to the pilots' locker room, where he shed his heavy winter gear and changed into clothing more suitable to the interior of a 'Mech cockpit, which was to say, as little as was practical and decent.

One of the primary limitations of BattleMech technology was heat. Driven by an internal fusion reaction, BattleMechs had almost limitless energy to power them. The trouble was, the flexing of myomer muscles and the firing of many powerful weapons tended to cause waste heat to build up inside the 'Mech's internal structure and cockpit. Heat sinks were installed along the surface areas, powerful coolant systems that labored to force heat out and keep the 'Mech's interior within operating tolerances. In frigid environments like Kore it was easier for 'Mechs to dissipate heat more quickly. Still, it often felt like an oven inside an operating BattleMech.

For that reason, MechWarriors wore fairly little while piloting their machines. Sturm's outfit consisted of a pair of padded shorts of a stretchy, breathable synthetic, along with rubber-soled boots similar to athletic wear. Over his bare chest, he slipped his coolant vest, a special garment woven from hundreds of thin plastic tubes. Coolant liquid circulated through the tubes, helping to keep the wearer cool as the cabin temperature increased. More than one MechWarrior had been defeated in battle, not because their weapons or armor weren't up to the task, but because they passed out from heat prostration and exhaustion in the midst of combat. The vest had a padded collar for the attachment of the neurohelmet that helped control and operate the 'Mech.

A combat knife went into the sheath in his right boot while a slim laser pistol went into the holster strapped to his left leg. Such weapons were largely a precaution in case the pilot was forced to eject from his BattleMech in hostile territory. The Lancers were hardly behind enemy lines, but Krenner drilled the importance of making such preparations a habit into all of his trainees. Likewise, Sturm would make sure to check the emergency supplies and other safeguards in his 'Mech before powering up the systems.

"These routines may save your life someday," Krenner always said. "That's when all the drilling pays off."

"What's your rush, kid?" came a voice that snapped Sturm out of his reverie. "The *Tammuz* is still a good hour or so out." Sturm turned to see the smiling face of Lon Volker, his fellow junior MechWarrior. Volker was leaning against the door of the locker room, a wide grin splitting his bearded face. Sturm returned the smile, trying to be agreeable, but try as he might, he just couldn't manage to like Volker.

"I'm sure Lieutenant Holt would appreciate it if we showed up for duty on time, Volker."

The other MechWarrior just kept on grinning. Volker was barely a year senior to Sturm, one of the first trainees from Kore and the first to become a MechWarrior. Still he acted like a veteran and treated Sturm like a naive younger brother he could tease and make fun of whenever the spirit moved him, which it often did. Volker was a good 'Mech pilot, good enough that he sometimes got away with pushing the limits of the regulations, on and off base. Whereas Sturm tried to maintain military discipline, Volker took advantage of the somewhat lax enforcement of regulations on Kore to have fun in his off-duty hours. Still, when he showed up for duty, he did his job well enough that nobody could complain, not even the exacting Sergeant Krenner. Sometimes Sturm found himself jealous of the other MechWarrior's easygoing attitude and manner.

"Yeah, it would do the lieutenant some good to lighten up. This isn't the front lines, kid, and all we're doing is unloading some cargo, not holding the line against a Clan invasion force. Holt treats everything like it's a matter of life and death."

"It's still our duty," Sturm said weakly.

Volker went over to his locker and started changing into his own 'Mech gear. He was in many ways typical of the Germanic stock of the Koran settlers: tall, broadly built, heavily muscled. His dark blond hair was cut close to his skull, but he sported a full, blond beard that he kept neatly trimmed. Curly blond hair covered his chest like a protective blanket. Volker always said it was in his Nordic genes to be able to handle the cold like a polar bear. Sturm, by contrast, could barely manage any facial hair (and what did grow always looked too scraggly, so he shaved it off) and his chest was bare. Volker always told Sturm he hardly needed a coolant vest, since he didn't really have anything to trap in the heat.

"Yeah, our duty. You know what our duty is, kid? Our duty is to find whatever way we can off this desolate rock and get ourselves out there where it's really happening. You know it, I know it, and even Lieutenant-freakin'-Holt knows it. Kore is a dead-end. It's where the 'Riders send their washed-up MechWarriors to finish out their time to pension and their malcontents to spend some time cooling off. Hell, it's gotten so bad they don't even bother to send relief troops out here anymore. They've got to recruit guys like you and me to do the duty. But I'm not going to stay buried here for the rest of my life. I'm getting off this rock sooner or later. The Lancers are just the first step in my ticket out of here." Volker slipped his coolant vest on and began adjusting the fit.

"Hey," he said, "did you hear? Old Hans says he saw the Ghost again."

Sturm glanced up from fidgeting with the ties on his holster.

"Really?"

"Yeah. Of course, I'll bet he had at least a little nip of something before that. Probably a big nip, if I know Brinkmann." Volker mimicked throwing back a bottle with a laugh. Hans Brinkmann did have something of a reputation as a drinker. He was the oldest MechWarrior in the unit, older even than Lieutenant Holt. Sturm had heard that he'd ended up on Kore as a result of some disciplinary action, but Brinkmann never talked about it and nobody else in the unit seemed to know much or, if they did, they weren't saying.

Of course, it wasn't the first time someone had mentioned a "ghost sighting." In fact, the Ghost of Winter was a regular story that circulated among the Lancers during long duty-shifts and off-duty drinking bouts. The story said that one or more of the Clan warriors left behind to defend Kore when the main invasion force moved on fought so fiercely when the Storm Riders came to retake Kore that he (or she, the story varied) swore to defend Kore against all invaders even after death. MechWarriors told stories about strange sensor readings and even sightings of a ghostly BattleMech out on the tundra or in the Jotun Mountains late at night.

Sturm remembered laughing off the stories at first, although secretly he did sometimes find himself double-checking his 'Mech's sensor readings on night patrols. Sturm mentioned the stories to his father once. Dr. Kintaro dismissed them as "ignorant superstition" and rambled on about how the metal deposits and some of the volcanic steam vents might create a kind of false reading of a large, hot, metallic object that sensors could mistake for another 'Mech at first glance. Still, there was something almost mystical about the Clans and their legendary ferocity, their code of honor, their willingness to fight to the death, that gave the story some weight. Sturm wondered if every MechWarrior and soldier on Kore didn't look out across the dark tundra some nights and wonder. Volker probably didn't, he guessed.

Sturm shrugged off the thought. Stewing about Volker or wondering about the Ghost was a waste of time and energy when he could be out there in his 'Mech where he belonged. He stowed the rest of his gear in his locker and turned to head out of the locker room.

"Hey, tiger," Volker called after him, "don't kill all those cargo modules. Leave a few of them for the rest of us to handle. Don't want you hogging all the glory." His bitter, mocking laughter followed Sturm out into the hall.

5

Kore Lancers Command Base
Outside Niffelheim, Kore
The Periphery
11 April 3060

Sturm climbed up the chain-ladder to the *Thorn*'s cockpit, shivering a bit from the icy wind that blew in through the bay doors. He swung into the cockpit and settled into the padded command chair. He triggered a switch and the cockpit hatch hissed shut with a thunk and the internal cabin lights came on, bathing the interior in a pale light. The main viewscreen lit up with a split 360-degree view around the 'Mech, compressed into 120 degrees on-screen. A heads-up display providing technical information was superimposed over the screen, while secondary displays provided additional information on the 'Mech's weapons and other systems. Everything was in perfect ready condition.

Reaching up above him, Sturm pulled down the neurohelmet, a key command element of a Battle-

Mech. The helmet was a bulky affair with an open faceplate in front and thick cables connecting it to the *Thorn*'s onboard computers.

One of the early design flaws with BattleMechs was the problem of keeping such giant machines standing upright. BattleMech myomer fibers worked similar to human muscles, contracting and relaxing in response to electrical current passing through them, allowing 'Mechs to move much like living beings. Still, a ten- or twelve-meter tall BattleMech lacked the balance and coordination of even a five-year-old; 'Mechs would simply topple over if their movements weren't carefully coordinated. Part of that coordination came from an internal gyroscope and a sophisticated series of computer movement-models, allowing the 'Mech to function in ways similar to a humanoid.

The rest of the balance came directly from the MechWarrior piloting the machine. In more ways than one, a 'Mech pilot was the real "brain" of the BattleMech. Contact pads inside the neurohelmet fitted tightly against the wearer's scalp. They conducted neural impulses from the brain to the 'Mech's control systems. The main functions of the 'Mech were still controlled manually; the lack of effective neuro-feedback limited the system's effectiveness as a primary control mechanism. But it did allow the BattleMech to tap into its pilot's own sense of balance and equilibrium. With the aid of the neurohelmet BattleMechs moved almost like living things, directed by the manual control inside the cockpit.

Sturm lowered the neurohelmet into place and inserted the medsensor plugs into the four sockets at the helmet's throat. The board showed green and he felt the familiar odd sensation in the back of his head as the neural systems linked in, connecting his balance-centers to the drive systems of the *Thorn*. The helmet also ran a security scan of Sturm's brainwave patterns, which served as part of the "key" to his 'Mech. He fastened the helmet down on the padded shoulders of his coolant vest.

The primary viewscreen lit up with a flashing status monitor and the words INPUT PASSCODE.

"Jenna's Dream," he said. The screen flashed PASSCODE VALID, and the massive war machine came to life. The screen filled with a view of the 'Mech bay as Sturm ran a systems check and cleared all of the 'Mech's connections with its maintenance cocoon. He pushed the command stick forward and the metal giant began slowly walking forward, footsteps booming against the ferrocrete floor. Sturm guided the *Thorn* out of the 'Mech bay and began moving at a brisk pace toward the landing pad.

He keyed open his comm channels with the touch of a button.

"C&C, this is Kintaro, I'm heading out to the landing pad. Over." There was a crackle of static in Sturm's ear on the channel.

"kkkzzzzrtttt . . . Roger that Kintaro . . . bzzzzt . . . proceed *zzzzzzzztttttt"*

"Come again, C&C. I'm having trouble reading you."

"Sorry, Sturm . . ." The voice crackled from the speaker in his helmet. ". . . we're having some . . . *kkkzzzzzttt* . . . trouble with the comm system . . . *kkkkkrrrrrrrrkkk* . . . trying to track it down now."

"Might be some kind of magnetic interference," Sturm offered. His father was always talking about Kore's unusually strong magnetic field, which sometimes caused trouble for electronics. Sturm had certainly been fooled more than once by false magnetic readings caused by the high-density metal ores in some of the local rocks.

"Probably all the second- and third-hand crap gear command keeps sending us," another voice cut in.

"Hey, Volker," Sturm responded, "glad you could be bothered to join us out here." He zoomed his 'Mech's sensors onto the profile of Volker's *Panther* emerging from the 'Mech bay. The sleek gray 'Mech was humanoid like the *Thorn*, but weighed in a bit heavier and mounted a large particle projection cannon on one arm.

"Couldn't let you face those cargo containers all alone, kid," Volker shot back. "Thought you might need a hand."

"Then the both of you can cut the chatter and get your butts over here," interjected another voice. "The *Tammuz* is hitting its final approach." The tone was friendly, but still carried a hint of steel.

"Yessir," Sturm responded. Volker shot back with a jaunty "Yes, sir!"

"And Volker," Lieutenant Holt continued, "don't forget that you haven't been in a 'Mech cockpit much longer than Kintaro, and that he beat you on the last training exercise by a good margin." Sturm grinned at the sudden silence on the commline. Volker apparently didn't have any smart remarks about that.

"C&C," Holt said over the channel, "keep working on the comm system. We're going out to meet the *Tammuz*. Maybe they can spare us a couple of techs to help out. We'll keep you apprised. Over."

"Roger that," the radio crackled. "Over."

Sturm walked his 'Mech toward the landing pad, with Volker's *Panther* close behind. Suddenly the other 'Mech sprinted forward, moving quickly across the frozen terrain.

"You heard the lieutenant," Volker said. "Let's go!"

Sturm smiled and shook his head. Volker just wouldn't give up. There was no need to move so quickly, and it was often dangerous to travel too fast across the frozen terrain of Kore. Even something as big as a BattleMech could slip or skid across the snow-covered ground, as Sturm knew from his training. He let Volker go and picked up his own pace slightly. Better to do the job right and get there in one piece than to grandstand. Let Volker have his fun, if that would make him feel better.

Already he had a visual on the *Tammuz*. The DropShip was descending toward the broad ferrocrete landing pad on final approach. Nearby were two other BattleMechs, standing like silent sentries watching the sky. The first was Lieutenant Holt's *Centurion*, the same 'Mech design in which Sturm had trained that morning. The fifty-ton 'Mech carried a decent array of armaments, particularly its arm-mounted autocannon. Hans Brinkmann's *Javelin* stood nearby. The thirty-ton 'Mech was squat and broad compared to the *Centurion*, its chest puffed out to contain racks of short-range missiles that let it pack a wallop at close range. Both 'Mechs were painted in the standard white and gray cammo of the Kore Lancers.

Technically, the Lancers would be classed as a scout lance by most Inner Sphere units. The *Centurion* was their heaviest 'Mech and it was classed as medium, almost puny compared to monsters like the *Atlas* or the *Banshee*. None of the others counted as more than light 'Mechs. Still, they were all Kore had, since it made little sense to assign a full twelve-'Mech company or even a medium or heavy lance to such an isolated world on the edge of known space, with little strategic value.

The Alfin Corporation wanted Kore protected, but they also had to be cost-conscious. That was why the Lancers often had to make do with less than top-line equipment and supplies. Kore simply wasn't a priority garrison. *Volker's probably right*, Sturm thought. *The comm system is second-hand junk. That's why it's not working right.*

The Tammuz *isn't in much better shape*, Sturm mused, as the giant DropShip resolved itself from a rapidly growing dot to a familiar outline. The ship was a giant metallic sphere some eighty meters in diameter, with a flattened tail mounting four powerful guidance thrusters around the central fusion drive. It had already turned so the thrusters pointed downward, firing controlled blasts to slow the descent of more than three thousand tons of metal through the atmosphere of Kore. The metal plates making up the ship's hull were dented and pitted from micrometeorites and atmospheric debris. The paint job was patched and scuffed, giving the ship a battered appearance. Still, it was an impressive sight. Used to working in and around giant BattleMechs, Sturm was still stunned by the sheer size of the DropShip.

Normally, *Union* Class ships like the *Tammuz* weren't used to visit planets like Kore. The *Tammuz* had room enough in its cavernous hold to carry a full company of BattleMechs and support fighters, more than enough space to carry supplies to a small colony like this. But supply ships arrived on Kore infrequently, and there was always a full load of processed ore to be taken back to Alfin facilities in the Inner Sphere, so those huge cargo bays were filled with ore carriers rather than 'Mechs. Sturm watched the ship descend as his 'Mech walked across the frozen tundra, thinking of the day when he might be able to board a DropShip like this and travel out across the stars.

The *Tammuz* fired its thrusters again and settled majestically into the landing pit in the center of the platform on a giant pillar of smoke and flame, resting on a set of four landing-columns that extended from the lower sides of the sphere like tiny legs. Sturm thought the whole thing was a strange cross between impressive and almost comical.

"Wait until they give the all-clear," Lieutenant Holt said over the comm. Then he began to move his *Centurion* around the outskirts of the landing pit, toward the *Tammuz*'s massive hatchway.

The next moment, a blazing bolt shot out from the DropShip, striking the *Centurion* in the torso. The PPC blast melted armor and sent the 'Mech staggering backward. Lasers mounted on the

DropShip's outer hull followed the blast with several blazing crimson beams that sliced into the 'Mech's armor.

"What the hell . . . ?" Sturm said.

"C&C, I'm under attack!" Holt was shouting over the comm. "Some kind of ambush! C&C, come in!" Only static filled the airwaves where the response from the Command and Control Center should be. Something was very wrong. Sturm pushed the control stick forward, driving the *Thorn* up to its maximum speed, closing in to help provide some cover for the *Centurion* to withdraw. Holt's voice came over the comm system again.

"All 'Mechs, *Tammuz* is considered hostile! Repeat, *Tammuz* is considered—" A burst of hard static cut off the communication as another burst from the DropShip's PPC struck the *Centurion*. The lieutenant's comm system might be damaged, or just temporarily overloaded by the charge of the particle blast.

As he closed in, Sturm thumbed the firing button at his left, and the *Thorn* spat a volley of LRMs from its right-side launcher. They streaked in toward the DropShip and impacted on the hull with a dull boom. The heavy armor, designed to withstand battles in the depths of space, held against the attack, although Sturm registered some new scarring on the hull plates. It would take forever to blast through that armor. He had to try and target some exposed system, like one of the weapons pods.

Brinkmann and Volker had also opened fire on the DropShip. In the smoke wreathing the ship's hull, Sturm could just make out the other 'Mechs falling back from the ship, trying to cover the lieutenant's more damaged 'Mech. The crackle of radio static filled his ears as his sensors began to pick up something else.

"Enemy 'Mechs!" Brinkmann shouted over the com. "We've got enemy 'Mechs incoming!"

Sturm zoomed the *Thorn*'s scanner in on one of the open cargo hatches of the DropShip and saw several giant, metallic forms emerging from it. On each of them, painted on the limbs and torso, was the crest of Clan Jade Falcon. Sturm's heart froze in his chest as the last of the invading BattleMechs stepped out of the DropShip. It was a massive seventy-five-ton *Mad Cat*.

The Clans had returned to Kore.

6

Kore Lancers Command Base
Outside Niffelheim, Kore
The Periphery
11 April 3060

Hans Brinkmann was the first to die. Enemy missiles screamed in toward his *Javelin* and exploded in a shroud of smoke and flames.

"Critical damage to the reactor!" Brinkmann yelled over the commline. "I'm not going to be able to keep it under control!"

The enemy *Puma* leveled both arms toward the *Javelin* and there was a boom like thunder as artificial lightning lanced from the 'Mech's twin PPCs. The blue-white beams of energy struck the *Javelin*'s cockpit and it exploded. A cloud of smoke and fragments showered over the area, leaving the rest of the 'Mech standing out on the ferrocrete landing pad, frozen in the midst of its last motion, as if it were as dumbfounded as the rest of the Kore Lancers at the sudden and savage attack.

"Bastards!" Sturm yelled and slammed down

on the firing stud. A cluster of LRMs streaked toward the enemy 'Mechs, and twin lances of crimson fire shot out at the *Puma*. The *Puma* was already moving and the missiles went wide, exploding against the ferrocrete, while only one of the lasers scored a hit, melting and burning some armor on the 'Mech's arm. Off to Sturm's right, the PPC of Volker's *Panther* gave a crack of thunder as he fired his own energy weapon at the invaders.

"Pull back!" Lieutenant Holt ordered. "Volker! Kintaro! Fall back toward the mountains and keep trying to get in contact with C&C."

"But Lieutenant, what about . . ."

"That's an order, Kintaro! GO!"

Sturm hesitated for only an instant. The lieutenant was right. There was no way they could defeat the more powerful Clan 'Mechs, especially not without Brinkmann. He turned his 'Mech around and began heading toward the Jotun Mountains, pushing the control stick forward and coaxing the *Thorn* up to its maximum speed. In moments he hit the edge of the landing pad and braced for the jolt as the 'Mech went from the hard, level ferrocrete to the snow-covered tundra. Fortunately, Sturm was practiced at piloting a 'Mech across the often treacherous terrain of Kore. He only hoped that the Clan pilots weren't as prepared for the slippery surface; it might slow them down just enough to buy the Lancers some breathing space. Then they could regroup, contact C&C, and find out what the hell had happened. Assuming C&C wasn't already under enemy control. But how could that be?

Sturm forced himself to push aside all of his questions and concerns for the moment. Right now he needed to focus on the matter at hand. He checked his display. Volker's *Panther* was right behind him. The heavier scout 'Mech wasn't as fast as Sturm's *Thorn*, so Sturm had a good head start on the other pilot. As for the *Centurion* . . .

Sturm slowed his 'Mech as quickly as he could on the frozen terrain.

"Kintaro! What are you doing?"

"Lieutenant Holt—he's . . ."

"There's nothing you can do for him, kid," Volker said, "except to do as he ordered. Now keep going, damn it!"

Sturm took another look at his display. Holt's *Centurion* was moving, but not to escape from the Clan 'Mechs. Although the *Centurion* was about as fast as the *Panther*, the lieutenant wasn't following his two MechWarriors. He was moving to cut off the invading 'Mechs and keep them from going after the rest of his lance. It was one medium Inner Sphere 'Mech against four vastly superior Clan 'Mechs. The lieutenant didn't stand a chance. He had to know that.

He does know it, Sturm thought as he pushed the *Thorn* up to top speed again. *He knows he can't win, but he wants us to get away.*

The young MechWarrior glanced at the information his sensors were relaying. The *Centurion* was moving in an arc around the enemy 'Mechs, using evasive maneuvers to try and avoid their fire. Fire spat from Holt's arm-mounted autocannon as a stream of heavy shells roared toward the enemy 'Mechs. Sturm saw as the fire stitched across the heavy armor of the *Mad Cat*, leaving pockmarks in its cerametallic skin, but otherwise causing no serious damage. The heavier 'Mech retaliated with four emerald lances of light from its blocky arms. The powerful lasers seared across the *Centurion*, melting and vaporizing armor plating, searing artificial muscles and internal structure.

Lieutenant Holt barely even slowed down. He let loose with everything his 'Mech had. The autocannon spat again, concentrating a stream of fire at the lead 'Mech, while Holt's torso-mounted laser returned a red beam of coherent light at the larger 'Mech's shoulder, aiming for the missile pod mounted there. The beam burned and scored armor, but didn't damage the missile rack, as far as Sturm could tell. The *Centurion* sent a flight of LRMs arcing toward the *Mad Cat*, but Holt was too close for the unguided munitions to be very accurate. They overshot their target to explode uselessly against the ferrocrete. Sturm thought one or two of the LRMs might have hit the DropShip, but he doubted that a couple of missiles could have done more than dent the *Tammuz*'s heavy armor plating.

Holt was going all out, moving rapidly and firing all the *Centurion*'s weapons at once. The heat in his cockpit would be nearly intolerable by now. Sturm himself was covered in a light sheen of sweat from pushing his 'Mech's speed, but he knew that was nothing compared to the oven the *Centurion* had to be. Even the superior heat-dissipating properties of Kore's frigid environment wouldn't be enough to reduce the 'Mech's heat buildup.

"Volker, we're gonna have company," Sturm said as he watched the monitors.

"I see them," Volker responded.

Two of the other Clan 'Mechs were breaking off from the fight and heading toward them. There was no way Holt could contain them; he had his hands full against the *Mad Cat*. Sturm ID'd them as the *Puma* and the *Uller*. Both were low-slung, crab-like designs, well-suited to the rough terrain and slippery ground. They were starting to move at a pretty fair clip, despite the heavy layer of snow. Sturm glanced at his own readings; he was at top speed now, moving at over ninety kilometers per hour. Volker's *Panther* was lagging behind. The larger 'Mech's top speed was only about sixty-five kph at best, and Volker seemed to be having more trouble with the terrain than Sturm. The enemy 'Mechs were gaining fast.

The commline crackled in Sturm's ear, and he could hear Lieutenant Holt's voice, as if from far away.

"Volker, Kintaro, it's up to you. Try to send for help. Signal the company. They're not—" The signal was cut off in a burst of hard static. Sturm looked at his heads-up display at the battle going on at the landing pad, now falling away in the distance. He could make out the *Centurion*, still moving, although its comm system must have been damaged. It was hemmed in, cornered near the DropShip by the *Mad Cat* and another Clan 'Mech, a *Fenris*. The *Centurion* showed up on the infrared scans like a small nova, its heat levels surely near critical, and there were indications its reactor was damaged. The 'Mech let loose at its tormentors with everything it had, but the two Clan 'Mechs were already closing in for the kill.

What are you doing, Lieutenant? Sturm thought. *Eject!* It was obvious Holt wasn't going to be able to win the fight. It was over. If the lieutenant ejected from his 'Mech, he might just be taken prisoner. Why the hell didn't he bail out?

The *Mad Cat* closed in like some kind of monstrous animal and swung one of its heavy arms like a club, striking the *Centurion* a mighty blow and sending it toppling over on its side.

C'mon, Lieutenant, Sturm thought, *get out of there, get out of there before . . .*

Standing over the fallen 'Mech, the *Mad Cat* leveled its arms toward it. A hellish green light flared, and the *Centurion*'s upper body was slagged by the tremendous heat of the powerful lasers. Sturm double-checked, thinking maybe Lieutenant Holt had bailed out before . . . no. There was no way. The commander's 'Mech was totaled and no one could have survived the damage. Lieutenant Holt was dead. For just a moment Sturm wondered if that was how his mother had died, sacrificing herself to give the warriors of her command a precious few more seconds.

Sturm also saw the two other Clan 'Mechs still closing in. He read their speed at nearly equal his own, much faster than Volker's *Panther.* There was no way Volker could outrun them. He had a head start, but the Clan 'Mechs would overtake him.

Suddenly, an indicator flared on Sturm's monitors as the *Puma* opened fire on the *Panther.* With incredible accuracy, the Clan 'Mech's twin PPCs sent blue-white bolts of energy slamming into the

Panther's back, where its armor was weakest, shearing off both left and right torsos with savage fury. The 'Mech's internal gyroscope fought to maintain its balance, but the blast caused Volker's *Panther* to lose its traction on the slippery ground and the devastating loss of so much structural weight threw the 'Mech completely off balance.

Sturm started to slow his *Thorn* and turn back. Volker was a sitting duck. His rear armor must have been vaporized by the blast, and the enemy 'Mechs were closing in on him fast. There was no way he could survive unless . . .

"Don't be stupid, kid." Volker's voice came over the commline, almost like he was reading Sturm's mind. "Keep going. Get out of here, while you still can!"

"I'm not going to leave you, too!" Sturm said.

"There's nothing you can do! Listen, I'm giving you an order, mister. Get the hell out of here. If you can, find some way to contact the 'Riders. Get some help. I can take care of myself!"

Sturm hesitated. The Clan 'Mechs would be on top of Volker any second. He might be able to help hold them off, help Volker to get clear, but the Clan 'Mechs were about as fast as the *Thorn.* Unless he could seriously damage them, it was highly unlikely either of them would escape if Sturm slowed down to the *Panther's* top speed, especially if that PPC blast had damaged any of the *Panther's* internal systems. If he went back to help Volker, it was far more likely they would both end up dead or captured.

"Only an idiot stays and fights when he knows he can't win," Krenner had said. *"A MechWarrior is also*

expected to know when he can serve himself and his unit better by retreating.''

Sturm recalled the sergeant's words to him earlier that morning and forced himself to fight down his desire to go back and help Volker, to throw everything he had at the invaders who killed his lieutenant and his fellow MechWarrior. Volker was right: Sturm couldn't do any good against those Clan 'Mechs but, if he escaped, he might somehow be able to warn the rest of the company about what was happening on Kore. As long as Sturm stayed free, there was a chance.

"Good luck, Volker," he said into his helmet mike as he turned the *Thorn* toward the mountains and pushed it as fast as it would go. He heard Volker answer him as the *Panther* rapidly fell away behind him.

"You, too, kid. Good luck." The Clan 'Mechs slowed as they approached the fallen *Panther*. Volker didn't even try to right his 'Mech as they trained their weapons on him. There was nothing he could offer except a meaningless act of defiance.

Sturm turned away from the scene and focused his attention on the dark peaks of the Jotun Mountains rising in the distance, offering the hope of sanctuary, for a while at least. He had to reach the mountains, and he had to find some way to send out a call for help.

He was on his own.

7

Jotun Mountains
Kore
The Periphery
11 April 3060

It seemed to take hours for Sturm's *Thorn* to cover the twenty or so kilometers to the Jotun Mountains, even though he actually made the distance in less than twenty minutes at top speed. By the time the high mountain peaks loomed overhead, Sturm was starting to feel the initial adrenaline surge from the battle at the landing pad—if such a slaughter could be called a battle—beginning to wear off. He was covered in sweat from the heat in the cockpit, and the *Thorn*'s armor had suffered some minor damage from a near PPC hit during his flight.

Sturm checked his display. His pursuer was still there, following only a few kilometers behind now. Both pursuing Clan 'Mechs had stopped to assess Volker's situation when his damaged *Panther* fell onto the snowy tundra. The *Uller* apparently remained behind to finish Volker off or to capture him, Sturm didn't know which. Meanwhile, the *Puma* resumed chasing Sturm's *Thorn*.

The Clan 'Mech was just as fast, even though it outweighed the *Thorn* by a good fifteen tons. It mounted an extended-range PPC on each arm, and it was damned accurate with them. Sturm probably would have reached the mountains sooner but for the need to follow a zigzagging course across the tundra, attempting to avoid incoming fire from the enemy 'Mech. Sturm remembered learning that *Puma*s usually carried advanced Clan targeting systems, making their weapons more accurate than the manually targeted weapons of most Inner Sphere 'Mechs. It was little wonder the *Puma* had been able to hit Volker's *Panther* in the back while going full tilt.

Fortunately, Sturm was able to stay at the extreme edge of the PPC's range, making it more difficult for the *Puma* to tag him. Still, he'd suffered some minor damage to his armor already, and his left-rear torso was entirely gone from a glancing shot. Sturm was only grateful that the shot hadn't hit the missile launcher mounted in his right side. Had a PPC beam cut through his armor there it might have detonated his remaining missile ammo, finishing him for sure.

To Sturm's advantage, the *Puma*'s PPCs seemed to generate a lot of waste heat, which sometimes forced the 'Mech to slow its pursuit a bit until its heat sinks could compensate. Sturm maintained a steady lead all the way to the mountains. He was also more experienced than the Clan pilot at handling his 'Mech over the snow-covered terrain, having logged hundreds of hours of simulator time and plenty of field experience. The *Puma* pilot occasionally slipped or faltered, although never enough to seriously damage his 'Mech or slow him down sufficiently for Sturm to escape. Out on the open tundra of Kore there were very few places a 'Mech could hide. Sturm knew of a few: crevasses and canyons covered with layers of snow, but he never gained enough distance to make use of them without the *Puma* spotting him.

He tried to lure the other 'Mech into one of the larger crevasses, running toward it at full speed, then dodging around it. That didn't fool the *Puma* pilot, who simply followed Sturm's course. Had the *Thorn* been equipped with jump jets, he might have been able to pull it off, but his 'Mech wasn't jump-capable. Sturm was just grateful the *Puma* wasn't either.

I've got to find some way to shake him, he thought for maybe the hundredth time. He keyed open the commline.

"C&C, this is Kintaro. Do you read? C&C, come in. This is Kintaro, under attack by enemy 'Mechs showing Clan Jade Falcon colors. Repeat, under attack. Do you copy?"

Nothing but static came in response. Sturm had been trying constantly to raise someone in Command and Control, but with no success. Either C&C was being jammed by the Clan invaders, or it had already fallen and the only people around to listen to his calls for help were the enemy. In either case, Sturm couldn't expect any help from the Lancers' ground forces and he definitely couldn't expect any help from his fellow MechWarriors. He was on his own.

He needed breathing room, a chance to hide out somewhere, take stock of his resources, and come up with some kind of a plan. To do that, he needed to deal with the *Puma*. The other 'Mech outclassed Sturm's *Thorn*. There was practically no way he'd be able to take the heavier Clan 'Mech in a straight-out fight. He had to use his other advantages against the Clan machine. The *Puma* might have the edge in armor and armament, but Sturm knew the terrain. The trick with the crevasse didn't work, but maybe something else would.

Sturm angled the *Thorn* toward Giant's Pass, as he himself had named it. His father had sent him through that pass into the mountains several times in the past few months to gather geological data. The pass was just wide enough to allow something as massive as a BattleMech through it, and Sturm had mapped the whole area and maneuvered through several times, so he knew the best route to take. The satellite and computer maps of the pass were still loaded in the *Thorn*'s computer systems, in fact, since the survey wasn't yet complete. Sturm had figured he'd be visiting the pass again, although he'd never expected it would be with an enemy 'Mech close on his tail.

Kore had a lot of metallic ores and deposits, which made it attractive to the mining corporation. Those same metallic ores were found in abundance in the mountains. Dr. Kintaro speculated that they were responsible for some of the unusual magnetic flux readings Sturm had picked up in his surveys. Additionally, the Jotun range was still volcanically active to some degree; geysers and hot steam vents were common. The combination of the powerful magnetic fields and the extremes of heat and cold played merry hell with a 'Mech's sensors. Sturm knew that. If he could make it through the pass, there was a chance he might be able to confuse his pursuer and throw him off the trail.

Sturm entered the pass and moved as quickly as he dared between the looming black cliffs above. The floor of the pass was worn smooth by some ancient glacier, covered with scattered rocks and boulders that could become treacherous if stepped on the wrong way. Sturm once slipped on a mass of loose, icy rock and his 'Mech took a spill that damaged one of the arm actuators. Krenner had him pulling extra hours in the simulator in addition to helping the techs replace the actuator. Lieutenant Holt really chewed him out for that mistake.

Holt. Sturm couldn't forget the sight of his commanding officer's *Centurion* lying on the ferrocrete landing pad near the DropShip as the giant *Mad Cat* loomed over it. Lieutenant Holt had given Sturm the chance to become a MechWarrior, accepted him as an apprentice with the Lancers, and given him the opportunity to fulfill his dream. He'd sacrificed himself so the men of his command could get away and have a chance. Sturm wanted to make sure that sacrifice wasn't in vain.

The pass opened up into a mountain valley, a deep gash cut between the high mountain peaks overhead, filled with snow and ice and broken, barren stretches of gray rock. Small, twisted trees and ground-covering plants clung to the rocks wherever they could find purchase, and more foliage huddled near the steam vents, soaking in the moisture and the heat to sustain themselves. Checking his display, Sturm saw that he was out of the *Puma*'s sight for now, shielded by the rock of the mountains. He estimated that he had only a few minutes to put his plan into action before the *Puma* came through the pass.

He aimed his lasers at a steam vent on the far side of the valley he'd mapped out previously. Twin beams of ruby light speared out for a split-second, superheating the rock around the vent and sending powerful gouts of steam shooting upward.

He moved the *Thorn* over to the edge of a crevasse he'd also mapped out in the valley. It was about seven meters deep and filled to the top with snow, almost invisible to the naked eye, but his sensors were just barely able to make it out. Sturm had nearly stumbled into it before, but his earlier experience in the pass made him more wary of potential pitfalls. This time, however, he deliberately walked the *Thorn* out onto the crevasse, holding tightly to the controls and praying for the internal gyroscope to keep the 'Mech upright.

The packed snow was not nearly strong enough to support the weight of a twenty-ton BattleMech, and the *Thorn* sank rapidly. Sturm managed to keep the 'Mech upright as it slid down into the hard-packed snow until it stopped sinking. He crouched the *Thorn* down as much as possible, keeping its head just at the edge of the crevasse.

Painted in arctic camouflage, the *Thorn* practically disappeared against the frozen terrain. When the *Puma* came into the valley, its scanners would pick up all sorts of magnetic and temperature anomalies, any one of which could be a concealed BattleMech, while the metallic rock strata shielded the *Thorn*'s own signals.

Sturm quickly powered down all of the 'Mech's non-essential systems to minimize its profile and shut down the heat sinks. The heat from the *Thorn*'s hull was already melting the snow around it, and Sturm knew he didn't have long. The temperature in the cabin was hot from the long run to the mountain, and Sturm sat in the dimness, sweating and watching his displays for some sign of his opponent.

There he is, he thought as the *Puma* came through Giant's Pass. The wide, low-slung Clan 'Mech was obviously having some trouble maneuvering through the pass, although not as much as Sturm had hoped. It stopped near the entrance to the valley and began to turn from side to side. It was scanning for him. Sturm held his breath as if that might help keep him hidden from the enemy 'Mech's sensors. Time ticked by with painful slowness. If the *Puma* pilot discovered him and moved in for the kill, Sturm was in a lousy position to do anything about it. He just had to hope his enemy would take the bait.

The other 'Mech turned toward the steam vent. It was the most powerful heat source at the moment, and the aftereffects of Sturm's lasers clearly showed. The geysering steam was creating a dense fog at the far end of the valley, an ideal place to hide something as large as a BattleMech. With a lurch, the *Puma* began stalking toward the mist.

That's right, Sturm thought, *keep going, just a little further.* The *Puma* stepped into fog and was quickly lost from sight, becoming a faint shadow moving through the mist. The *Thorn's* scanners were barely able to track it through the interference. Sturm doubted he could hit the *Puma* reliably at this distance, even with his LRMs, which would never do enough damage in one shot to disable the other 'Mech. He bit his lip and waited as the seconds ticked by. He had to time this exactly right. If he estimated the other 'Mech's speed correctly, the *Puma* should have arrived near the steam vent, and its pilot was probably just starting to figure out that Sturm wasn't there.

Now.

The *Thorn* rose up just above the crevasse, and Sturm fired both lasers while mashing his thumb down on the firing button for the LRMs. The lasers and missile fired, not at the mist-shrouded *Puma*, but at the mountainside high above it. Beams of coherent light slashed across an ancient glacier, turning snow and ice to superheated steam as a flight of five missiles impacted the mountainside with a boom.

There were a few brief seconds of silence, then suddenly a groaning sound, like the mountain was crying out in pain. The groan became a deafening roar as a thousand tons of snow and ice dislodged themselves from their resting place on the mountainside and slid down into the valley like a giant white tsunami.

The *Puma* didn't even have a chance to move

before the avalanche crashed over it. The giant BattleMech vanished under the torrent of snow in an instant. Sturm's last sight of it was the force of the avalanche knocking the *Puma* off its feet before burying it.

"Yes!" Sturm let out a whoop of triumph and began slowly moving the *Thorn* out of the icy crevasse. The avalanche probably didn't destroy the *Puma*, although it might have seriously damaged it. Sturm needed to make sure the clan 'Mech wasn't going to be coming after him again. He started moving toward the other side of the valley as the cloud of snow kicked up by the avalanche was beginning to settle. There were no signs of movement from under the avalanche itself.

That was when the powerful laser cored into the *Thorn's* left side, vaporizing armor and setting alarms to shrieking inside the cockpit.

What the hell . . . ? Sturm thought as he quickly turned to face the *Uller*, coming out of Giant's Pass. *Damn!* He didn't think the other 'Mech would follow so quickly. The *Uller* must have hung back and waited to see what the *Puma* would do. Sturm responded by firing his lasers at the Clan 'Mech, but the *Uller* dodged one and its armor held against the other. It responded with another deadly blast from its pulse laser that cut through the *Thorn's* torso armor. Myomer muscles and titanium bones melted under the emerald heat of the laser, and superheated steam gushed out of the rents in the 'Mech's armor.

WARNING, REACTOR SHIELDING DAMAGED, read Sturm's readouts, flashing red across his vision. His clever plan had trapped him in the valley. The *Uller* was covering his means of escape. There was nowhere to go. The *Thorn*'s reactor could go critical at any moment. Sturm watched the lifeless visage of the enemy 'Mech on his heads-up display as it raised its arms to fire on him again. He was certain this attack would be the one to finish him.

With a curse, Sturm slammed his hand down on the ejection switch. Explosive bolts blew off the top of the *Thorn*'s cockpit, and the frigid air slapped Sturm in the face. A moment later, he was pressed down into his chair by the force of the acceleration as the booster rockets launched him out and away from the dying BattleMech.

The last thing Sturm saw as he spiraled up and away was the *Uller*'s lasers and autocannon clobbering the *Thorn*. Black smoke streaming from its head and torso, the 'Mech fell backward and crashed into the ground. A miniature sun blossomed in its chest as the *Thorn*'s fusion reactor went critical, leaving a blackened hole and a melted mass of limbs and myomer muscles. Then the black cliff face rushed in at him and Sturm's world was swallowed up in darkness.

8

Kore Lancers Command Base
Kore
The Periphery
11 April 3060

The Command and Control Center of the Kore Lancers command base was in enemy hands. Volker recognized some of the grim-faced soldiers standing guard in the corridors as he was led through them by his captors. Many of them he knew as part of a maintenance crew from Niffelheim, techs and other workers at the base. He'd seen a few others in the city itself, indicating that someone had been planning this operation for some time.

There was one thing he was sure of: whoever they were, they weren't from the Clans. The 'Mechs that took down Volker's *Panther* and killed Brinkmann and Lieutenant Holt were definitely Clan 'Mechs, but the troops in the Command Center weren't Clanners unless everything Volker had ever heard about the Clans was a gross exaggeration. These troops lacked the crisp military efficiency and decorum of the Clans. Their "uniforms" were mismatched collections of cast-offs, and so was their equipment, for the most part. Their manner wasn't that of trained and disciplined military men and women from a society that glorified war and battle above all else. They were more like down-on-their-luck mercenaries, or maybe even pirates.

After his 'Mech was hit fleeing from the invaders, Volker didn't have a whole lot of choice but to surrender. His *Panther* was laid out on the tundra, most of its rear armor burned away by a double PPC blast, and two Clan 'Mechs were moving in for the kill. With his 'Mech's head resting against the ground, he couldn't even bail out. The best his ejection system would do is slam him into the ground and probably break every bone in his body. Volker was a survivor. He wasn't willing to commit suicide for the defense of a frozen rockball like Kore, not like Lieutenant Holt. He'd fought until his dying breath for nothing. The invaders still controlled Kore anyway. No, Volker was alive, and he aimed to stay that way.

He broadcast a surrender to the invaders and powered down his 'Mech's systems. For a moment, he thought they would kill him anyway simply on principle, but from all he'd heard about the Clans he didn't think that was their style. It turned out that he was spared. Though his *Panther* was savaged, the most critical sections—such as engine, gyro, and cockpit—were still intact and salvageable; significant salvage by anyone's measure. And no pirate or mercenary would destroy that amount of C-bills if the 'Mech could be salvaged.

Volker was removed from his 'Mech and brought back to the Command and Control Center, which was already under the control of the invaders. They placed him in a room under guard, with the rest of the Lancers who were on duty when the C&C was taken. A few minutes ago the guards had shown up to escort Volker out of the room. He kept his eyes open for opportunities to escape, but there were armed men everywhere and not a whole lot of places to go.

Even if he did manage to disable the guards, then make a run for it and steal a jeep or a hovercraft to make it back to Niffelheim, it wouldn't gain him anything. He figured the invaders would control the city in fairly short order as well. After all, they had 'Mechs and the resources of the command base and they'd neutralized the 'Mechs of the Kore Lancers. All Niffelheim had for protection was some ground vehicles and infantry, no match for the power of the giant death machines. No, it was better to find out all he could about the invaders, keep his eyes open and watch for an opportunity to present itself.

The guards led Volker to another room where a grizzled man with a three-day growth of gray and black beard tossed him a bundle of clothing.

"Get dressed," the man grunted at him. Volker was still wearing what he'd had on in his 'Mech cockpit: a tight-fitting pair of shorts, high boots, and his coolant vest. He shrugged out of the vest and put on the khaki shirt, then pulled the pants on over his shorts. The man handed him a Lancers-issue parka.

"Let's go," he told Volker, who knew better than to ask where. Obviously it was somewhere outside and, for the time being at least, his captors didn't want him to freeze to death. That was useful information in and of itself.

The guards brought him just outside the Command Center, where the broad ferrocrete compound stretched between it and the 'Mech bay, now empty. Two of the invading BattleMechs were in the compound, the *Fenris* and the *Mad Cat*. Volker had been around BattleMechs for years, but he was still in awe of the size of the fearsome *Mad Cat*, standing no more than fifty meters away from him. Usually he only saw another 'Mech this close up from the cockpit of his own 'Mech or a simulator. Seeing one in person from the ground made him realize how tiny he was in comparison, how easily that 'Mech could crush him, like an insect, underfoot.

The *Mad Cat* came closer, covering the distance in a couple of giant strides that shook the ground and made Volker's heart rise into his throat. The 'Mech stopped a scant five meters away and seemed to be looking down on him. Then the cockpit hissed open and a figure emerged. Although the newcomer was wrapped in a long, hooded coat designed to protect against the bitterly cold wind whistling across the compound, Volker was sure he caught a glimpse of shapely, muscular legs clad only in a tight-fitting pair of shorts as the figure descended the chain ladder hanging from the cockpit of the *Mad Cat*.

Reaching the ground, the pilot of the *Mad Cat* turned and came toward Volker, clutching the coat against the cold. Dark hair spilled from inside the hood, framing a face that was both cruel and beautiful, and as cold as the wind cutting across the tundra. Her features were pale and flawless, except for the black eye-patch that covered one eye, the faint edges of an old scar peeking out from either side of it. Under the coat, Volker could see that she wore the fairly standard MechWarrior uniform of shorts, combat boots, and a tank top under her coolant vest. What he could see of her body was clearly in excellent shape, but Volker remained captivated by her face and the penetrating gaze of her good eye, which was a pale, icy blue.

She stopped just a meter or so in front of him, looking him up and down. It was Volker who spoke first.

"Susie Ryan," he said, then just as quickly regretted it when a rifle butt slammed into his gut. He doubled over, crouching on the cold ferrocrete, and tried not to retch.

"So," Ryan said with a wicked smile, "my reputation precedes me, even out in the hind-end of the galaxy. If you know me, 'Mech-boy, you should know better than to speak unless you're spoken to. Don't forget that *I'm* the one who's in charge here and the only reason you're still alive is because your 'Mech is worth a hundred times more than your worthless hide."

She scarcely raised her voice the entire time, but Volker got the message loud and clear. He slowly got back to his feet, never taking his eyes off Ryan the entire time.

Susie Morgraine Ryan, the legendary pirate queen of the Periphery. The daughter of two of the most infamous pirate-mercenaries in the region of space on the outskirts of the Inner Sphere, orphaned by the Clan invasion.

"I might be more valuable than you think," Volker started.

The guard raised his weapon again, but Ryan stayed him with a wave of her hand. "Oh? And just how do you think *you* might be useful to me?" she said, arching the brow over her good eye.

Volker tried to offer the most convincing smile he could, the one he'd used to win over many a local girl in Niffelheim, although he doubted it would melt the heart of an ice queen like "One-Eye" Ryan.

"I know Kore," he said. "I've lived here all my life, and I'm a trained MechWarrior."

Ryan smirked. For a moment, Volker thought she was going to make some disparaging comment on his abilities as a MechWarrior, considering the fact that he was in her custody. Instead, she looked him up and down, like she was sizing him up.

"Hmmm, you might just be useful at that," she said, almost to herself. "But what about your loyalty to your unit, to your home? You said you grew up here. You should know that I'll lay waste to this entire rock if that's what it takes to get what I want. What do you think about that?"

Volker swallowed. Ryan's voice never wavered from a polite conversational tone while she talked about mass mayhem and destruction. Still, what did it matter to him? His parents were dead, killed during the Clan invasion, and he had no other family on Kore, no one who really mattered. All he wanted was a way off this desolate iceball and into the Inner Sphere where things were really happening. He'd believed that the Kore Lancers were his ticket, but they were done. As far as he knew, he was all that was left of the unit, apart from the ground-pounders.

"I think you're a woman who always gets what she wants," Volker answered carefully. Ryan favored him with her wicked smile again. "It doesn't matter to me what you do with this place. I just want out of here."

"Good attitude," Ryan said. She looked around at the desolate, snow-covered terrain. "I can see why you're not too sentimental about this ice cube. What a pit."

That piqued Volker's curiosity. "Then why come here? And why the Clan-marked 'Mechs?"

"You're just full of questions, aren't you?" Ryan countered. For a moment, Volker thought he'd made a mistake, but Ryan simply folded her arms across her chest.

"Well, the 'Mechs are a little something I've got to show for busting so many Clan heads. They sure as hell strike the fear of God into people, and if they chalk things up to another Clan raid rather than to little ol' me, so much the better. As for the rest, all in good—"

A beeping sound interrupted, and Ryan pulled a small field communicator from inside her coat and held it near her lips.

"Ryan, go."

"Cap'n, this is Yaeger, we caught up with the last local 'Mech, the *Thorn*."

Kintaro, Volker thought. He knew the kid would never manage to get away. He shouldn't even have hoped it.

"Report."

"We're in the mountains, about twenty klicks out from the 'Mech base. The *Thorn*'s totaled, coupla hits and the reactor went critical, but before he went down the damn git triggered some kind of avalanche up here in the mountains, buried Darnell's *Puma* under a ton of snow. He's okay, but it knocked him flat. We're diggin' him out now."

"What about the *Thorn* pilot?" Ryan asked.

"Looks like he bailed out. I saw the hatch blow off before the 'Mech blew. You want us to look for him?"

Ryan considered for only a second before replying. "No, don't bother. No need to waste the ammo. If he bailed out that far away from here, the weather will take care of him for us. And even if he does manage to make it back here somehow, he'll have to surrender to us anyway. Get Darnell's 'Mech out of there and tell him if there's any damage to it I'm going to take it all out of his hide. Ryan out."

She pocketed the communicator and turned back to Volker.

"Well, it sounds like the rest of your lance is accounted for. Too bad about the 'Mech, but that's what happens when you're stupid." She studied him for a moment. "What's your name?" she asked suddenly.

"Volker. Lon Volker."

"Well, Volker, you're not an idiot, I'll give you that. You know when to give up and how to stay alive. Keep acting smart and you might just manage to live through this.

"Put him back with the others," Ryan told the guards. "I may want to talk with him later." She turned her attention back to Volker. "You'll get your chance to prove your worth to me, 'Mechboy, sooner or later."

As the guards led him away, Volker looked out across the tundra at the distant peaks of the Jotun Mountains and thought about Kintaro out there, alone and without his 'Mech. *Personally, I hope you managed to splatter your brains against a rock or something, kid. I sure as hell wouldn't want to die like you will otherwise.*

No. Lon Volker was a survivor, and he meant to get out of this alive, no matter what.

9

Jotun Mountains
Kore
The Periphery
11 April 3060

It was Sturm's shivering that woke him. As the dark haze around his brain slowly cleared, consciousness returned, and with it, the realization of his situation. In those first few moments of awareness, Sturm knew he was probably a dead man.

He woke up on a ledge a decent way up the side of the valley. He had no idea if he'd guided his ejection module there or if it had been mere dumb luck. He was still strapped into the padded command chair that had launched free from his dying 'Mech. It was lying on its side and the straps were digging unpleasantly into Sturm's shoulders and there was stabbing pain in his left side. He reached up and disengaged the release buckle, sliding out of the chair onto the frozen rock. When he tried to roll over and stand up, the pain in his side turned into white-hot needles poking into his shoulder joint.

Damn! I must have wrenched my arm good in that fall, he thought. He carefully probed his left shoulder and upper arm where the pain was focused. Nothing felt broken, so it was probably just a sprain or a pulled muscle. He tried to roll over again, this time favoring his other side and cradling his injured arm against his body. He was able to sit up and take stock of the situation. Other than the sprained arm, all he had were minor cuts and bruises from the bail-out and the landing. All things considered, he was damn lucky.

When he looked down into the valley, however, Sturm didn't consider himself quite so fortunate. The remains of his 'Mech lay there, still smoking. The overload of the *Thorn*'s small fusion reactor didn't leave much more than a tangled mess of burned and melted limbs and a big blackened hole where the 'Mech's torso used to be. Whatever the reactor didn't wreck, the detonation of the 'Mech's remaining missile ammo probably did. Even if he'd been able to climb down there, Sturm was certain there was nothing worth salvaging from his old 'Mech. The only good thing was that the Clan invaders wouldn't get anything, either.

Sturm looked up toward the other side of the valley. The tons of snow from the avalanche he'd triggered had been dug up and melted, leaving a half-frozen mess of slush and jagged ice. Deep depressions showed where the Clan 'Mechs had passed through but, other than that, there was no sign of them. Clearly the *Puma* had dug itself out, probably with some help from the *Uller,* and then both 'Mechs withdrew.

Sturm started to wonder how long he'd been out and realized he was still shivering violently. The temperature was well below freezing, and he was clad only in a thin pair of shorts and his coolant vest. His extremities were already starting to feel numb, and Sturm knew he was in serious danger of frostbite unless he got himself under some shelter, and fast.

Leaning on his fallen command chair for support, Sturm pulled himself slowly to his feet and went around to check his emergency supplies. *Thank god, they're still here,* he thought as he pulled out the narrow box from under the back of the chair. In it was a rolled-up pair of insulated pants, which he quickly pulled on over his boots and shorts, and a lightweight, insulated jacket that he put on over his coolant vest. Without the circulation pumps running, the vest would actually help to trap some of his body heat as it warmed the liquid inside the tubes, so Sturm left it on as he rummaged through the survival kit for anything else that might be of use. He took the emergency kit, including the medical supplies, and drew the web belt that held it around his waist. He also had his laser pistol and the combat knife in his boot-top, both of which had managed to stay with him during his ejection from the *Thorn.*

Properly equipped, Sturm started to consider the question of shelter next. Although he was feeling a bit warmer already, it would be nightfall soon, and then the temperature would *really* start to drop. There was no way he could remain outside and survive. He needed some place out of the wind where he might possibly build a fire.

He very briefly considered the *Thorn*. No, there wasn't enough left of the 'Mech to give him shelter, even if Sturm could risk climbing down into the valley to reach it. He also thought about trying to build an igloo or an ice shelter. He'd had to learn to do so during the arctic survival course that was required for all of the Lancers on Kore, but again, he wasn't sure about climbing down into the valley.

His only other option was to climb up. The sides of the valley were fairly steep and he didn't have any climbing gear, plus his sprained arm would slow him up. Sturm knew from his father's research, however, that the Jotun Mountains were riddled with caves and tunnels. The elder Kintaro spoke often of the many geological features on Kore that were volcanic in nature. The mountains were full of old lava tunnels and steam vents, often with spectacular crystal and metallic formations. Sturm could take shelter in one of those and, if he was lucky, he might find a live steam vent or hot spring to which he could draw close enough to stay warm without boiling himself alive. That would give him a chance to consider what to do next.

For a moment, as he stood on the ledge, looking up the rock face, the enormity of his situation almost overwhelmed him. Even if he did find shelter, he was still stranded nearly two dozen klicks from home base in a hostile environment, with the Clan raiders awaiting him back home. Assuming they didn't simply massacre everyone and. . . .

No! He shook his head to clear it. There was nothing to be gained by such thoughts. He had to focus on the matter at hand. He remembered what Krenner had taught him. *"First, stay alive, then you can worry about your other problems."* Sturm gritted his teeth and started making his way up the rock face.

It was slow going. Several times, he nearly lost his grip on the slippery rocks and fell, but he managed to hold on. After only a few minutes his shoulder was throbbing and burning with pain, but Sturm grabbed hold of the pain like he'd been taught and used it to keep goading himself upward, to keep himself awake and alert. The pain was like a wave of warmth spreading through the rest of his body. In a strange sort of way, it was almost pleasant.

Sturm pulled himself up onto another ledge and flopped down to rest there for a few moments. He couldn't take long; it was already starting to get dark. If he stopped for too long, he might not be able to get back up again. He had no idea how long he'd been climbing, but it seemed like an eternity. He just lay for a moment on his side, his breath puffing small clouds of mist in the frigid air.

Suddenly, Sturm heard something nearby, a low, growling noise. He lay perfectly still for a moment, trying to figure out where the sound was coming from, then suddenly realized he was lying on top of the laser pistol strapped to his hip. As he started to roll over, Sturm looked up and saw a large, white-furred shape emerge from a dark cleft in the rock face. It was big, almost as big as

Sturm was, walking on all fours and covered in pale fur that matched the patches of snow on the ledge. It had a long snout filled with sharp white teeth and framed by black lips and a black nose as it began to snarl and bare its fangs.

A winter wolf! Sturm thought. They were a local Koran life form. The eggheads in life sciences speculated that they, along with several other life-forms, had been introduced to Kore centuries ago by a failed colony, engineered from Terran stock to survive in the harsh wilderness. Winter wolves were some of the largest, most savage predators on Kore, equipped with broad paws that let them race across fields of packed snow in pursuit of their prey and to navigate the rough terrain of the mountains where they sometimes laired. The wolf was less than four meters away from Sturm, and it looked hungry. Winter wolves didn't normally attack settlements, but they were known to attack people alone out in the wilderness.

And I must look like the lame member of the herd, Sturm thought. He rolled over slowly and carefully, reaching for his laser pistol. He popped open the holster and wrapped the numb fingers of one hand around the grip. With one arm sprained, he had to use his off-hand to draw the pistol. As the wolf growled gain, Sturm threw himself to the side and yanked the pistol out of its holster as fast as he could.

The wolf charged. Sturm fired. The laser scored across the animal's right flank with a crack of superheated air and the smell of burning fur and flesh. The hundred-kilo beast crashed into Sturm, and the two of them went rolling across the ledge, perilously close to the edge.

Sturm tried to stiff-arm the wolf in the throat, but his bad arm was too weak to pull the move off effectively. The wolf lunged for his throat, its fangs bared, and Sturm managed to bring up his laser and fire again. A glowing ruby beam of light speared out, lancing directly through the winter wolf's neck. There was a terrible sizzling sound following the crack of the laser beam, then the wolf's howl of pain was cut short as the beam cauterized its throat and vocal cords. A massive weight slumped onto Sturm's chest, and he fought down the urge to gag from the smell of burning fur and flesh.

Sturm managed to kick the winter wolf's body off of him, rolling to the side. He lay there, gasping for breath, then checked to see if he was hurt. The wolf's claws and teeth had left some minor cuts and gashes on his arms, and he had a long, bloody scratch where the wolf's rear claws tore his pants, but otherwise he was unhurt.

Kintaro, you are one lucky bastard, he thought. Better get moving before he started pushing his luck too much, though. He managed to get back on his feet and stood looking down at the dead body of the winter wolf before he remembered something.

He looked back toward the dark cleft where the wolf first appeared. A cave! A cave meant shelter, and warmth, and survival. Of course, if the winter wolf was using it as a den, the cave might also mean the additional danger of a mate or cubs, but at that point Sturm was past caring and not too choosy. He moved over to the dark opening and crouched down to crawl inside. The failing light from outside the cave showed that it was fairly narrow—Sturm's outstretched arms could touch either side—but it extended back into the mountain a good distance, fading into darkness. The floor of the cave was worn smooth and littered with the bones of some of the winter wolf's kills.

Working almost on auto-pilot, Sturm set up a small proximity sensor from his survival kit near the cave entrance and used his laser to heat a small pile of loose rocks to provide some warmth. Then he collapsed, slumping up against the wall. He knew that he should clean the cuts from his fight with the winter wolf as soon as possible, and that he should probably try and treat his injured arm, but he was too tired to even care. His last thoughts before sleep claimed him were to hope that the wolf was alone and to wonder why the Clans would want to return to claim Kore. Then everything was swallowed up by oblivion.

10

Niffelheim
Kore
The Periphery
11 April 3060

Laura Metz's world was being turned upside-down, and there wasn't a whole lot she could do about it. As she stood in the narrow alleyway, her breath making frosty clouds in the air in front of her, she tried to gather her wits and figure out what to do next. They were supposed to fall back to some defensible buildings further into the city, but was there really any defense against something like *that*?

Four Clan BattleMechs were moving into the city. They were led by a massive seventy-five-ton *Mad Cat*, a hunched-over design with club-like arms, bristling with heavy weapons. Alongside came a *Fenris*, a *Puma*, and an *Uller*. The *Puma* and the *Uller* were similar to the *Mad Cat*; hunched over, with birdlike feet that shook the ground as they moved. The *Fenris* was a blocky, humanoid design, one arm ending in a hand and topped with a missile-launcher, the other arm ending in the barrel of a particle projection cannon.

Laura was a ground-pounder, a member of the Kore Lancers' small infantry division, and one of the few who happened to be in Niffelheim when the whole thing hit the fan. Most of the Lancer personnel were unavailable. They were either being held prisoner at the command base or they were already dead. Laura thought about some of her friends who were on duty and what might have happened to them, but there was no time for grief or worry. The primary concern was survival, and the chances for that looked slim.

The Clan BattleMechs had attacked without warning, seizing control of the command base and destroying or disabling Kore's own BattleMech defenders. Without 'Mechs, or the mechanized infantry vehicles kept at the base, all the city of Niffelheim had to defend itself was a small collection of vehicles, some off-duty soldiers, and a scant local militia that was poorly trained and equipped. Against the might of four of the most powerful war machines ever devised by human technology, they didn't have a prayer.

Still, Sergeant Krenner had organized the remaining troops to mount a defense of Niffelheim when the Clan BattleMechs came to the city, and come they did, shortly after nightfall. Their running lights made the fearsome 'Mechs clearly visible as they crossed the few kilometers between Niffelheim and the Lancer base. Some of the infantry was set up on the outskirts, armed with short-range missile launchers, heavy machine guns, and whatever else they could find in the armory. Weak weapons against multi-ton walking tanks packing lasers and PPCs, but it was all they had.

Laura watched the 'Mechs approach, moving almost sedately toward the city. They were in no hurry, and they had to know the demoralizing effect the sight of such huge war machines would have on the troops and the locals. They took their time. After all, there was nowhere for anybody to run. Niffelheim was the sole city on Kore, and the rest of the planet was icy wasteland and wilderness. People were trapped in the city, just waiting for the 'Mechs to arrive.

Krenner ordered everyone to hold their fire until the 'Mechs got into optimum range; ammo was precious and not to be wasted. The BattleMechs grew larger and larger as they got closer and closer to the city, until Krenner gave the order to fire.

Several of the SRM launchers were loaded with inferno rounds. The rockets covered the 'Mechs with sticky, flaming gel that damaged their armor and forced their heat sinks to work overtime to deal with the tremendous heat. The infernos sent great clouds of steam rising into the frigid night air of Kore, but they barely even slowed the 'Mechs down. The raider machines took the worst the Lancers had to throw at them and kept coming.

Retaliation was swift. Laserfire from the raider 'Mechs swept through the ranks of the troops. Even the lightest 'Mech laser was capable of nearly vaporizing a human being; all the water in the body instantly turned to steam, and people struck by the lasers literally exploded, instantly turned to charred ash and bones. Laura saw several of her comrades burned up by the hellish green bolts of light that swept across the battlefield. An autocannon blast from the *Uller* destroyed a jeep, flipping it up into the air to land some eight meters away, torn to shreds by the high-explosive shells.

Sergeant Krenner ordered a retreat almost immediately, and Niffelheim's defenders fell back into the city itself. The streets were mined with explosives in various places, designed to be tripped only by something as large as a BattleMech. The blasts destroyed several buildings, and Laura saw one of the 'Mechs—she thought it was the *Uller*—falter a bit, staggered by the collapsing rubble before it righted itself. The four enemy machines kept wading through whatever was thrown at them, like unstoppable juggernauts. They just kept coming.

The Lancers resorted to urban street-fighting techniques, sniping at the 'Mechs with machine guns and man-portable inferno launchers. They were like a swarm of insects, stinging the metal giants wherever they could to force them to retreat. Occasionally, a BattleMech would swat at the troopers, demolishing a building with a sweep of one giant arm, or annihilating its targets in a blaze of laserfire. It wasn't long before the remaining troops were in full retreat, ordered by Sergeant Krenner to fall back to the government buildings in the heart of the city. There they would make their last stand against the invaders.

Laura turned the corner of the alley and looked

out into the street. It was mostly deserted. Alarm sirens whined in the distance and she could make out one of the 'Mechs, standing just taller than the nearby buildings, slowly lumbering through the streets several blocks away. The footfalls of the giant machines shook the ground as they moved, like the rapid beating of Laura's own heart. Clutching her assault rifle tightly, she began running down the street, stopping to duck into alleys and doorways to check for any signs of the approaching 'Mechs or indications that they had ground troops following them into the city. There didn't appear to be any.

Thank God for small favors, she thought, as she made sure the coast was clear again before making a mad dash to another doorway. The outer areas of the city had already been evacuated, the soldiers were the only ones left. Laura managed to get separated from the rest of her small unit when a building nearly collapsed on them. In the chaos and confusion, with the dust and smoke filling the air and one of the Clan 'Mechs hot on their heels, the Lancers scattered and Laura found herself alone, making her way through an abandoned section of the city.

Suddenly, she saw bright lights coming quickly down the street. For a second, she thought it might be an approaching 'Mech, but they were headlights from a small vehicle. Laura decided to take a chance that it wasn't the Clans sending their own vehicles into the city and stepped out of the shadows to flag the vehicle down. It came to a quick stop a few meters away, and she ran up to the passenger-side door.

The older Japanese man behind the wheel looked at her in surprise. A civilian? What the hell was he doing out here?

"Sir," she began, "what are you . . . ?"

The man just shook his head.

"Get in," he said. Laura sure as hell wasn't going to argue. She pulled open the door and climbed into the small hovercar. She'd barely had time to settle into the seat before the driver accelerated again and they shot off down the street.

"Thanks, Mr. . . . ?"

"Doctor, actually," he said. "Dr. Hidoshi Kintaro."

"Corporal Laura Metz," she returned, sliding her rifle onto the seat where she could get at it. "You must be with the geoplanetary research division. I thought all of you people were evacuated already."

The doctor grimaced a bit. "We were, but I couldn't leave behind all of my notes and research materials." He gestured to several plastic boxes stacked in the back seat. "They represent years of work. I couldn't risk them being destroyed."

"You risked your life for a bunch of research data?" Laura asked. *This guy must be tougher than he looks*, she thought.

Dr. Kintaro just nodded.

"Where are we headed?" Laura asked.

"To the government center. That's where everyone is being evacuated to, isn't it?"

"Yeah, for all the good it'll . . . LOOK OUT!"

As the hovercar turned a corner, a giant metal foot slammed down into the street almost in front of them. It was the *Puma*, looming overhead, its flattened torso swiveling toward them.

Kintaro slammed the wheel hard to the side, sending the vehicle skittering around the giant foot and shooting through the intersection. He floored the accelerator and the hovercar shot ahead down the empty street, turbofans whining.

The *Puma* turned and, like a predator attracted by the sudden flight of its prey, began to follow.

"He's coming after us!" Laura yelled over the roar of the engine.

"I can see that!" Dr. Kintaro shouted back. "He's also cut us off from our most direct route to the center. We'll have to go around."

"Cut through there!" Laura said, pointing to a side street. Fortunately, Dr. Kintaro wasn't in the mood to argue. He simply slammed the hovercar into a hard right-hand turn, the rear fishtailing for a moment before coming back under control. The 'Mech would have a harder time taking such a sharp turn, and they might be able to lose it in the maze of narrow city streets. Laura only thanked God the *Puma* wasn't using its massive PPCs; one blast from them could turn the vehicle into smoking fragments.

He isn't bothering, Laura thought. *He's playing with us, like a cat with a cornered mouse and he doesn't want to spoil his fun. That was, until he got bored with the chase, then he'd probably vaporize them, car and all.*

The hovercar slid sharply through another turn as the *Puma* came down the street. The 'Mech was moving at a decent clip, occasionally brushing past buildings, knocking down walls, and crushing everything else in its path. It was heedless of everything except its quarry, and Laura thought they might be able to use that to their advantage.

"Over there!" she shouted to Dr. Kintaro. "Through that street!" The doctor compliantly took the turn and sped down the street. Laura narrowed her eyes and tried to pierce the darkness that cloaked the city. With all the lights out, there was nothing to help her see but the headlamps of the vehicle. It should be right about . . . there. She spotted it, a narrow wire strung between two buildings about three meters off the ground. The *Puma* was closing in as the hovercar sped under the wire down the street.

"Stay low and hold onto your hat, Doc," she said as the BattleMech raced down the street after them.

Moments later the *Puma* hit the wire and triggered the explosive charges planted by the Lancer troops earlier. The shaped charges blew outward, and the force of the blast rocked the street. Chunks of masonry and shrapnel pelted the BattleMech, and the walls on either side of the street collapsed, raining ferrocrete down on the *Puma* and kicking up a thick cloud of dust.

Caught off guard, the *Puma* was moving too fast when it hit the blast. It stepped forward, and its mammoth foot came down on a mass of rubble, thrown off balance by the force of the explosion. The *Puma* pitched forward and slammed into the pavement with a loud crash, heavy chunks of debris pelting its vulnerable back armor.

"Whooo-HOO!" Laura whooped at the sight of the fallen BattleMech. "Take that, you Clan bastard!" The blast and the fall certainly wouldn't have disabled the *Puma*, but it would take the pilot a little while to right his 'Mech and get it back on its feet, and they'd at least done some damage.

"Very clever," Dr. Kintaro said with a wry smile. Laura returned it with a grin of her own. Her teeth were very white against her sweat- and grime-streaked face.

"Unfortunately, a celebration may be a bit premature," the doctor said as the hovercar turned the corner into the government center and nearly ran straight into the towering legs of the seventy-five-ton *Mad Cat*. The monster BattleMech tilted downward to look at them, and Laura thought she could almost see the damn thing smiling.

11

Jotun Mountains
Kore
The Periphery
12 April 3060

Sturm woke up the next morning knowing he wasn't dead. *Being dead couldn't possibly hurt this much*, he thought. He was cold and stiff and sore from his night in the cave, but he was also grateful to be alive, and his injuries didn't seem too severe in the light of day, which came pouring in through the entrance of the cave.

He gingerly levered himself up into a sitting position and hauled the emergency medical kit out of his survival pack. First aid and field medicine were part of the training drilled into him from the beginning of his apprenticeship with the Lancers, and Sturm was grateful for it now. He carefully cleaned and dressed the cuts and scratches he'd received from the ejection and from the winter wolf's claws, hoping the claws weren't dirty enough to cause an infection. The antibiotics from the kit should help take care of that, however. He also taped up his arm—mildly sprained rather than broken—and began to take stock of his situation.

It was pretty bleak. His 'Mech was destroyed. He might be able to make it down to where the remains of it lay and salvage a bit more useful gear, but it was doubtful much would have survived the reactor overload. Even if he did go back, he'd have to make his way back down into the valley with an injured arm, and it was likely the avalanche he'd triggered against the *Puma* had left other parts of the snow-packed slopes unstable. Plus, if the enemy was out looking for him, they would certainly start with the remains of his 'Mech, although at this point, Sturm highly doubted anyone was out looking, friend or foe. He was on his own.

He was cut off from the command base. His small comm unit couldn't carry far enough through the interference of the magnetic fields and metallic ores in the mountains to reach it, assuming there were any members of the Lancers still alive to reach. Even then, the frequencies would all be monitored by the enemy and they would find out that he was alive, and probably be able to figure out where he was. Then again, capture was looking like a pretty good option at this point, he thought glumly. At least then he'd probably be warm and fed.

He pulled a ration bar out of his survival pack and tore it open, chewing slowly on the pastelike food concentrate while he thought. It tasted like wet cardboard and did little to settle the rumbling in Sturm's stomach. He sincerely wished he hadn't

skipped lunch before his training session yesterday. He'd been looking forward to a decent dinner
after off-loading the cargo from the *Tammuz*. How
far away that time and those concerns seemed, in
light of his current situation.

I might be able to reach Niffelheim on foot, he
thought. It would be a long trek across the frozen
tundra of Kore to get there, more than twenty kilometers, and the terrain was full of snow-covered
crevasses and pitfalls that, while they were no
more than potholes to a BattleMech, could become
deathtraps for someone on foot. *Still, I can't hide
out in a cave forever and hope someone comes and finds
me*, Sturm thought. His filtration canteen and all
the snow in the mountains could provide him
with fresh water almost indefinitely, but the ration
bars would only last a few days, maybe as much
as a week if he stretched them out carefully. After
that there would be nothing to eat unless he
started hunting. His thoughts turned briefly to the
carcass of the winter wolf he'd killed outside, assuming that other scavengers hadn't already taken
it. It wasn't a pleasant thought, but when it came
to survival, unpleasant things were sometimes
necessary.

A concern even more important than food was
the fact that his laser pistol had only a limited
charge. It was his only weapon, apart from the
combat knife in his boot-sheath, and his only
means of staying warm. He might be able to
gather some wood from the trees and scrub in the
mountains to build a fire, but out on the tundra
there was nothing to burn. His lightweight cold-

weather gear wasn't suited for long-term exposure, either.

Going back to the city and getting captured definitely beats out freezing or starving to death, he thought. That was, of course, assuming the Clan invaders weren't simply planning to slaughter everyone on Kore just on principle, in which case Sturm could be walking right into his own execution. Still, a quick, clean death was better than slow starvation or exposure. Sturm also didn't think the clans would kill people without cause. They would definitely kill without mercy; almost everyone on Kore had lost someone to the last Clan invasion. But it wasn't in their character to kill without a reason.

In fact, the more Sturm thought about it, the less the whole invasion seemed to add up. Why would Clan Jade Falcon invade Kore? Yes, their occupied territory was closest to the planet, but what value could Kore have to them? He grabbed his canteen and made his way over to the entrance of the cave while he thought about it. Scooping up some patches of snow near the cave mouth, he filled the top chamber of the canteen. The snow would melt and the filters in the canteen would provide clean water to quench his thirst and wash the taste of the ration bar out of his mouth.

The last Clan invaders were from Clan Steel Viper, Sturm knew. Perhaps Clan Jade Falcon invading Kore was some sort of matter of honor. The Vipers had failed to hold it, so another Clan had to step in. The Clans had very elaborate codes of honorable behavior, and they often seemed to be trying to one-up each other. Still, it seemed like a minor victory at best, capturing a mining world protected by a single lance of light 'Mechs. The Clans liked their victories to be more challenging. Or so Sturm had heard.

The way the raid came off seemed all wrong, too. When the Steel Vipers had invaded ten years ago, they didn't try to conceal their arrival, or to surprise their enemy. Their DropShips simply landed on Kore and the Clan BattleMechs and Elementals moved in, taking whatever they wanted. Sturm recalled reading that the Clan commander had even gone so far as to send a message to Sturm's mother, who'd been commander of the Kore Lancers then, asking where she wished to do battle and what forces she intended to bring. It was all very straightforward: no deception to it at all. So why hijack an old DropShip like the *Tammuz* and use it rather than a Clan DropShip or even an atmospheric drop of BattleMechs from high-altitude to the surface?

And there were only four 'Mechs, Sturm thought. The Inner Sphere armies arranged BattleMechs in groups of four to make up a "lance," the smallest BattleMech unit. The clans didn't use the lance arrangement. Their units were made up of "stars" of five 'Mechs, not four. *So why only four 'Mechs on board the* Tammuz? *Maybe there was a fifth 'Mech I didn't see,* Sturm thought, but that seemed unlikely. *Why would one of the 'Mechs stay inside the DropShip? Perhaps it was some Clan idea of honor, pitting only four 'Mechs against the Lancers' four, but it still didn't add up.*

Sturm knew he wasn't going to get anywhere just sitting around here thinking about it. He was just delaying the inevitable. What he had to do now was to figure out his next move and it looked like he didn't have much choice. He had to get back to Niffelheim, maybe hook up with some of the militia or something like that, assuming he could even make it back without getting caught, or killed.

He decided to try and salvage the pelt of the winter wolf and use it for additional warmth. He might also be able to cure some of the meat and take it with him, just in case. He doubted it would taste very good, but it had to be better than the ration bars. Pulling his light coat tightly around him, he emerged from the cave into the bright morning sunlight. The air was cold, but the wind wasn't too strong.

The other predators had apparently left the winter wolf's corpse alone. It lay on the ledge where Sturm had left it, quite frozen. He grabbed it by the back paws and dragged it into the cave. It would need to thaw out a bit before he could do anything with it, so he also gathered some wood and scrub brush from outside and used it to start a small fire. His laser was able to get the damp wood burning, the fire sending up a steady stream of smoke. It was possible that someone might see the smoke, but Sturm wasn't too worried. He doubted the raiders would be anywhere near the mountains.

They've probably already moved on the city, he thought, or they will be soon.

He also decided to explore further into the cave to see if the winter wolf's lair contained anything usable, either bones or the possibility of a hot spring to provide some warmth. The cave was fairly narrow and extended back for some distance into the rock, far enough that Sturm needed the small flashlight from his survival pack to see clearly.

The light glimmered off something at the rear of the cave, and Sturm moved toward it carefully. At first he thought it was ice or some kind of crystal or metallic deposit, but as he drew closer he could see that it was a metallic wall, stretching from floor to ceiling and side to side, curved outward slightly, like the side of a metal cylinder.

What the hell . . . ? Sturm thought. He knocked on it gently, and the sound seemed to echo inside. It was probably hollow. There was no apparent way around or through it. It was solid metal, with no seams or joints visible. *Who would put something like this here, and why,* he wondered, running a gloved hand over the cold metal. Sturm briefly thought it might have something to do with the mineral surveys, but he'd never heard his father mention anything like this, and Sturm had worked many of the surveys in this area of the mountains. He'd never been asked to place anything or to check up on any kind of instrumentation like this. Besides, the metal extended straight up and down into the solid rock. It would take something like an industrial laser to cut through the rock for something like this.

Suddenly, Sturm's options expanded. *Could this have something to do with why the Jade Falcons had decided to come here,* he wondered. Whatever lay behind the metallic wall might be something useful, might even give Sturm a better chance of survival. He decided to investigate.

The metal was completely smooth and showed no signs of any way through it. There were no apparent mechanisms or ways of opening it, so Sturm decided the only way he was going to find out what was on the other side was by cutting through it. He set his laser on a low setting and began using the beam as a cutting torch. It sliced through the metal like a hot knife as he slowly traced a roughly circular path, cutting a hole almost a meter wide, going from one side of the wall to another. The work was painstaking, and Sturm had to hold the laser in his good hand. Finally, he finished and quickly stepped back as the cut part fell out onto the floor with a loud clanging sound that echoed in the dim cave.

Sturm shined his light through the hole. The metal was part of a cylinder all right. It was some kind of shaft, sunk through the stone of the mountain. A cold, gentle breeze flowed out from the newly cut hole, and the cut edges were already beginning to cool. Sturm carefully avoided them as he stuck his head into the shaft to get a better look. The shaft extended off into darkness up and down. The flow of air seemed to be moving downward, making him wonder if it wasn't a ventilation shaft of some kind. Sturm had seen similar things in Niffelheim's mines—but ventilation for what?

There was only one way to find out for sure. He checked and found the edges of the hole cool enough to touch. Slinging his survival pack in front of his body, Sturm swung one leg, then the other, over the edge of the hole. Bracing his feet against one side of the shaft and his back and shoulders against the other, he'd be able to climb down it slowly. He wished briefly for some rope in his survival pack, but there was none. He'd have to manage without it. Still, the shaft wasn't too wide, so he could climb down this way, provided it didn't widen or narrow much.

He'd probably end up breaking his fool neck, but the shaft represented a complete wild card in his whole situation. He couldn't pass up on finding out what it was for. It might just provide him a way out of all this.

Ouch, easy does it there. Sturm's sprained arm started to throb a bit and he tried to use mostly his good one, pressing it against the side of the shaft as he started to slowly shuffle downward, like a crab or a spider crawling on the inside of a pipe. The metal was icy cold to the touch, and his skin quickly began to feel numb from rubbing against it, but the exertion of the climb helped to keep him warm and Sturm soon found himself sweating under his winter gear.

He went down a good eight meters or so, he estimated, the faint light from the hole above fading quickly. The shaft was almost pitch-black, and Sturm didn't have any hands free to hold his flashlight, stowed in his survival kit along with the rest of his gear.

Suddenly the surface of the shaft became colder and Sturm noticed that the metallic walls were becoming covered with a layer of ice, probably accumulated from snow or water coming in from the top of the shaft, wherever the air entered. It was getting slippery as the heat from his body started to melt the surface layer of ice.

Damn! he thought. That would make getting all the way down a lot harder, if not impossible. *Maybe I should head baaaaaaa . . . oh no!* Suddenly Sturm's right foot slipped on an icy patch and he lost his grip against the walls of the shaft. He scrambled to right himself, but he could find no purchase on the ice-covered surface. Pain lanced through his arm as Sturm started sliding down the shaft in a freefall.

Unable to halt or even slow his plunge by much, the young MechWarrior fell into darkness.

Some distance from the cave, on the side of the mountain, a cleverly hidden rock panel slid open. A complex array emerged, unfolding like a metallic flower with dark petals, greeting the sun and the sky. The device whirred and clicked into place with mechanical precision, sending forth a silent call into the void, then folded back into itself, withdrawing into the mountain like it came, the rock closing up behind it, leaving no sign of its presence. Then all was silent once again.

12

Alfin Corporation Research Lab
Niffelheim, Kore
The Periphery
12 April 3060

Doctor Hidoshi Kintaro looked across the room at the woman who was very likely responsible for the death of his son. As of the previous night, Susie Ryan and her pirate crew were the undisputed rulers of the planet Kore, and Doctor Kintaro was among the thousands of people whose lives were controlled by their new conquerors. There was no sign of the MechWarriors of the Kore Lancers, and all reports said that they'd been killed in the pirates' initial attack.

The battle of Niffelheim was over quickly. Although the remnants of the Kore Lancers and the local militia had put up a good fight, they were simply no match for the powerful BattleMechs at Ryan's command. Shortly after Dr. Kintaro and Corporal Metz managed to escape from the *Puma*, the other pirate 'Mechs closed in on the government center and seized control. Dr. Kintaro thought for certain that they were going to be crushed under the heel of the giant *Mad Cat*, but Susie Ryan, unlike some of her followers, knew that needless killing wasted potentially valuable resources.

Still, that didn't mean the pirate queen was any less ruthless. Ryan issued an ultimatum to the planetary governor: surrender, or her 'Mechs would level the city, starting with the most inhabited areas. There wasn't much choice. As with the Clan invaders ten years previously, the government of Kore surrendered to the pirates.

Only then did Ryan's ground troops enter the city. The remaining military forces were quickly rounded up and imprisoned, while the civilian population was allowed to go about their business normally, under the watchful eye of Ryan's own troops. The governor met with Susie Ryan to hear her demands. Surprisingly, one of her first orders as the new ruler of Kore was for the governor to arrange a meeting between her and the director of geoplanetary research, Dr. Kintaro. Ryan smiled when she saw who Kintaro was.

"Ah, Doctor," she said, "you look much taller than you did last night."

Kintaro was amazed that Ryan actually remembered him from when her 'Mech stopped his hovercar, with himself and Corporal Metz inside. From the high vantage of the *Mad Cat*'s cockpit, they must have looked like ants, but she still managed to recognize him.

Ryan met with the doctor in his office at the geoplanetary research facility. She was accompanied by two guards, but they were ordered to wait outside. Hidoshi briefly considered and discarded the idea of trying something against Ryan; she was here alone and armed only with a holstered pistol at her hip, but he quickly realized there was very little he, a scientist and researcher, could do against a trained soldier and a cold-hearted killer like Ryan. For a moment, he thought of his son and considered whether it might still be worth it.

"What do you want of me?" he said, eyeing Ryan coldly as she picked through some of the scattered papers and survey maps on his desk with a cool mask of disinterest. She brought her gaze up to capture his, her one good eye narrowing. Hidoshi didn't shrink from that withering glare, but sat, straight and tall.

Ryan smiled slightly at his show of defiance and sat down on the edge of the desk. "You've done a great deal of research on this planet, Doctor. What can you tell me about it?"

Dr. Kintaro cleared his throat a bit. He was amazed at how Ryan could speak so casually after having forcibly taken control of an entire city. What was this woman after?

"Well," he began, "Kore is a rocky planet, smaller than Terra, but with a roughly similar gravitation because of the high concentration of metals and heavy minerals in the planet's core and crust. The planet was highly volcanically active at some point in the past, leading to the formation of extensive geological phenomena like the nearby mountain ranges, and exposing some of the metallic deposits and rock strata during earthquakes and eruptions. There is still considerable geological activity, although not nearly as much as must have existed in the past."

Ryan seemed focused intently on his words, so Kintaro continued.

"The planet is rich in various metallic ores, particularly aluminum, iron, nickel, and tungsten. The heavy metallic deposits contribute to Kore's unusually strong magnetic field, which makes survey work more difficult; the magnetic fields interfere with most scanning equipment. Likewise, many areas of the planet are still volcanically active, and active steam vents and lava tubes cause some problems with our infrared and seismic sensors."

"What about life?" Ryan interrupted. "Any native life-forms?"

"Yes, there are some," the doctor said, pushing his chair back from the desk. "Mostly plants and simple animal life, small mammals and such, adapted to exist in the cold environment. There are also life-forms we believe were introduced to the planet and engineered to survive in the environment."

"Introduced? By who?"

"We're not sure. Some Koran life-forms are clearly descended from Terran stock. The genetic similarities are simply too great for it to be anything else. The winter wolf, for example, is a Koran animal engineered from the Terran *lupus*. The animals have been here since long before the start of this colony by the Alfin Corporation, probably a century or more. Our best theory is that they were brought here by other colonists. There are indications Kore was colonized a long time ago. The colony probably wasn't able to survive, but some of the life-forms they introduced into the biosphere were able to do so."

"This . . . colony," Ryan said. "Are there any ruins? Any evidence?"

"Very little," Kintaro replied. "We've found some indications on one of the southern continental plains that may be ruins of some kind on our mapping surveys, but they're buried under a heavy layer of ice and snow. Even close fly-bys can't make out whether or not they're the remains of structures or simply unusual rock formations."

"When would this colony have been here?"

"Difficult to say. Anywhere from a hundred to two hundred years ago, maybe even more. If a jump-drive malfunction caused a colony ship to end up out here, it could have come from almost anywhere. If they were unable to resume their original course, they might have tried to settle here. Honestly, we haven't devoted much effort to it. Alfin Corporation is interested in Kore's metallurgical resources, not in archeology or history, so the whole thing was written off as a minor mystery for us to look into later, once more of the planet was explored." He paused and looked at Ryan. "Is this what you came to Kore for, information about a colony that might once have been here?"

Ryan's good eye again narrowed dangerously.

"I'm the one asking the questions here, Doctor. Your job is simply to answer them, completely and to the best of your ability. As long as you continue to do that, you're useful to me, and that means you get to stay alive, understand?"

Dr. Kintaro nodded, his lips compressed into a grim line. "Yes, I believe I do," he said.

"Good. Now, are there any other signs of habitation on this planet?"

Kintaro shook his head.

"No, none. Niffelheim is the only settlement anywhere on the surface of Kore, and we have satellite scans of the entire planetary surface."

"I'll want to see them," Ryan said. "What about under the surface?"

"Under the surface? Well, as I said, Kore was quite volcanically active in the past. The surface crust is prone to valleys, crevasses, and a large number of caves."

"How many caves?"

The scientist shrugged. "Thousands, perhaps hundreds of thousands. The Jotun Mountain range nearby has numerous caverns, mostly steam vents and ancient volcanic lava tubes, along with glacial formations and openings created by ground-quakes. We've only really started to map and survey them."

"How big are these caves?" Ryan asked. Her questions were becoming more probing, more urgent. Dr. Kintaro sensed that the conversation was drawing closer to the information she was really looking for.

"They vary," he replied. "Some are quite small, nowhere near large enough for a human to fit through. Others are quite large, as many as five to ten meters in diameter, perhaps more."

"I see," Ryan said, leaning back. Her expression was thoughtful as she glanced around at the survey maps tacked up on the walls of the room.

"You said you'd gathered this data using satellite imaging?" she said, gesturing at the maps.

"Most of it, but we performed ground surveys as well, using aircraft . . . and some of the BattleMechs from the Lancers' command base."

"Can our own 'Mechs be used to continue to survey the area?" Ryan asked.

Kintaro shrugged again. "I suppose so. I'm not terribly familiar with the sensor capabilities of Clan BattleMechs, but I must assume they're at least as sophisticated as those used by the Lancers, if not more so. It would require re-tuning the sensors somewhat."

"Good," Ryan said. "That's what you're going to do."

"May I ask what it is we're looking for?" Dr. Kintaro asked.

"Large concentrations of metal, Doctor. I'll give you all the specifications. You and your staff will gather your research information and whatever else you need to make the necessary adjustment to the 'Mech sensors. I'll have you brought out to the command base in one hour."

Ryan turned to leave. She paused at the door, her hand resting on the handle, and glanced back at the scientist.

"If you defy me," she said, "or if I discover that any information you've given me is inaccurate, I will have a member of your staff killed. I'll continue to do so until I get what I want. Is that clear?" Kintaro nodded and Ryan smiled. "Good, I will see you shortly, then. I'm about to give you the opportunity to make quite a discovery, doc."

With that, the pirate queen walked out of Dr.

Kintaro's office and gave her instructions to the guards outside. Hidoshi began gathering his notes and materials and picked up the comm unit to give instructions to his assistants.

He paused for a moment, holding the comm in his hand as he considered his conversation with Ryan. *What is she looking for,* he wondered, *and is it really worth so many lives?* He thought about his wife, and now his son, both killed in the defense of an isolated world on the edge of known space, and he wondered about the point of it all.

Then he opened the commline and began giving instructions. There was a great deal of work to do.

13

Jotun Mountains
Kore
The Periphery
14 April 3060

Karl Yaeger hated grunt work. It was boring, repetitive, and pointless, not the sort of thing for a MechWarrior, even a pirate, to be doing. Hell, he didn't become a MechWarrior to tromp through some frozen wasteland gathering scientific data for a bunch of eggheads. He was trained to pilot the most dangerous war machines of the thirty-first century. His BattleMech carried enough firepower to lay waste to a city, but here he was, playing scout on some frozen hellhole of a planet without any real idea what he was looking for.

On the other hand, Yaeger was a soldier, and he followed orders. Especially when those orders came from a woman like Susie Ryan, his commander and the "queen" of what remained of the Bandit Kingdoms after the Clans blew through them like a hurricane ten years ago. "One-Eye"

Ryan was the toughest and meanest MechWarrior Yaeger had ever met. She'd managed to pull together the remnants of the old Bandit Kingdoms with nothing more than her charisma, strength of will, and keen knowledge of combat tactics, which she'd used to good effect against the Clans.

Ryan's Rebels had managed to pull off several victories against Clan Jade Falcon using inferior 'Mechs and superior cunning. It was those wins that had netted the Rebels 'Mechs like the *Uller* Yaeger piloted now. He had to give them credit; those Clan bastards might not know a thing about being human anymore, but they did build the best 'Mechs, more advanced than anything seen in the Inner Sphere. The *Uller* beat the hell out of the old *Commando* Yaeger used to pilot. He was fond of his old 'Mech, but it had nothing on this baby. Inner Sphere 'Mech designs had fallen behind over centuries of warfare, while the Clans just kept on advancing. It was only now, years after the Clan invasion, that the nations of the Inner Sphere were starting to catch up.

And what do we do with all this hot tech, he wondered. *We use it to take over some iceball out on the edge of nowhere, kick around some light 'Mechs, then spend a few days running surveys and sensor sweeps of a bunch of frozen mountains.* But if Captain Ryan wanted it done, Yaeger would do it. He might not understand it, but he knew the captain had to have some sort of purpose in mind. He'd never known Susie Ryan to lead her men wrong, or to do something without a plan that would net her and the Rebels a tidy profit, probably a major profit, when all was said and done.

Whatever it was, it would be some of the easiest money the Rebels ever earned, that was for sure. The attack on the lance of 'Mechs defending the planet had gone off exactly as planned, smooth as silk. *They never even knew what hit them. Sure, that last 'Mech managed to get away for a little while, but he didn't get too far.*

Yaeger smiled and chuckled, showing a gleaming of gold from one of his teeth as he thought about finishing off the *Thorn. That was a sweet kill. Too bad we didn't get the pilot, too. Still, he has to be dead by now anyway. There's no way anyone could survive on a planet like this with no real supplies and his 'Mech destroyed.* He almost felt sorry for the guy. That wasn't how Yaeger wanted to die, alone and trapped in a frozen hell. If he had to go out, it'd be in a fight. He'd heard there were wolves and other critters living in the mountains, too. The guy might have gotten eaten by something before he ended up freezing to death.

In fact, that wasn't all Yaeger had heard. Some of the techs and even the other MechWarriors had heard a local legend that the Jotun Mountains were haunted. The tale was that, after Clan Steel Viper forces were defeated by the mercenaries who protected Kore, people saw ghostly images of a Clan BattleMech in and around the mountains. They said one of the Clan MechWarriors swore with his dying breath to avenge his own and those of his people, that he haunted the mountains in the dead of night, waiting for the day when his vengeance would come.

The wind howled outside the *Uller's* cockpit, and Yaeger found himself shivering despite the heat inside. The sensor readings showed the outside temperature well below zero. *This planet gives me the creeps,* he thought, checking the scanners again. The modifications made by that Japanese doctor were supposed to help pick up large metallic deposits; he'd said something about them being used to find places to mine ore. Yaeger didn't know what Captain Ryan was looking for with them, but he hoped they'd find it soon so they could boost off this godforsaken place and head for home. Yaeger preferred to be out where the action was, not hanging around these looming black mountains, thinking about old ghost stories. *I mean, it's the thirty-first century. Who the hell believes in ghosts anymore?* Still, he checked his sensors again.

Hey, what was that? Yaeger opened up his commline.

"*Uller* to base. I've picked up some kind of unusual heat trace. Going to check it out."

"Roger that, Yaeger," came the voice over his headset.

"Probably just another steam vent or animal or something," Yaeger said. "I'll let you know. *Uller* out." *This damn planet is making me jumpy,* he thought. *No wonder people think they see ghosts, with all of this magnetic and thermal junk messing up sensor readings.* He was getting false readings by the boatload and this was probably just another one of those. Still, it was something to break up the monotony. He turned the *Uller* around, its massive feet thudding against the frozen ground, and maneuvered it toward the source of the reading.

It was buried under some snow in what looked

to be a good-size crevasse not far from the mountains. That probably made it some kind of steam vent. It had to be, from the amount of heat it was putting out. As the *Uller* came closer, Yaeger wondered what it could be, until he thought about a similar heat trace he'd seen. It was in the mountains, just before the *Thorn* ambushed Darnell's *Puma*. It was the heat trace of a 'Mech buried under a layer of snow to hide its heat signature.

Suddenly, the snow and ice exploded upward and a giant, bone-white BattleMech rose up out of the crevasse like an apparition. It was a Clan 'Mech, a *Goshawk*, bearing the silvery snake-head symbol of Clan Steel Viper. Its heavy shoulder flanges and hooded cockpit made it look like a bird of prey. Its right arm ended in the barrel of a large pulse laser, while its left hand gripped a heavy arrangement of three machine gun barrels. Additional laser and machine gun barrels poked out of the 'Mech's torso, and small, boxy missile packs sat on its shoulders. Framed against the black mountains and the white snow, the pale 'Mech looked like a metallic skeleton, the front of its cockpit painted like a grinning skull.

The *Goshawk* leveled its right-arm laser at the *Uller*. Bolts of hellish green light shot out in rapid succession from the heavy laser and from the two smaller pulse lasers on the 'Mech's right torso. They slammed into the *Uller*, vaporizing armor with their tremendous heat as red warning lights flashed all across Yaeger's damage display.

The sound of the alarm signals snapped him out of his sudden shock at the sight of the 'Mech. He grabbed the controls, stepped the *Uller* to the side, and brought his own laser to bear. At the same time, he opened a comm channel back to the command base.

"*Uller* to base! I'm under attack by an enemy 'Mech! *Goshawk* with Clan Steel Viper markings! Repeat, I am under attack!"

"*Uller*, we are dispatching reinforcements!" came the voice over the speakers.

Yaeger barely heard it as he lined up a shot with his 'Mech's large laser and fired. A green beam stabbed out, but the *Goshawk* was already moving. It came surging up out of the crevasse and began running across the tundra. The laser bolt missed it cleanly. The *Goshawk*'s medium pulse laser fired, slagging armor on the *Uller*'s torso and coming perilously close to damaging the internal systems.

Yaeger spun his 'Mech to track the *Goshawk* and opened up on it with his autocannon and SRM-pack, sending a stream of rapid-fire shells and several missiles streaking toward the enemy 'Mech. He saw at least one of the missiles impact the *Goshawk*'s extended shoulder flanges, denting and scarring armor plating there, but the autocannon missed completely. Most of the *Uller*'s weapons were too long-range. Yaeger needed some more room to maneuver if he was going to use them to full effect.

Incoming missiles, his sensors warned him, as the other 'Mech fired its shoulder-mounted SRM-packs. The missiles screamed in and impacted dangerously close to the *Uller*'s cockpit. Yaeger was shaken by the blast and slammed against his safety harness as the *Goshawk* triggered its jump jets. Like a mechanical phantom, it leapt into the air on streamers of fire and vanished from sight. Yaeger struggled to regain his wits as his status indicators all screamed for attention. There was structural damage from the missile hit; parts of his 'Mech's torso armor were completely gone. He was vulnerable.

Where did he go? Yaeger thought. His scanners weren't much help. The local magnetic and thermal interference created numerous false readings and ghost-images. Yaeger scanned the external cameras to try and get a visual on the enemy 'Mech, but it was too dark. The *Goshawk* could be hiding among the craggy outcroppings of rock or in another chasm or crevasse. It seemed to have vanished into thin air. As he searched, Yaeger's thoughts were screaming, *Who is this guy? Where did he come from?*

Then a laser bolt struck the *Uller* in the back. It blew through the thin armor there, and the damage displays showed internal structural damage to the 'Mech's left side. It wasn't critical, but it was pretty bad. Yaeger turned his 'Mech to face his opponent and fired his lasers and autocannon simultaneously. He scored a hit with the autocannon, pocking and scarring the *Goshawk*'s torso armor, but the heat level inside the *Uller*'s cockpit was starting to rise. Sweat was pouring off Yaeger's body as his coolant vest worked overtime to keep his body temperature down. He'd lost a heat sink to the *Goshawk*'s last attack.

The enemy 'Mech was in motion again, moving swiftly across the tundra. Yaeger tracked it and fired the *Uller*'s large laser again. The green beam narrowly missed the *Goshawk*, which was moving too fast. Suddenly, the other 'Mech turned and began running directly at the *Uller*, growing larger and larger on Yaeger's monitors as it charged toward him at almost ninety kph.

It was too late to get out of the way, so Yaeger let loose with everything he had. Laser and auto-cannon fire slashed across the *Goshawk*, leaving black scars on its white-painted armor. The attacks did some damage, but nothing to slow the fifty-five tons of BattleMech from its charge.

The *Goshawk* rammed one of its shoulder flanges into the *Uller* like a rushing football player. Yaeger fought to control his 'Mech and barely managed to keep the *Uller* from falling on its back, which would have left him almost helpless. The *Uller* took a step back to stabilize itself, standing peril-ously close to the crevasse from which the *Goshawk* had emerged. The *Goshawk* also took a step backward, looking almost like it was assuming a martial arts stance. The Clan neurohelmets made the movements of the 'Mechs seem almost lifelike.

The *Goshawk* leveled its arms toward the *Uller*, one ending in the barrel of a large laser, the other holding the rifle-like arrangement of heavy ma-chine-gun barrels. Yaeger's sensors screamed a warning as the *Goshawk* achieved a targeting lock. Yaeger started to move, to get out of the way, but too late. The pulse laser fired, followed by the machine guns roaring to life a split-second later. A rapid succession of emerald bolts came straight at the *Uller*'s cockpit, boiling away armor and re-flective layers of shielding before a hail of gunfire penetrated the outer hull and riddled Yaeger's body with high-caliber bullets.

The last thing Karl Yaeger saw was the grinning skull-face of the *Goshawk* and the emblem of Clan Steel Viper. The last thing he thought was how he'd always hoped to go out in battle. At least he wouldn't die on the ground, frozen to death or eaten by some animal. He would die like a warrior.

By the time the *Puma* and the *Fenris* arrived near the mountains, there was no sign of an attacker, only the *Uller*, standing alone and silent on the frozen tundra, like the remains of some ancient statue. Its armor was pitted, melted, and charred, leaving myomer muscles and endo-steel skeleton exposed to the freezing air in places. The cockpit was a ruined mass of blackened metal and plastic, riddled with bullet holes. Steam still rose from its wounds and from the rapidly cooling body of its pilot.

And there, on the ground in front of it, was laser-burned a crude representation of a snake's head, fangs bared. The symbol of Clan Steel Viper.

14

Kore Lancers Command Center
Outside Niffelheim, Kore
The Periphery
16 April 3060

Susie Ryan was *not* a happy woman. After five days on a desolate planet on the edge of the Periphery, all her efforts to find what she'd come for had been for naught. She might even have wondered if the rumors and stories she'd been hearing were true, except for one thing. Over the past two nights, her forces had been attacked by Clan BattleMechs of unknown origin, bearing the emblem of Clan Steel Viper. But who were these newcomers? Were they *really* from the Steel Vipers? How did they get to Kore and what did they want here?

So far, there were at least two Clan 'Mechs involved in the attacks on the Rebels: a *Goshawk* and a *Hellhound*, both known to be Viper designs, both painted bone-white and bearing skull-motif designs. Two nights ago Karl Yaeger had died at the hands of the *Goshawk*, and his *Uller* left crippled.

No one else even saw the 'Mech; it was already gone by the time help arrived. The only reason they knew it was a *Goshawk* was Yaeger's last transmissions to the command center that he was under attack.

The *Hellhound* attacked the Rebels' *Puma* on patrol the following night. This time, Ryan made sure help was closer at hand. She arrived in her *Mad Cat* and caught a glimpse of the snow-white 'Mech before it disappeared into the mountains. She briefly considered going after it, but not without knowing whether it had allies waiting somewhere to carry out some sort of ambush. The *Puma* wasn't critically damaged, but it would still take time to replace its destroyed armor. At least the techs had the *Panther* they'd captured working again. It could fill in for the *Uller* for the time being, and Ryan had brought along MechWarriors enough to do the job she'd come for. It was no problem replacing Yaeger, but that didn't solve the question of where the attacks were coming from.

Ryan wasn't foolish enough to assume that the mysterious 'Mechs were from the Clans. After all, hadn't she used Clan 'Mechs bearing a Clan crest to fool the defenders of Kore? Someone else could be doing the same thing. But what if they *were* Steel Vipers? What if they'd returned?

"No, impossible," Ryan thought aloud, as she paced the length of the commander's quarters in the Kore Lancers' command center. "It can't be the Clans."

She'd taken over these quarters shortly after the base was secured. They were spartan, but she'd occupied worse. All the various personal items and garbage that had belonged to Lieutenant Holt, the Lancers' commanding officer, had been tossed into a box to get them out of the way. A table currently held survey maps of Kore, with various areas where her 'Mechs had found unusual magnetic readings marked in green, and the places where the mysterious 'Mechs had attacked marked in red.

"It couldn't be the Clans," Ryan repeated to herself, almost like a mantra. She'd received no word from the *Inanna* of another JumpShip arriving in the Kore system. It was possible that a Clan ship could have entered at the system's zenith jump point on the opposite side of Kore's sun, where it would be hidden from her JumpShip. Even then, she'd received no warning of any DropShip landings, either from her JumpShip or the planet's satellite network. Of course, the network was far from comprehensive. It was possible that a small DropShip might be able to slip through, but . . . no. There was simply no way the Clans could have landed BattleMechs on Kore without her knowing about it.

There was always the possibility that the Clans had resources and technology completely unknown to the Inner Sphere, but she was sure that, if they had the capability of achieving planetfall without anyone the wiser, she would have heard about it by now. She'd been fighting the Clans for ten years, and she knew them as well as anyone. Besides, guerrilla warfare and sneak attacks weren't the style of the Clans, not even the Steel Vipers. They preferred a straight-up fight. If the Clans had

'Mechs on Kore, they wouldn't be wasting time sniping at the Rebels, they would simply move in and attack, especially if they had the advantage. Even if it was only a single Star of 'Mechs, they'd outnumber the Rebels' single lance, so why wouldn't they attack, especially now, with the *Uller* out of commission?

If the Clan 'Mechs didn't arrive *after* the Rebels, there was only one other possibility: they were on Kore *before* Ryan and her men arrived. That led her to suspect that her reasons for coming to Kore were sound, but that her prize might have been snatched away from her. There was still time to turn the tables and grab a victory out of all this, but first she had to be sure she was right.

She sat down on her bunk and touched a button on the intercom. A voice responded immediately.

"Yes, Cap'n?"

"Have the techs made any progress in accessing the base's computer files?" she asked.

"Umm, no, not yet, Cap'n. They've been busy repairing the damage to the 'Mechs and there hasn't been—"

"Don't give me excuses!" Ryan broke in. "Get me those files! Take some of the techs we've got locked up and put them to work on it. Do whatever is necessary to pry the passcodes out of them or I'll come down there and demonstrate some new interrogation techniques on *you*, understand?"

"Yessir!" came the voice from the intercom. "I'll get right on it."

Susie Ryan gave the device a tap to shut it off and slumped back onto the bed.

Dammit! she thought, slamming a fist down on the hard mattress. *Everything was going perfectly. They'd carried off the plan flawlessly, from hijacking the DropShip that visited Kore to using it to land their own 'Mechs on the planet and deal with the local forces quickly and cleanly. They'd secured the city and its scientific resources to aid in the search. Everything was going according to plan, until the "ghosts" showed up.*

Look at me, she scoffed inwardly, *even I'm referring to them as ghosts.* The rumors were circulating among her men that the mysterious BattleMechs attacking the Rebels weren't even 'Mechs at all, but some kind of spooks out of a local legend. MechWarriors, in general, were a superstitious lot, and pirates even more so. Some of them actually believed that Kore was cursed or haunted or whatever and wanted to lift off as soon as possible. Ryan didn't believe such nonsense herself, but she had to deal with her men. The longer this went on, the more the rumors and stories were likely to grow and the harder it would be to convince her people to continue what they saw as a fool's errand. She might even have to tell them the real reason she'd come to Kore. The lure of potential gain might quell some of the grumbling in the ranks.

What was really needed was swift and decisive action, something to put things back on track and convince the men of her ability to handle even this "ghost." As a knock sounded at the door, Ryan smiled and sat up on the bed.

"Enter," she said.

Lon Volker stepped into the room, followed by an armed guard. Volker was wearing civilian clothing, but he'd managed to keep himself presentable. His blond beard was neatly trimmed and he looked cleaner than the guard was. The pirates had allowed their prisoners access to the necessary facilities, on Ryan's orders. She wanted to encourage the impression that they would be allowed to live if they continued to cooperate.

She nodded toward the guard. "Wait outside, and see to it we're not disturbed." The man nodded in return and withdrew, closing the door behind him.

Volker eyed her warily as Ryan gestured to the chair next to the table.

"Sit down," she said. A look of defiance flashed briefly in the man's eyes, but then he came and sat down, gripping the arms of the chair with his hands.

"You wanted a chance to prove yourself to me," she told him. "Now you've got it."

"What do you want?" Volker asked.

"Information," she said. "Tell me about the MechWarrior who piloted the *Thorn*."

Volker's eyebrows raised in surprise. "Kintaro? Why?"

"Because I asked you politely," Ryan said in a dangerously low tone. "Don't make me ask you again."

Volker swallowed a bit and looked down at the floor, then back up at Ryan.

"He was a kid," he began. "He became an apprentice a few years ago. The lieutenant and Sergeant Krenner sponsored him on account of his mother—she was commander of our unit until she got killed fighting the Clans when they hit Kore ten years ago."

"How good a pilot is he?"

"Not as good as me," Volker said, daring to smile. Then, more soberly, "He was all right, I guess. He did okay in training exercises and simulations, but he'd never seen any real action."

It was Ryan's turn to smile. "Neither had you until a few days ago, 'Mech-boy," she said. "Was he checked out on all of the unit's 'Mechs?"

"Yeah, we all were, trained on different classes and types. Krenner wanted us to be familiar with how all kinds of 'Mechs worked so we'd know how to handle them, from the inside and the outside."

"What about the Clan 'Mechs?"

"Clan 'Mechs?" Volker asked. "Well, we fought a lot of clan 'Mechs in simulations, based on data the Storm Riders acquired from the FedCom military. I don't know how accurate it was, though."

"Could Kintaro pilot a Clan 'Mech?"

Volker's brow furrowed a bit in thought.

"I guess so, I mean, a 'Mech is a 'Mech. I know I could pilot one, so Kintaro might have been able to, I suppose."

Ryan stood up and paced over to the small table, where she picked up a model of a *Centurion* that rested there, turning it over in her hands idly.

Volker turned his head to look at her. "Why all the questions about Kintaro? What's the point? He's dead."

"I'm not so sure about that," Ryan said, more to herself than to Volker.

"What are you talking about? He's got to be

dead! He was out there on his own for days with no more than basic survival gear, and your guys blew his 'Mech right out from under him. There's no way he could have survived."

"You may underestimate him," Ryan said, "but I cannot."

Volker jumped up out of his chair, his mouth a hard, angry line.

"Me? Underestimate that pip-squeak? Listen, the only reason he was even *in* this unit was—"

"I'm not interested in your opinions, Volker." Ryan's voice was sheer ice as she turned the full force of her gaze on her prisoner. "Only in your answers to my questions."

"Well," Volker said, "I'm telling you that Kintaro is the least of your worries . . . unless he's come back from the dead as a ghost."

Ryan spun toward Volker as the 'Mech model snapped under the pressure of her grip with a loud crack that sounded like a gunshot in the small room.

"That's it, isn't it?" Volker dared to smile again. "You think Kintaro has something to do with the attacks on your men." At Ryan's slight look of surprise he just shrugged and said, "We still hear rumors, even in lock-up. I know all about those 'ghost' 'Mechs."

"What do you know?" Ryan asked. She tossed the broken pieces of the model onto the table and dusted off her gloved hands.

"I know that your guys are scared," Volker said. "Some of them think there really *is* a ghost."

"But you don't?" Ryan sneered.

"Hey, if it's a 'Mech, that means it's solid, and

that means I can kill it. Put me in the cockpit of a 'Mech and I'll take on your 'ghost' any day."

"Interesting idea," Ryan said, "but I have other plans for you."

"What plans?" Volker asked warily as Ryan took a step closer to him and smiled wickedly.

"Like I said, you wanted to prove yourself to me, and I'm going to give you a chance." She gripped Volker's shoulders and gave him a firm shove backward. He stumbled back a few steps before the backs of his knees hit the edge of the bunk. They buckled and Volker went down onto the mattress.

Before he knew it, Ryan was on top of him, pressing her mouth against his. She kissed him hungrily and felt him responding to her. He reached up to put his arms around her, but Ryan grabbed his wrists and pinned them over his head on the bed. She looked down at him and smiled.

"So, do you think you're ready?" she said. She laughed softly at Volker's silly grin and his attempts to keep his cool in the face of her advances. Some interrogation techniques are more fun than others, she thought. Soon enough, she would have what she needed to take care of any and all obstacles and achieve her goal. For the time being, she'd let Volker show her just how good he thought he was.

15

Kore Lancers Command Center
Outside Niffelheim, Kore
The Periphery
16 April 3060

Laura Metz sat, her back propped up against the wall of the room the pirates were using to hold the two dozen or so remaining members of the Kore Lancers. They'd been here for days, ever since Ryan's Rebels took over the command base and the city. They were being held in one of the storage buildings of the command base. All the various supplies were moved out, and the prisoners moved in. They were being fairly well-treated, all things considered. They were fed regularly (the command base stocked plenty of food, and the pirates' control of the city ensured that it kept coming). All they had were blankets on the floor to sleep on, but the pirates allowed them out in shifts each day to shower. As far as being a P.O.W. went, it wasn't bad.

Ha, prisoner of war, Laura thought. *That's a laugh.*

As if you could call this whole thing a war. It wasn't even close. Still, the pirates were certainly acting strangely. Susie Ryan apparently didn't want her "guests" mistreated—at least, not until she got whatever she was after.

That was the part Laura didn't get. What did Ryan want on Kore? If her only aim was to conquer the planet and take control of the mining operations, why keep any of the Lancers alive? There wasn't any point in holding prisoners, unless perhaps Ryan wanted to make sure she had trained people around, in case her crew had any difficulties dealing with the command base's systems. That would make sense, but it just didn't sit right.

The Rebels clearly weren't after the BattleMechs on Kore. They'd destroyed all but the *Panther* while taking the command base. The techs had reported that the *Centurion* and the *Javelin* wouldn't be much use for anything but scrap and spare parts, and she'd heard that Kintaro's *Thorn* was scattered across a mountain somewhere. Pretty poor showing, if salvage was what they were after. Volker was the only MechWarrior who'd survived the attack, and the pirates had just come and taken him away "for questioning," adding to Laura's concerns about the whole thing.

No, Ryan was after something else. Maybe it was the mining operation. Kore was rich in a lot of minerals, particularly materials useful for manufacturing 'Mechs. Maybe the pirate queen wanted to supply her own 'Mech factory or something like that. Still, Laura didn't know of any 'Mech-production facilities out in the former Pirate Kingdoms that Ryan might control. It just didn't make sense.

"What are you thinking about, Metz?" came a voice from just overhead. Laura looked up into the grim face of Sergeant Krenner. She started to rise, but he waved her down and moved to sit next to her.

"At ease, Corporal," he said. "No point in snapping to attention 'round here right now. You just looked like you could use some company."

She smiled weakly. "Thanks, Sarge."

"You worrying about Volker?" he asked.

"Yeah, some."

"Girl, I don't know what you see in him."

"What are you talking about?" Laura asked.

Krenner only laughed, a deep chuckle. "Don't give me that innocent routine, kiddo. Everyone on base knows that you and Volker are an item." Laura flushed a bit and Krenner smiled wider. "Hard to keep secrets on a post this small. Soldiers and mercs gossip worse than old ladies."

"We're not exactly an 'item,' Sarge. We're just . . . enjoying each other's company," she said slowly.

"You know, I always wondered if you and Sturm might end up getting together?"

"Kintaro?" Laura said. "Um, I never really thought about it, Sarge. I mean, Kintaro seems like a good kid but he was always so . . . intense, I guess, so wrapped up in training and stuff that I never really thought about him."

"He was a good kid," Krenner said quietly.

"Yeah, I'm really sorry, Sarge. You tried to look out for him."

"Not well enough," Krenner said, shaking his head. "I promised his mom I'd keep an eye on him."

"Wasn't anything you could do, Kren," Laura said quietly. She wanted to reach out to Krenner, but she didn't think it was appropriate. Not here, in front of everyone. "Kintaro knew the risks. That's part of being a soldier, especially a Mech-Warrior. When it comes right down to it, there's nothing we can do about that."

"Yeah, you're right," Krenner said. "And now you're worried about Volker, huh?"

"Yeah, a bit." Actually, Laura didn't know how she felt about Volker. He'd come on to her pretty strong from the moment they'd met. At first, she'd rebuffed his advances. She knew all about Volker's reputation as a ladies' man; every woman on Kore probably did by now. Still, there was something roguish and charming about the young MechWarrior, something Laura found intriguing. It wasn't like there were a lot of great opportunities for romance on a world like Kore, and one day she'd decided to give him a chance. That was a few months ago, and the two of them had "enjoyed each other's company," as she put it, since then.

"He'll be okay," Krenner said. "Volker's a survivor. He can take care of himself."

"That's for sure," Laura said. "I'm sure he'll be fine." She decided to change the subject. "I've really been wondering what this is all about. I keep going over it in my head: what the hell does Susie Ryan want with a place like Kore?"

Krenner shook his head slowly. "Damned if I

know. It doesn't make any sense. Only thing I know is that we've got to stay alive and figure out how to get control back from those pirates. Another supply ship isn't due for months. By the time the rest of the Storm Riders figure out what's going on, it might be too late."

In other words, we'll probably be dead, Laura thought. It wasn't a pleasant idea, but she was a soldier and she was prepared for it.

"Sure, but how can we do that?" she said. "We can't even get out of here, much less tangle with four Clan 'Mechs." There were guards outside the door at all times, armed with heavy automatic rifles. The door was locked. Someone like Krenner could probably bust it down with a couple of tries, but he'd be riddled with bullets before he could even finish. They didn't have much chance against the pirates, much less their 'Mechs.

"Don't be so sure," Krenner said quietly. "There are ways to handle 'Mechs, girl. We just have to wait for the right opportunity to come along. Sooner or later, Ryan or her people are going to make a mistake. They may have the hardware, but they don't have the discipline. They'll make a mistake. We just have to be ready when it happens."

"You can count on me, Sarge."

"I knew I could, Metz. This ain't over ye—what the hell?"

"What?" Laura asked.

"Do you hear that?"

"I don't . . ." Then she paused and listened. "Wait, yeah."

"It's a 'Mech," Krenner said. "Coming in fast."

"Probably one of the Rebels' 'Mechs," Laura said, but Krenner shook his head.

"I don't think so. It sounds like it's moving at near top speed. Why would one of their 'Mechs come in running?"

"Who else could it be?" she asked. "The 'ghost'?" The Lancers had heard the pirates talking about the mysterious attacks that had been occurring. Krenner made sure his people repeated any stories they'd heard about the Ghost of Winter to their captors at every opportunity and to each other when they thought the pirates were listening. He even made up a few guaranteed to make your hair stand on end. Anything that unnerved the pirates was a potential weapon for the Lancers. Still, Laura had never believed any of the stories until just that moment.

The rest of the Lancers could hear the incoming 'Mech now, and an alarm klaxon howled somewhere inside the command center, echoing across the compound. Everyone was on his feet now, alert and ready for whatever happened. Krenner exchanged a few meaningful looks with the higher-ranked men and women in the room, including Laura. Without speaking a word the Master Sergeant told them all to be ready. The opportunity they'd been waiting for might have come sooner than anyone expected.

"They're moving out the troops," Krenner said quietly, but his voice carried in the near-silence of the room. "They're under attack."

"The 'Mech is getting a lot closer, too," Laura said. The thundering footfalls of the giant war machine could be felt as vibrations through the ferrocrete floor. Every member of the Lancers had spent enough time around BattleMechs to know when one was practically right on top of him or her. The roar of gunfire sounded outside the building, and Krenner moved to press his ear against the door.

"I think the guards have gone for a look," he said. "Looks like our chance."

Before the burly sergeant could slam his shoulder against the door, a loud, booming noise came from the ceiling of the room.

"What the hell is *that*?" Tom Flannery said, looking upward.

"It's the 'Mech," Krenner replied quietly.

"What, is he knocking to come in?" Flannery quipped, as everyone in the room got nervous. What was going on?

"That's it . . ." Krenner said quietly to himself, then he barked, "Okay, everyone back away from the wall! Get back!"

The Lancers scrambled away just in time as a pair of metallic protrusions came crashing through the opposite corners, just below the roof. Ferrocrete blocks, support materials, and clouds of dust sprayed into the room. Laura suddenly felt like a mouse trapped in a hole with a giant cat outside, clawing to get in. She wished she had just about any sort of weapon to hold onto, even though she knew it would do her no good.

With a thunderous tearing sound, the roof of the building peeled back, showering loose dust and debris down into the hole, along with a scattering of snow and ice. A blinding light stabbed down, and Laura threw up her arms to shield her eyes as they adjusted to the brightness.

Framed in the hole in the roof, looming against the blackness of the night sky was a BattleMech. It was a Clan 'Mech, a *Goshawk*. Its lights illuminated the bone-white hull, blackened in a few places by weapons fire. It was broad-shouldered, with heavy shoulder flanges and a sort of hooded cockpit painted in the likeness of a grinning skull. The spotlights threw it into a harsh relief of black and white.

There was a moment of silence as everyone in the room simply stared at the 'Mech and it seemed to stare back. Then a sound came from the metal giant's external speakers and a voice boomed out.

"What are you all standing around for? C'mon, Lancers, let's blow this firetrap!"

"Sturm . . . ?" Krenner breathed, then a broad smile split his dark face and he let out a whoop. "You heard the man!" he yelled to the rest of the crew. "Let's get the hell out of here!"

A ragged cheer went up from the Lancers as the *Goshawk* swung one arm at the wall and knocked it down in one blow, leaving a gaping hole leading to the outside. Krenner immediately took charge and began shouting orders.

"Get moving!" he shouted. "Head for the 'Mech bay and get your hands on whatever vehicles they've got. We've gotta clear out of here pronto!"

The Lancers immediately moved to obey, swarming out of the hole as the 'Mech took a step back, then strode toward the other storage building, where it did the same as before, liberating the other members of the Lancers held there. Krenner stepped out of the hole in the wall, with Laura close behind.

"Stick with me, Metz," he said and headed at a run for the other building to rally the rest of the troops. Laura responded with a quick "yessir," and moved to follow. As they covered the space between the two buildings, she saw at least two dozen pirates, armed with assault rifles, running across the compound.

"Sarge!" she called out. Krenner didn't even slow down, he must have seen them.

So did the *Goshawk*, it seemed. The pale giant straightened up from knocking down part of the building's wall and leveled its left arm at the oncoming pirates. It carried a long-barreled weapon that contained three heavy machine guns. The three barrels spat fire, and a stream of high-caliber rounds sprayed across the compound. The pirates yelled and ran for cover while several others danced and jerked as they were slammed by the hail of bullets, which dropped them where they stood. The gunfire sparked and ricocheted off the 'crete, forcing the other pirates to keep their heads down.

"Go!" Krenner shouted to the others in the building. "Go for the bay! He'll give us cover!"

The remaining Lancers sprang into action and started running across the compound as the BattleMech opened up with another round of machine gun fire to keep the pirates at bay. A few of them fired their rifles from cover, but they aimed at the 'Mech rather than the retreating Lancers, and even the assault rifles weren't powerful enough to damage a BattleMech's armor. The rounds only sparked and pinged harmlessly off the metal giant's shoulders, torso, and head.

A jeep carrying a heavy machine gun came roaring across the compound, but the 'Mech only turned slightly toward the newcomer. Twin bolts of blazing green light shot out from the ports on its torso, slamming into the vehicle. The pulse lasers almost instantly turned the jeep into a fireball that boiled up into the darkness of the night, casting a ruddy glow over the compound and sending more pirates scattering for cover.

When the last of the Lancers were clear of the buildings and heading for the 'Mech bay, Krenner turned toward Laura and nodded, then the two of them were off and following the others. Behind them, the 'Mech turned and took a couple steps out into the compound, careful to give the running figures below a wide berth.

Laura could feel the vibrations as the gigantic feet impacted with the ferrocrete. In only a few strides, the 'Mech was moving ahead of the group of Lancers toward the bay, laying down another barrage of machine gun fire to scatter the remaining pirates. Some of them didn't move quickly enough and were cut down by the gunfire.

Where the hell are the pirate 'Mechs? Laura thought as she ran. She looked around the compound and saw the pirates regrouping, saw the burning wreck of the jeep and a few other small vehicles the ghost 'Mech must have encountered on its way in, but no sign of the enemy 'Mechs. Something was definitely going on. The *Goshawk* pilot must have some kind of a plan.

Kintaro, she thought. *Krenner said it was Kintaro.*

Could it be? Could Kintaro still be alive? There was no time to wonder as she ran as quickly as she could. She paused only to bend down and grab a fallen assault rifle from where a dead pirate had dropped it. She worked the slide and checked to see that it was working, then held it in a ready position as she charged forward again.

16

Kore Lancers Command Center
Outside Niffelheim, Kore
The Periphery
16 April 3060

Corporal Laura Metz leveled her assault rifle and fired a burst as some pirates rushed toward her. The hail of gunfire caught one and sent him spinning onto the ferrocrete. The others scattered for cover as Laura kept running for the 'Mech bay, following the rest of the Lancers. The white BattleMech stood overhead like a protective arch, straddling the entrance to the bay and holding off the remaining pirates with its heavy machine guns.

Metz and Krenner rounded the edge of the open bay doors and snapped off a few shots at the few pirate guards on duty inside. The pirates began to return fire, but the technicians working in the bay were mostly members of the Lancers. They took up wrenches and other tools and used them as weapons to knock rifles aside and to strike pirates upside the head, giving the other Lancers time to rush them. The pirates who fought were shot or knocked out, their weapons clattering to the floor, where the Lancers picked them up. Then they headed for the vehicles stored in the bay.

"Stick to the hovercraft!" Sergeant Krenner shouted over the alarm klaxon and the rattle of gunfire. "We're going to have to go out overland and the wheeled vehicles will never make it!"

Laura didn't know exactly what the pilot of the 'Mech who'd liberated them from the makeshift prison had in mind, but she was fairly sure who was inside the cockpit and she knew that Krenner trusted him with his life. If getting away from the command base was part of Kintaro's plan, Krenner would do everything he could to help pull it off.

The *Goshawk* stood near the entrance to the 'Mech bay, using its triple heavy machine guns to keep the pirates at bay. Most weren't willing to get too close and the bodies of the few pirates who tried were scattered across the ferrocrete floor. Still, it was only a matter of time before the pirates brought in heavy weapons capable of hurting even a BattleMech or, worse yet, before their own 'Mechs arrived on the scene. Powerful as it was, Laura knew that one Clan BattleMech didn't have much of a chance against two or three of the pirate 'Mechs, which were also Clan designs. The Lancers needed to pull out quickly or not at all.

A motion out of the corner of her eye caught Laura's attention. She turned to see a pirate guard, either someone they'd missed or one who'd taken only a glancing blow. He was crouched behind a rack of maintenance tools and parts, leveling his rifle directly at Krenner. She tried to bring her own assault rifle to bear as she yelled out a warning.

"Sarge, look out!" Krenner spun around and spotted the shooter, but too late to do anything about it.

A single shot rang out, and the pirate slumped forward over the tool rack, knocking it over and spilling tools over the floor of the bay. A tall, blond figure emerged from the shadows of the bay, holding a smoking service pistol in one hand. He waved toward Krenner and Laura with a jaunty smile.

"Volker!" Laura shouted. He was alive! She wanted to rush over and give him a hug for that, but for now she stayed where she was and kept an eye out for any other unseen hazards. For his part, Krenner stayed under cover and shouted back over his shoulder.

"Thanks, Volker!"

Volker moved up to the mouth of the bay as the engines of two Winterhawk hover APCs roared to life, the turbo-fans scattering clouds of dust and snow as they rose up on powerful cushions of compressed air. The Lancers piled in through the open troop doors of the twin hovercraft.

"Nice to see you still alive," Krenner said to Volker.

"Same to you," Volker replied. "When all the alarms started going off, I saw my chance and took it. I figured you'd do the same and head for the bay, so I came to see if I could hitch a ride."

"Good timing," Laura said with a smile that Volker returned. "We were about to leave without you."

"Glad you didn't have to." Volker nodded his head to indicate the *Goshawk*, which was still holding off the pirates.

"Who's that?" he asked.

It was Krenner's turn to smile. "Who do you think?" he replied. "Kintaro."

"Kintaro?" Volker shook his head in disbelief. "No way."

"Believe it, boy," Krenner said. "I don't know how, but it's him. Let's go, our ride's leaving." With that, the three of them headed for the nearest Winterhawk. The moment they were inside, they pulled the hatches closed and headed for the front of the hovercraft.

Volker looked down at the corporal sitting at the controls and the man moved aside without protest as Volker took his place. Krenner took the co-pilot position while Laura slid into one of the crew seats and quickly strapped in. Volker pulled on the radio headset and was running a quick visual check of the instrument panel in front of him.

"May not have legs," he said, "but I can pilot it." He placed his hands on the controls and eased the Winterhawk forward. The other hovercraft followed suit, and the multi-ton vehicles glided out of the vehicle bay on cushions of air, engines whining. As soon as they were clear, Volker opened the comm.

"All right, let's punch it!" He pushed the control stick forward, and the powerful thrusters on the Winterhawk fired up, sending the hovercraft shooting out across the compound toward open ground.

An armored jeep equipped with a swivel-mounted machine gun roared across their path. A pirate manning the gun fired a long burst right across the front of the lead Winterhawk. The rounds sparked and ricocheted off the APC's armor plating and reinforced windscreen. Volker didn't even flinch as the gunfire spattered the screen in front of him. He only pushed the Winterhawk forward and shot toward the oncoming jeep. As they drew closer and closer, Laura dug her fingers into the edge of her seat.

It was the jeep that turned away first. At the sight of the huge APC bearing down on him, the pirate driver tried to swerve out of the way, but he was a moment too late. The Winterhawk struck the left fender of the jeep with a dull thud, followed by a crash as the jeep flipped and rolled a short distance across the compound.

The Winterhawks reached the edge of the ferrocrete and shot out across the grounds, reaching the area of the perimeter fence, which looked like it had been stepped on a couple times by the *Goshawk*. By the time the hovercraft hit the open tundra of Kore, they were doing nearly one hundred kph and still accelerating.

Laura looked at the heads-up display above the console in the Winterhawk's cockpit and saw the *Goshawk* fire a last blast from its lasers and machine guns to clear the area immediately in front of it. It turned to the side and raised its right arm. Rapid pulses of blazing green light shot out, aimed directly at one of the fuel-storage tanks near the vehicle bay. The outer metal of the tank melted instantly and the fuel inside went up like a bomb. The blast shook the Winterhawks slightly from nearly two hundred meters away, and a red-orange ball of fire boiled up into the sky on a pillar of black smoke.

Then the 'Mech turned from the scene of carnage and began racing away from the command base at top speed. It accelerated rapidly, nearly keeping pace with the hovercraft.

Krenner turned to Volker as they began to pull away. "Ease off a bit, hotshot. Let Kintaro keep up. These rigs don't have much more than popgun turrets. We're meat if we get caught out in the open with no protection. 'Sides," he said, smiling broadly, "Kintaro's the only one who knows where we're going."

Volker grunted and eased off the throttle somewhat reluctantly, although the hovercraft still flew over the frozen terrain at a decent clip. The command base was rapidly falling away behind them.

In short order, the Goshawk came up alongside the two hovercraft, moving at a rapid pace between them. It was a testament to the training of the Kore MechWarriors that Kintaro was able to keep the giant humanoid BattleMech running across the icy surface and still keep up with the faster hovercraft.

The Winterhawk's commline crackled, and Kintaro's voice came from the speakers.

"Kintaro to Lancers. Hello, folks, glad you could join the party. What's your status? Over."

Krenner spoke before Volker could even begin

to reply. "Sturm! Damn, kid, you had me worried! What the hell happened to you and where did you find that little Clan toy? Over."

Kintaro's grin was almost audible over the channel. "Hey, Kren, sorry to make you worry. Had a little problem with my old 'Mech so I decided to get me a new one. It's a long story, but I'll fill you in soon as we get where we're going. Over."

Volker chose that moment to break into the conversation. "And where exactly is that? Over."

"Volker? Glad you made it, man. I owe you one for that save back with the raiders. I'd rather not talk about it over comm, not unless we can be sure no one's listening in. It'll be a lot easier to show you. Over."

Krenner nodded to Volker, then returned to the commline. "That's affirmative, Kintaro. You lead the way and we'll keep an eye out for any company. Over."

"Will do, Sarge," Kintaro said. "But we shouldn't have too much to worry about. I rigged up another appearance by the 'Ghost of Winter' at a ridge about eighty klicks north of here. Two of the pirate 'Mechs went to check it out. By the time they figure out it's just a bunch of junk and head back here, we'll be long gone. Only thing we have to worry about is the *Mad Cat*. Over."

Now it was Volker's turn to smile. "Not a worry, Kintaro. The *Mad Cat* is Susie Ryan's 'Mech, and she won't be a problem for a while. I took care of that. Over."

"Really?" Sturm said. "Then it sounds like we've both got some stories to tell. I'm going to radio-silence for now. Follow me in and you can tell me all about it later. Kintaro out."

Krenner reached out a hand to close the comm-line as Laura glanced over at Volker. Something about the way he said he'd "taken care of" Susie Ryan made her uncomfortable. She knew that she and Volker weren't exactly . . . well, she wasn't sure what they were exactly, but there was something about it that bothered her. She decided to set her worries aside for the time being. Right now, the Lancers were free and they had a chance, where things had looked hopeless before. The surprise appearance of Kintaro in a Clan 'Mech completely turned things around. Maybe Krenner was right, maybe she had underestimated Sturm Kintaro.

The *Goshawk* led the Winterhawks on a course for the Jotun Mountains. Kintaro brought them in close, where the profiles of the peaks, along with the metallic deposits and thermal vents, could baffle any sensors that might be tracking them. They hugged the mountains for a short distance before coming to a pass leading into the peaks themselves.

Kintaro's 'Mech took the lead, the hovercraft following close behind. The pass was narrow, just wide enough for a BattleMech to squeeze through. It opened into a broad, long valley, surrounded by high mountain peaks capped with heavy blankets of snow and ice, their lower slopes covered with scrubby trees and other hardy Koran plants. The *Goshawk* waded through the deep snow in the valley while the hovercraft floated about a meter above the ground, kicking up clouds of sparkling snow, which made it more difficult to navigate and follow, since the other sensor systems didn't work terribly well surrounded by the mountains.

Still, they were enough to follow along as the *Goshawk* approached a sheer black cliff-face, where it paused, standing silently at the base of the cliff.

"What's he doing?" Laura started to say, but she was cut off by a faint rumbling from the cliff-face itself and then the rock split apart. A dark, narrow crack split down the front of the cliff from top to bottom. It quickly began to widen into a straight, black separation as two halves of a giant door slowly swung inward into the mountainside.

"Well, I'll be damned . . ." Krenner said quietly under his breath.

When the doors disappeared into the darkness beyond the opening, the *Goshawk* took a step forward, turned slightly and gestured with its laser-cannon arm, waving the hovercraft to follow. The 'Mech stepped through the cavern-like opening and vanished.

Krenner clapped Volker on the shoulder. "All right, then, let's go," he said.

The Winterhawks glided into the entrance and, immediately after they entered the darkness, the giant doors swung shut again and closed with a dull thud, the cleverly designed artificial rock blending perfectly into the cliff-face, making the entrance disappear back into the terrain of the valley.

Powerful lights came on near the roof of the vaulted cavern some fourteen meters above the heads of the Kore Lancers. They illuminated a giant cave, its smooth walls cut out of solid stone by powerful drilling lasers. The cavern was tall enough for Sturm's BattleMech to stand upright in it, with a few meters of clearance between its head and the ceiling. It was roughly oval-shaped, some eighty meters long.

Running along the walls of the cave was a complex series of metallic scaffolds, cables, and panels that formed compartments, deep niches. In each niche stood a tall, silent metallic figure, painted a stark white that gleamed dully in the light of the overhead lamps. BattleMechs. Four of them in all, plus Sturm's *Goshawk*, each 'Mech bearing the emblem of Clan Steel Viper.

Sturm's voice crackled over the commline again.

"Welcome to Shangri-la, everybody. Welcome to the lair of the Ghost of Winter."

17

Shangri-la
Jotun Mountains, Kore
The Periphery
16 April 3060

"Well, I'll be damned," Sergeant Krenner repeated, stepping out of the hovercraft and looking up and around at the interior of the vast cave. The remaining two dozen Lancer personnel were doing likewise.

Sturm walked the *Goshawk* to the empty niche in the cave wall and settled it into place, powering down all the 'Mech's systems. The cockpit hatch opened with a hiss of air and a cloud of steam escaping into the cavern's chill air. Sturm pulled off his neurohelmet and climbed out, clad only in his MechWarrior shorts, a coolant vest, and a pair of combat boots. He dropped a chain-ladder down the front of the 'Mech and clambered down to meet the rush of people who came to greet him.

Krenner was at the front of the group and the first to grab Sturm's hand and shake it firmly before pulling the young MechWarrior into a bear-hug.

"Damn, boy, am I glad to see you again! I was sure you'd bought it!"

Sturm smiled. "Not so long as I kept following your advice, Kren. It kept me alive and may have given us all a chance."

"So, what happened?" Krenner asked, taking in the whole of the cavern with a wave of his hand. "Where did this place come from?"

Sturm took a deep breath and ran one hand through his damp hair, pushing it back from his face.

"Well, as near as I can tell, this is some sort of Clan 'Mech depot. It must have been set up by the Steel Vipers when they came to Kore ten years ago. People thought they were doing some kind of research or scouting out in the mountains, but actually they must have been setting up this place. From what I've been able to gather, that was part of the Vipers' job. They were second-line forces, coming in behind the main Clan thrust into the Inner Sphere. After the Clans took a planet, the Vipers moved in to set up supply lines in case they were ever forced to retreat back beyond the Periphery. This must be one of them."

"But what happened? Why didn't the Clans hold on to it?" Laura asked, coming to the front of the group.

Sturm shook his head. "I'm not sure. Once they set up the depot, the Vipers moved on to the next world, leaving a small force behind to defend the place, mostly Elementals, those Clan warriors in power armor. The invasion was rolling right along back then, and the Clans were virtually unstoppable. The Vipers must have been under a lot of pressure to get these depots set up, then move on. They probably never figured they'd have to worry about any kind of counter-attack this far out on the Periphery."

"Trouble was," Krenner said, "the Inner Sphere forces *did* manage to halt the Clans' advance. That ended up in a stalemate for the last ten years."

"In all the fighting," Sturm continued, "maybe the Steel Vipers who set up this particular depot were killed or something, or the location of the depot was simply lost. After the Storm Riders came back in and kicked out the remaining Clan garrison, the Vipers decided not to come back, for some reason. Nobody knew about the depot, so it just sat here."

"But somebody did find out about it," Volker put in. Sturm glanced over at him and nodded.

"Yeah, that's what I figure. Susie Ryan and her men didn't come to Kore for any mineral resources or to salvage a few old mercenary BattleMechs. They wanted these." He took in the 'Mechs with a sweep of his hand. "There's a whole Star, five Steel Viper 'Mechs, along with tons of ammo and supplies, and a lot of other equipment here. It'd be worth a lot to just about any regular or merc unit, especially an operation that needs 'Mechs as much as the old Pirate Kingdoms do. With these 'Mechs, Ryan could probably do a lot of damage and better arm her MechWarriors to take on more Clan 'Mechs."

Volker cocked his head and looked at Sturm curiously. "How did you know that Susie Ryan was behind the raiders?" he asked. "We didn't know it ourselves until after we got captured. From the outside their 'Mechs look just like Jade Falcon 'Mechs."

Sturm grinned and shrugged. "Sometimes there are advantages to being 'dead,' I guess. After they wrecked my *Thorn* in the mountains, Ryan's men left me for dead, figuring the weather would finish me off."

"Yeah," Volker interjected. "I heard her say as much."

"Well, it nearly did," Sturm continued. "I managed to find shelter in a cave not too far from here. In the back of it there was a ventilation shaft they drilled to bring fresh air down into these caves. I cut through the shaft with my laser and started to climb down." His face was still flushed from the heat of his cockpit, but he felt his cheeks grow even hotter with embarrassment. "Parts of the shaft were covered in ice. I slipped.

"I slid most of the way down to the bottom when I could feel the movement of the air getting more powerful. There was some sort of fan at the bottom of the shaft, pulling in air from the outside. I nearly ended up chopped meat, but I managed to shoot the fan with my laser and burn it out before I hit. Then I knocked out a maintenance panel and crawled out. That's when I found this place.

"That was almost a week ago. As soon as I found the Clan 'Mechs, I realized what the raiders must be after. At first, I thought the Vipers had simply come back for their 'Mechs, but I used the comm system in one of them to monitor the pirates' broadcasts. There was a lot of interference, so I couldn't make things out too well, but it was enough to figure out they weren't Clanners. When I heard Susie Ryan's name, I started to figure out what they'd pulled off, and why.

"The 'Mechs were all still in perfect working order. The only problem was getting past the security systems. At first, I didn't think I'd be able to bypass the security lockouts in the BattleMechs. Turns out the Clans aren't as paranoid as we are about their 'Mechs being stolen. The security systems weren't as sophisticated as I thought, and had only a simple code-lock system. I managed to bypass the security lock-outs on the *Goshawk* and the *Hellhound*, with the help of some tools I found around the depot," he said with a grin. "There are Clan simulator systems here, too, for testing and training. I used them to get a feel for how the 'Mechs operated and to do some 'test drives' before I went out. Then I started hitting the pirate 'Mechs whenever I could.

"At first it was pretty easy, since I could monitor their communications and get a fair idea of what they were up to. I also painted the two 'Mechs so they'd be a little more scary. I figured some of the old stories would get around and it couldn't hurt to have the pirates good and scared. But pretty soon, it was getting a lot harder to catch them by surprise. I only managed to take out one 'Mech and damage another."

"Nothing to sneeze at, kid," Krenner said. "You did pretty damn good, all things considered."

"Figured I could use some help," Sturm said, "and that all of you had enough of a vacation in

'Casa de Ryan,' so I set up some spare 'Mech gear in a northern ridge to send out signals that would look like an active 'Mech was there. The pirates sent two of their 'Mechs, hoping to catch the 'ghost' in action while I came in and hit the command center. I was worried about the *Mad Cat*, but I decided the risk was worth it."

"You didn't have to worry," Volker said, folding his arms proudly across his chest. "That bitch Ryan was questioning me right when you attacked. When the alarms went off, I took my chance and punched her out. Then I grabbed her sidearm, took out the guards, and headed for the vehicle bay. I figured it was the best way out of the place."

"Why didn't you go after your 'Mech?" Sturm asked.

Volker shook his head. "It's still not operational yet, but Ryan told me the pirates are repairing it."

"Damn," Sturm said, almost to himself. "That gives them four functional 'Mechs."

"So?" Laura spoke up. "We've got *five* 'Mechs to their four, and one of theirs is Volker's old *Panther*."

"Yeah," Sturm said, "but how many MechWarriors do we have? Ryan brought extras along to pilot these 'Mechs when she found them, so she's got replacements. We've just got me and Volker. We can't operate five 'Mechs by ourselves."

"I bet I could handle one," Laura said.

"You? I don't—"

"Okay, people," Krenner broke in. "Time out. We're all tired and we just got away from those pirates. We need some time to recoup and plan our next move. Let's not go biting each other's heads off yet and try and focus on the enemy. Is this place secure?"

Sturm nodded. "You're right, Kren. Sorry, Corporal, but I'm operating on next to no sleep and Clan rations and, let me tell you, the Clans may know tech, but they're lousy cooks." That brought chuckles from some of the Lancers. "We should be pretty safe here for now. Seems like the whole depot is shielded to blend in with the rest of the mountain, and all the sensor interference makes it tough to pick up. All the surveys of the area found were some slightly unusual magnetic-resonance readings. As long as we keep quiet, I doubt the pirates will find us."

"All right then," Sergeant Krenner said. "You go and get some sleep, Sturm. I'll get some people and start taking stock of this place. Maybe we can find some other stuff we can use. Then we can talk about strategy when you're rested."

"Thanks, Kren," Sturm said. Krenner began barking out orders to the Lancer crew as Sturm began walking toward the barracks. He was just pulling open his coolant vest when Krenner's voice caught his attention.

"Sturm," the Master Sergeant said as he caught up in a couple of long strides. "I want you to know that you're not off the hook yet."

"Huh?"

"I mean, I'm not taking command here, MechWarrior. I'm just a ground-pounder, not a 'Mech jockey. You're still in charge. I'm just keeping things running."

"Me?" Sturm said. It came out almost like a squeak. "Krenner, I can't—"

"Damn right he can't!" Volker said as he stepped up to the pair. "Need I remind you that I'm the senior officer here, Mr. Krenner?"

"Yeah, by a whole couple of months," Krenner said.

"I've still got seniority over Kintaro," Volker insisted.

"Seniority doesn't mean squat to me, Volker," Krenner returned. "The point is that you don't outrank Kintaro. You're both MechWarriors. Lieutenant Holt is dead and Kintaro is the one who just saved all of our butts. He knows this depot and he knows the Clan 'Mechs. He's more familiar with the situation than you are and, right now, he's the god-damned hero of those people over there! Right now, they'll follow him, and that's the way it is!"

"I see you already forgot that Kintaro didn't save everyone's butt back there, Sarge. If it wasn't for me, you'd probably be a smear on the bay floor right now, but fine. I'll play it your way for now." Volker turned to Sturm, as if he'd just noticed him standing there. "Hey, Kintaro, if things get too rough, just let me know and I'll step in."

Up until that moment, Sturm had had his doubts about command but, for a second, they disappeared, replaced with anger at Volker's attitude. "Don't worry," he said quietly. "I can handle it." Volker just shrugged and walked away. Krenner clapped a hand on Sturm's shoulder.

"Go and get some sleep," he said. "I can handle Volker."

Sturm nodded and walked wearily to the barracks and the bunk he'd been using as his own since he'd found the depot. He smiled a bit as he noticed that he'd taken the senior officer's bunk. He'd just figured it was the most comfortable. *Now I'm not so sure*, he thought. Somehow he'd figured that freeing the other Lancers would let him turn over responsibility to someone else. Now Krenner was placing it firmly on his shoulders.

Sturm dropped onto the bunk without even removing his vest or boots. He lay there for a few moments, fingering the talisman of his mother's 'Mech that he wore around his neck. He couldn't help wondering what Jenna Kintaro would have done in this situation. Before any answers came, he drifted off into a deep and dreamless sleep.

Sturm was awakened sometime later by a touch on his shoulder. He started awake and reached down for his sidearm before a deep voice whispered to him.

"It's okay, it's me, it's Krenner."

Sturm relaxed and let out his breath, reaching up to rub the sleep from his eyes. Krenner's dark silhouette was framed in the faint light from the corridor outside.

"What is it?" Sturm asked. "Is it morning already?"

"No," Krenner said. "It's about 0400 hours. You need to get up. We've got a problem."

A few minutes later, Sturm was dressed in a Clan Steel Viper duty uniform with the insignia torn off and standing in a part of the depot he never even knew existed. The small chamber was located above the main depot area, close to the surface of the mountain itself. It was packed with sophisticated electronic equipment and had a smaller version of the main hatch that opened into the 'Mech bay.

In the middle of the room rested a large metallic turntable of sorts that held a central column with a metallic cylinder hinged to the center of it, like a stubby machine-gun mount. Tom Flannery was in the process of examining the computer readouts and displays on the nearby console.

"The techs found this a little while ago," Krenner said.

"What is it?" Sturm asked.

It was Flannery who answered, but he spoke without taking his eyes off the console. "Near as I can tell, it's a small, highly sophisticated hyper-pulse generator, similar to the ones used by Com-Star to send interstellar transmissions."

Sturm was familiar with the principle: HPGs transmitted packets of energy that traveled faster than the speed of light, allowing communications to be beamed across the vast distances between star systems. Many of the HPGs in the Inner Sphere were controlled by ComStar, but it made sense that the Clans would have ones of their own.

"Does this mean we can send a signal to the rest of the company?" Sturm asked. If they could signal the Storm Riders and let them know their situation, then the Riders could send reinforcements. All the Lancers would have to do is hold out until they arrived.

"I'm not sure yet," Flannery said, "but I think I can get it to work."

"How do you know so much about HPGs?" Sturm asked.

Flannery shrugged a bit and smiled sheepishly. "Before I joined the Storm Riders I was a ComStar acolyte," he said. "I was just a kid then, but I really believed in the Word of Blake and ComStar. When things inside ComStar started to fall apart, I saw the light and figured out that ComStar was just like everyone else in the galaxy, looking out for number one. I figured I'd do the same, so I left and signed up with the Riders. Still, I haven't forgotten what I learned from my ComStar training. I'm pretty sure I can use this generator to send a signal to the rest of the company."

"That's great!" Sturm said. He turned to Krenner. "You said there was a problem?"

"There is," Flannery said, answering for the sergeant. "It looks like this particular HPG is active, and that it was activated automatically several days ago, probably right after you broke into the depot. It activated and sent out a signal, some kind of automated message."

A cold feeling clutched at Sturm's stomach. "Where did it send the message?" he asked, already knowing what the answer would be.

"Right into the Clan Occupied Zone," Krenner said. "By now, the Steel Vipers know that someone broke into their toy box. The Clans are probably on their way here right now, and you can bet they're not happy."

18

Shangri-la
Jotun Mountains, Kore
The Periphery
17 April 3060

"People, we have a problem," Sturm said.

They were assembled in a meeting room in the Clan 'Mech depot, sitting around an oval-shaped table with a smooth black macroplas top, six members of a unit that currently didn't number more than a couple dozen people. Sturm stood at the head of the table, still wondering what he was doing in charge of this whole crazy situation. He looked out at the other members of the Kore Lancers who now formed what could be considered the unit's command structure.

Sergeant Aaron Krenner sat at Sturm's right, of course. Sturm didn't know what he'd do without Krenner's support and guidance. The Sarge had backed him as commander of the Lancers, firmly believing Sturm could handle the situation with the pirates, and now the looming threat of the

Clans. Sturm only hoped he could justify Kren's faith in him. The Master Sergeant didn't speak much, but allowed Sturm to take the lead, offering only the occasional suggestion.

On the other hand, Sturm didn't know what he was going to do about Lon Volker. He respected Volker's abilities as a MechWarrior, but he just couldn't find it in himself to like him. It was just as obvious that Sturm wasn't one of Volker's favorite people, either. Volker considered himself more experienced and senior to Sturm. But, as Sergeant Krenner pointed out, Sturm was more familiar with the 'Mech depot, more familiar with the terrain of the Jotun Mountains, and he had more of the respect and admiration of the other Lancers. Sturm hoped he could find a way to handle Volker diplomatically, because he certainly needed his help. He was the only other truly qualified 'Mech pilot left in the Lancers.

Next to Volker sat Corporal Laura Metz. Krenner had recommended that she be included in the meeting and Sturm agreed. He liked Metz, even though she'd rarely ever given him the time of day back before the arrival of the pirates. Still, she was a good and capable member of the Lancers. Sturm knew Krenner thought Metz had potential, and he could see some of it himself, but her involvement with Volker gave him pause. It could mean that Metz might side with Volker and make trouble over Sturm being in command.

Listen to me, Sturm thought. *Less than a day in command and I'm already starting to sound paranoid.*

Next to Krenner sat technician Tom Flannery. Flannery was definitely one of the best young techs the Lancers had. In a matter of hours he'd already figured out the Clan HPG system and was now working on getting them more technical information on the 'Mechs. Flannery was an invaluable resource as a tech, but Sturm knew he was going to need even more from him than that before all this was over.

Lastly there was Rachel Clancy, a grim-faced young woman with deep auburn hair cut military-short in MechWarrior style. Clancy, like a lot of the Lancers and other Korans, had lost part of her family in the Clan invasion. Her father was an infantryman with the Lancers who'd died defending Niffelheim from the invaders. She had only begun her training as an apprentice Mech-Warrior a few short weeks ago, but here she sat, looking composed and calm as she listened, as they all listened to what Sturm had to say.

I wonder if any of them are as scared on the inside as I am right now, Sturm wondered. If they were, nobody showed it, and Sturm knew that he had to do the same. He put aside his fears and concerns and got down to the business at hand.

"The good news," he said, "is that Flannery, our resident miracle worker here, has managed to rig up the clan HPG so we can send out a message to the rest of the Storm Riders back in Lyran space. We've already sent out a transmission informing them of the situation here on Kore and asking for reinforcements. Our best guess is that it'll still take at least a few weeks for them to get here, depending on which unit is the closest and has the fastest access to a JumpShip. We also haven't gotten a response yet, so we can't be sure the cavalry is on the way yet.

"The bad news is that the HPG has already transmitted a signal into the Clan Occupation Zone directed at Clan Steel Viper. We have to assume that the Vipers know that someone has broken into their 'Mech depot and that they're going to respond. For all we know, a Clan force is already on its way to Kore, which is why it's imperative that we move as quickly as we can."

"How much time have we got?" Metz spoke up.

Sturm shook his head. "There's no way to know. They might be here in a couple weeks or a couple months. Or they might never come. For all we know, the Steel Vipers might be busy with their own problems. Things in the Clan Occupation Zone aren't entirely stable, either. They might decide that Kore is too small and too far away to be bothered with. Hell, they may have already written the place off and maybe nobody's even listening for a message from here. But we have to assume the worst, which means we might have to deal with some angry Clanners as well as the pirates. That makes taking care of the pirates as soon as possible and regaining control of the command center our first priority."

"What about just talking with Susie Ryan?" Volker asked. "You said Ryan probably came here looking for these Clan 'Mechs. If we tell her we've got the 'Mechs and that there's a Clan force on its way here, maybe she'll decide it's more trouble than it's worth and just leave."

Sturm shook his head. "No. We can't do that. If we try to negotiate with Ryan, we're showing our hand too soon. Right now, the only thing stopping her from mounting an attack on this place and just taking those 'Mechs is the fact that she doesn't know where we are and she doesn't know our exact strength. If we give away our location or the strength of our forces, Ryan will take any opportunity to crush us and get what she wants."

"You seem to know an awful lot about a woman you've never met," Volker said. "But I have. I talked with her. She's ruthless, but she's not stupid. I think she might be reasonable. She probably doesn't want to deal with the Steel Vipers any more than we do."

Sturm was about to respond when Sergeant Krenner spoke up. "You're talking about the woman who staged a sneak attack on this planet and killed a lot of good people from this unit, Volker. Including Lieutenant Holt and Hans Brinkmann."

"So?" Volker said. "There's nothing we can do about that now. Do you want to be practical about this or are we just out for revenge?"

"This isn't about revenge," Sturm said before Krenner could reply. "It's about the fact that I don't trust Susie Ryan further than I can throw a DropShip. I believe she'll do anything she can to get her hands on these 'Mechs. She's already thrown away more than enough lives trying to get at them. What are a few more? I don't think Ryan will be reasonable any longer than it takes to get us to expose ourselves so she can strike. *If* we're going to negotiate with Ryan, we need to do it from a better position, or we need to be able to take back the command center ourselves. If anyone has a better idea, I'd love to hear it right about now."

"You know what I think," Volker said. "I think it's suicide to go up against Ryan's Rebels with what we've got, a couple dozen people against what, a hundred pirates? We're better off negotiating while we've still got a chance."

"Anyone else?" Sturm asked as he swept his gaze across the rest of the table. No one spoke for what seemed like a long time.

Finally Flannery said, "We're behind you, sir. What's the plan?"

"If we're going to take on Ryan's Rebels, we need 'Mechs. We've got them down in the 'Mech bay. What we need now are MechWarriors. That's where you all come in."

There was a moment of stunned silence in the room before anyone gathered their wits enough to speak. Flannery was the first.

"Us? MechWarriors? Kintaro I'm a *tech* . . ."

"And a damn good one," Sturm said, leaning forward on the table and bracing himself with his palms flat on the polished black surface. "I also think you could be a damn good MechWarrior. We also don't really have much of a choice. Volker and I are the only full 'Mech jocks left. Clancy knows enough that she can pick things up. But that still leaves us with two 'Mechs with no pilots, and we're going to need everything we've got to go up against Ryan's Rebels and have a chance of winning. They've got more experience and some heavier 'Mechs, but Kore is our home and the Korans our people. We're all this planet's got to protect it, and that's our job. Krenner and I know you can do it, but we don't have a lot of time."

"So what's the plan?" Metz asked. Unlike Flannery, she looked intrigued by the idea of becoming a 'Mech pilot. Krenner had predicted she would and thought she had the stuff to do it.

"There are simulator pods in the depot. The Clans probably set this base up for some long-term postings, and they wanted their warriors to keep sharp. Krenner, Volker, and I are going to train you to be MechWarriors. It's going to be fast, it's going to be hard, and it's going to be real basic, because we don't have time for anything fancy, but I think it's our best shot." There was another pause as everyone thought it over. They very quickly came to the same conclusion: there wasn't much choice.

"All right," Flannery said. "I'm in."

"Me, too," said Metz.

"You *know* I'm up for it," Clancy said with a small smile. "Just let me at 'em."

"All right," Sturm said, leaning back from the table into his chair. "Time to hit the simulators, people. As soon as you're ready, we're going to give Susie Ryan just what she wants: a shot at our 'Mechs, but she's going to find out she can't have them without a fight. Volker, get everyone down to the 'Mech bay and suited up for the simulators. Start them off with some basic mission scenarios and training runs."

"Yes, sir," Volker said quietly. He pushed back from the table and everyone else followed suit. As they filed out of the room, Sturm spoke to Krenner.

"Kren? Can you hold up a second?"

The big man paused by the door and waited for the others to leave before closing it and walking back over to the table where Sturm sat.

"Am I doing the right thing here?" Sturm asked, hanging his head and tracing patterns on the polished black tabletop. "I mean, is Volker right? Should we try talking to Ryan first before I start committing a bunch of green pilots with only a few hours of simulator training to fight trained pirate MechWarriors who probably have more experience than I do?"

"You said it yourself," Krenner said, looking directly at Sturm. "We can't trust Susie Ryan for a second. She'll turn on us at the first opportunity. The only thing we've got going for us is the element of surprise. Ryan doesn't know what we have here, or what we're going to do with it. That gives us an edge. We'd be stupid to give it away."

"I just wish I could see another way," Sturm said quietly, looking up from the table to meet Krenner's gaze. "What if we can't do it?"

Krenner's gaze never wavered. "Then we go down fighting," he said. "Sometimes, when you're in command, you have to make the hard choices, Sturm. You have to do what you think is right, no matter what." He came over and clapped Sturm on the shoulder with one massive hand.

"You're doing okay," he said. "I think your mom would be proud."

"Thanks, Kren," Sturm said. "You get going. I'll be right down to help out with the simulators." Krenner nodded and left the room, leaving Sturm alone with his thoughts for a moment.

I wanted to be like my mother, he thought, *but I never realized until just now what she faced.* His hand went to the metal piece around his neck. *I only hope I can be half as brave as you were when the time comes, mom*, he told her silently. His thoughts turned to his father, who was still in Niffelheim. Sturm hoped he was okay. There was so much he'd wanted to say to him in the last few days.

He pushed back from the table with a sigh. *With luck, I'll get the chance*, he thought. Then he got up and headed down to help supervise his new command.

19

Kore Lancers Command Center
Outside Niffelheim, Kore
The Periphery
20 April 3060

"Still no sign of 'em, Captain, and we're not too likely to find any out in this weather," Darnell said over the commline. "I can hardly see five meters in front of my face, and the sensors aren't much more accurate. They could be anywhere. Over."

"All right, all right, turn it around and head back to base. As soon as you get a clear channel, signal them that we're on our way back. *Mad Cat* out."

"Roger that, Captain," came the reply.

In the cockpit of her *Mad Cat*, Susie Ryan gave a deep and frustrated sigh. As much as she hated to admit it, Darnell was right. It had been four days since the *Goshawk* freed the Kore Lancers from the command center, luring two of the pirate 'Mechs off on a wild-goose chase to cover the raid.

The 'Mech and the Lancers had fled somewhere into the Jotun Mountains, but efforts to track them were first hindered by the mountains themselves and now by the foul weather sweeping down across Kore's northern plains.

The fierce storm dumped snow across the tundra and whipped it into a solid curtain of whiteness that visual sensors could barely penetrate. The Rebels were piloting their 'Mechs almost completely by instrument readings, which was dangerous this close to the mountains. The sensors were notoriously inaccurate. Already they'd hit upon half a dozen false leads that turned out to be metallic ore deposits or volcanic vents.

Darnell's *Puma* also nearly plunged into a crevasse that he didn't see until he was practically on top of it. It was fortunate he was able to avoid it. Ryan couldn't afford any more damage to any more of her 'Mechs at this point. The techs had the Koran *Panther* up and working again, but it was a poor replacement for the *Uller* they'd lost to the "Winter Ghost."

Since the surprise attack on the command center, the "Ghost" had vanished along with the Lancers themselves. Ryan was certain that the "Ghost MechWarrior" had to be Sturm Kintaro, the missing member of the Lancers, whose 'Mech was destroyed in the mountains. Somehow, Kintaro must have found the Clan depot she suspected was hidden on the planet.

On the one hand, Ryan was gratified to know that her suspicions were correct and the wild stories were worth what she'd paid for them. There *was* a secret Clan depot on Kore, set up by the

Steel Vipers in the early days of the Clan invasion and later lost to Inner Sphere mercenaries and either forgotten or abandoned. Such a collection of Clan technology and military hardware was a treasure-trove for the old Bandit Kingdoms, which desperately needed more 'Mechs to fight against the Clans. Ryan would like nothing more than to use those 'Mechs against their former Clan owners and grind them into the dirt with them.

But some wet-behind-the-ears MechWarrior, barely out of training, somehow manages to stumble onto them! And he's using them against me! The sheer nerve of this Kintaro made her blood boil. But, she did have to admit, the kid had guts, taking on a force like the Rebels on his own, and piloting an unfamiliar BattleMech to do it. Ryan couldn't help but be impressed by what Kintaro had managed to do to the *Uller*, not to mention the damage he'd also done to the command center.

And Kintaro's not alone anymore, is he, she thought. *No, now he had the rest of his unit to help him out, maybe even to pilot some of the other 'Mechs he'd found. That was a serious risk; Kintaro's people weren't trained, Ryan knew that. He and Volker were the only qualified 'Mech pilots left alive in the wake of the attack on Kore. Still, they might be able to tutor some of the more promising members of the unit to handle a 'Mech well enough to be a threat.* She was definitely taking a risk with every moment that passed.

The sooner those 'Mechs were in her hands the sooner she could get off this miserable rock. Ryan was eager to return home and start putting her new prizes to work. Already what was supposed to be a fairly short excursion into the Periphery and back was starting to run over schedule. Ryan's new pirate coalition certainly didn't run itself. She knew it was vulnerable to Clan attacks and to internal stresses. If she was away too long, her lieutenants would start stabbing each other in the back to claim control of everything, and all she'd built would be for nothing. Still, there was time before that became a real concern, and Ryan didn't plan on leaving Kore empty-handed. Not if everything went according to plan.

Still, she told herself as the *Mad Cat* lumbered over the tundra, it pays to have a little extra insurance, just in case things don't go as planned. She keyed open the commline to the command center.

"C&C, this is Ryan. Over."

"C&C here. Go ahead, Captain. Over."

"Send some men over to the research center and have them find Dr. Kintaro," she said. "I want them to make sure he stays there. If he's not there, tell them to find him and bring him there. And have a jeep waiting for me at the 'Mech bay to take me out there. I'd like to have a little talk with the good doctor. Ryan out."

"Roger that, Captain. I'll get some men out there right now. Over and out."

Ryan settled back into her command couch and allowed the rocking motion of the *Mad Cat* to calm her thoughts. Yes, everything would be just fine. It was simply a matter of pulling the right strings and setting things up so they fell her way. Those 'Mechs would belong to her soon enough, and then she could leave this iceball and get back to business. Sturm Kintaro and his little band she would leave out for the winter wolves, to show people the price of defying Susie Ryan.

She smiled to herself. Whether he knew it or not, Dr. Hidoshi Kintaro was about to be far more useful than she first thought.

20

Shangri-la
Jotun Mountains, Kore
The Periphery
22 April 3060

Laura Metz sat in the cockpit of a BattleMech, doing her very best to stay alive. But her opponents certainly weren't making that easy.

She was piloting a *Vixen*, a light Clan 'Mech, massing only thirty tons. The Clan designation called it an *Incubus*, but Kintaro preferred to go by the Inner Sphere names for the Clan 'Mechs. The *Vixen* was considered a "second-line" design by the Clans; a 'Mech kept in reserve while the front-line models handled an initial assault. It wasn't anywhere near the class of medium 'Mechs like the *Goshawk*, much less heavy 'Mechs like the *Mad Cat*, but the *Vixen* still looked plenty tough. Laura recalled the awe she'd felt standing at the foot of the giant war machine and thinking about being in control of it.

"Keep moving, Metz!" came the voice from her

headset, and Laura focused her attention on the matter at hand. She was slowing down, and one of the enemy 'Mechs, an *Uller*, was starting to get her in range. She pushed the control stick forward and sped up. Speed was definitely one of Lady Fox's advantages (as Laura had decided to name her 'Mech). She knew that choosing a name for a 'Mech she only barely qualified to pilot was an act of hubris on her part, to say nothing of using it when she wasn't even in the 'Mech, but sitting inside a simulator pod. Still, somehow it made the whole thing feel more real to her, made the *Vixen* seem more like it was *hers*.

At top speed, the Lady Fox could do just over one hundred fifty kph. Laura was nowhere near that speed. She was still getting a feel for moving quickly across the frozen terrain. The ice and snow made things considerably trickier. They'd started out operating on clear terrain, but graduated up quickly to tundra, since Kintaro and Krenner thought it was important they be able to handle the conditions.

"This whole thing'll be over real quick if we get everybody falling on their faces out there," Krenner had said. So they fought on a simulation of Kore's terrain, covered in ice and snow, which was amazingly slippery, even to a giant humanoid war machine. *Especially* to a 'Mech, as a matter of fact.

The heads-up display flashed a warning of incoming missiles. Laura dodged left, following the evasive maneuvers she'd learned. Her 'Mech's limbs pumped and responded to her commands, sprinting across the snow. The missiles missed by a fair margin, and Laura started to give a whoop of relief, but it quickly turned into a startled cry.

"What the . . . agh!" she yelled as the Lady's foot hit the edge of an ice crevasse she hadn't noticed. She fought with the controls to swerve away from it as the signals feeding through her neurohelmet tried to use the *Vixen*'s internal gyroscope to maintain its balance in the way no other machine could. But it was too little, too late. The 'Mech windmilled its arms, then slid down the slide of the icy pit, dislodging a mass of snow and sending chunks of ice pinging off the hull.

Laura managed to land the Lady relatively upright. The padding of her command chair and harness absorbed the impact, leaving her only slightly jostled. She quickly checked the status display for signs of damage and saw only some minor loss of armor on her right leg, no internal or structural damage.

The next problem was getting out of the crevasse. It was about thirteen meters deep, just a scant few meters above the *Vixen*'s head. The 'Mech's arms could reach out of the pit, but the *Vixen* had only one free hand, the other taken up holding its primary weapon, a large pulse laser. The easiest solution would be to simply jump clear of the pit, but the 'Mech also lacked jump jets, unlike the *Goshawk* or the *Hellhound*.

Suddenly, from her external pickups came a deep booming noise and snow and ice shivered down off the sides of the crevasse. Laura turned her 'Mech around as best she could and focused the sensors up toward the edge of the pit just in time to see a giant BattleMech step close enough to the edge to be seen and recognized by its bird-like shape, club-like arms, and the missile pods on each of its shoulders: a *Mad Cat*. The 'Mech leveled its weapons down at her, and Metz reached for the firing button for her own weapon systems.

A voice from her headset interrupted her. "Bang," it said. "You're dead."

She let go of the controls and slumped back in her command couch, throwing her head against the raised back in frustration, as far as the neuro-helmet would allow. "Dammit, not again," she moaned.

The door of the training pod opened with a *thunk* and Sturm Kintaro leaned in to offer her a hand.

"Time to eject, MechWarrior," he said with a grim look on his face. Laura reached up and pulled off the neurohelmet, and shook out her sweat-soaked hair. She swore that the sadistic Clan technicians who designed the simulator pods intentionally made them run hotter than a real 'Mech just so trainees would get used to the heat, or else pass out, making it easier to cull out the weakest of the herd.

She took the proffered hand gratefully and climbed out of the pod. Clancy was waiting, and she gave Laura a nod before sliding into her place for another training session. Laura was really starting to like Clancy. Even though she had a bit more training than either Laura or Flannery, she never looked down on them and always treated them as equals. In fact, Laura discovered that she liked that about Kintaro as well, although he had a harder time being friendly with any of the trainees.

"Not so good?" she said to him, anticipating a critical analysis of her performance.

"You didn't do too bad," Kintaro said to her surprise. "Until, of course, you ended up dead." Seeing her face fall, he smiled a bit. "Don't worry about it," he said. "You're still doing a hell of a lot better than I was after a couple days in training. Hell, I didn't hit arctic terrain until I'd been doing simulations for *weeks*.

"Just keep a closer eye on the terrain when you're moving, especially when you're moving fast," he said. "It helps to get a feel for where you're going, and then look at your sensor data before you move. Think one move ahead all the time and you'll end up with fewer surprises." He held a plastic bottle out to her.

Laura accepted it gratefully and took several long, deep swallows of the water inside. It was tepid, but still far cooler than she felt at the moment. "Thanks," she said.

"No problem." He started back toward the control console for the simulator pods, whose monitors displayed a pilot's-eye view along with an overview of the battlefield.

"Sir?" Laura asked. It was a second before Kintaro turned around. He clearly wasn't used to being called "sir" by anyone. "Do you really think we've got a chance against Ryan's Rebels?" she asked. He looked at her for a long moment, like he was trying to think of what to say.

"If I didn't, Laura," he said, "we wouldn't be doing this." It was the first time he'd ever used Laura's first name. When she nodded, Kintaro turned back toward the console and she watched him for a moment, wondering how she'd never really noticed things about him before.

She felt a bit guilty just then, and flicked her eyes down to the floor. *What would Lon think about me checking out Sturm Kintaro*, she wondered. *Probably nothing good. He doesn't like Kintaro, but then, I don't belong to him. It's not like we're anything serious.* Still, she felt guilty. Since they'd gotten away from the command base and into training to fight the pirates, she'd seen next to nothing of Volker. They were both extremely busy, of course, but it was more than that. Volker seemed preoccupied, wrapped up in his own thoughts, and he preferred being alone. The few times she tried to talk to him about it, he brushed her off.

Laura knew that having Kintaro for a C.O. was bothering him. Volker considered himself more experienced than Sturm, and he didn't like taking orders from a "kid" who was younger than him, even if it was only by a year or so. She wondered if maybe it had something to do with Volker getting captured by Ryan's Rebels while Sturm escaped. She knew that Volker thought Sturm had "lucked into" the 'Mech cache.

Glancing over at the chronometer on the wall, she noticed that she had almost an hour until it was time to report for another cockpit briefing on the *Vixen*. She decided to see what Volker was up to. Maybe he could use somebody to talk to, and she was feeling too wound up to relax anyway. Maybe Volker's up for a little mutual relaxation, too, she thought with a wicked smile.

Finding him, however, turned out to be harder than she first thought. Although every one of the Lancers had double-duty to perform, checking out the systems of Shangri-la and the 'Mechs, or training for taking on the Rebels, Volker still seemed to manage to slip off from time to time on his own. Probably because he wasn't required to log as much training time as the new recruits and because he wasn't a tech or a grunt but a Mech-Warrior. That gave him some additional leeway, although it was clear that Kintaro and Krenner were fed up with Volker's attitude.

She checked his quarters, but didn't find him, so she also checked the mess-hall, with no luck. It wasn't until she decided to head back to the 'Mech bay that she ran into him in the corridor outside.

"Hey, Lon," she said with a smile. "Been looking for you."

He returned the smile and shrugged. "I've been around. I was just checking out some of the systems on the Cerberus." Laura knew that was the name he'd given the Hellhound. Kintaro had assigned it to Volker because it was the second-heaviest 'Mech in the Star, fifty tons to the *Goshawk*'s fifty-five. "It's definitely a cut above my old *Panther*," he said. "I just hope we get a chance to hold onto these 'Mechs."

"You don't think we can handle Ryan's Rebels?" Laura said with a note of disapproval in her voice.

"Seriously? Think about it, Laurie. I mean, c'mon. Sure we've got them outclassed in tonnage, but only by about ten tons. *Ten tons*. Compare that to the fact that we've got only two experienced MechWarriors to their four and things don't look so good.

"Golden-boy Kintaro may think these Clan 'Mechs make us tough enough to take anyone on, but I think he's just fooling himself. He wants to be some big hero and come charging in to save the day. All he's going to end up getting is killed if he's not more careful."

"And what do you want, Lon?" she asked.

"Me? You know me, Laurie. I've always wanted to be a MechWarrior, to pilot a 'Mech and to be damn good at it. But I also want to stay alive. I've got nothing against a good fight, but I think going up against the Rebels with no training and no preparation, with the possibility of the Clans breathing down our necks, is just stupid."

"If you don't think we can win, why are you even here?" she asked angrily. She hated to admit it, but what Volker was saying made sense. Maybe they *were* just fooling themselves.

Volker shrugged. "Like I said, I like a good fight, and I like having a 'Mech of my own. The Rebels took my *Panther*, Laurie. I could have ended up dispossessed. I wasn't going to stay a prisoner, and I sure as hell ain't going to hang back and watch while Kintaro sends complete greenies into the field. So here I am. I may not like it, but you do what you have to do."

Laura thought about that. Volker's fears were certainly justified. Every MechWarrior's worst nightmare was the loss of his or her 'Mech. Battle-Mechs were a rare commodity in the thirty-first century, especially for mercenary units like the

Storm Riders. Mercs had to make do with what they had, and many 'Mechs were family heirlooms, handed down from one generation to the next. A MechWarrior without a 'Mech was a sorry sight. In some ways, an honorable death in battle was preferable to becoming dispossessed.

"Hey," she said, trying to change the subject, "I've got a few minutes before my next training session. Do you want to grab a cup of java?" She dropped her voice a touch lower. "Or maybe find a quiet spot away from everybody for a little while?"

Volker was about to reply when another voice cut into the conversation.

"Volker!" Sturm Kintaro said. "I've been looking for you."

"Didn't know I was lost," Volker said.

Kintaro's face showed that he wasn't amused. "You were supposed to relieve me on the training pods almost twenty minutes ago," he said. "Or did you just forget about that?"

"I had things to take care of," Volker said. "I was checking out the Cerberus and—"

"I really don't care what you were doing. I need you down there manning the training console. Now."

"I still think this is a complete waste of time," Volker said. The two of them were standing practically nose to nose. Laura wondered if they were going to come to blows. The tension in Kintaro's whole body practically vibrated like a guitar string.

"Your opinion is noted, MechWarrior, but right now, all I want—"

"Sturm!" came Sergeant Krenner's voice. The Master Sergeant came running down the corridor, calling out as he went. "Sturm! We need you in the communications center right now!"

"What is it?" Sturm asked, his confrontation with Volker defused, for the time being.

"It's Susie Ryan," Krenner said. "She has your dad, Sturm, and she's threatening to execute him."

═══ 21 ═══

Shangri-la
Jotun Mountains, Kore
The Periphery
22 April 3060

Sturm was the first one to reach the communications center, with Krenner, Volker, and Laura close on his heels. The comm center held the depot's various communications equipment, with the exception of the HPG gear, located further up the mountain. The Clan equipment was capable of breaking through some of the commline interference caused by Kore's intense magnetic field and the metallic ores in the mountains. The image displayed on the viewscreens occasionally crackled with static. Still, Sturm had no trouble making out who it was, or what she was saying.

"The command base just started broadcasting this, sir," the communications tech said to Sturm. "They've got it on a repeating loop."

"This is Captain Ryan, commander of Ryan's Rebels and military ruler of this miserable backwater planet," said the image of Susie Ryan on the viewscreen. She was dressed in a paramilitary uniform, and the patch over her left eye gave her face a sinister look. It was the first time Sturm had actually seen Ryan's face, the face of the woman responsible for the assault on Kore and the death of so many of his friends.

"This message is directed at the MechWarrior named Sturm Kintaro, formerly of the Kore Lancers. Kintaro, you have taken something that belongs to me and I want it back. If you do not surrender yourself and those former members of the Kore Lancers you are harboring . . ." As she spoke, the image panned back to include the rest of the room where Ryan was standing. Sturm saw his father sitting in a chair. A pirate standing beside him leveled a laser pistol at Dr. Kintaro's head. "If you do not surrender, your father will be executed. His execution will be broadcast so that you and everyone else can see the price of defying me and, I assure you, the execution will be very painful and will take a long, long time."

The image focused back on Ryan, whose face filled the display. "I don't give a damn about you, Kintaro, or your Lancers, your friends, or your family. If I have to burn down every damn thing on this planet, I'll do it, but give me what I want and I'll leave peacefully. Don't be a fool. You can't win. Give it up now before somebody gets hurt, and you have my word that this will all be over.

"If you're actually stupid enough to think that I'm bluffing . . ." There was a pause as the camera shifted to two of Ryan's men pushing a struggling man into the room. He was thrown onto the floor at Susie Ryan's feet, and Sturm recognized him as Derek Nordstrom, the Alfin-appointed governor of Kore. Ryan drew a slim laser pistol from a holster at her waist and leveled it at Nordstrom, who struggled to rise.

"No, no, please, don't!" the governor pleaded, and Sturm found himself biting his lip. "Please, NO!" Ryan coolly shot Nordstrom in the head, the ruby beam of light stabbing through his forehead and out the back of his skull, killing him instantly. The governor flopped onto the gray floor, smoke and steam pouring from the exit and entry holes left by the laser beam. Ryan indicated the body with a nod of her head, and the pirates moved quickly to haul it out of the room while she holstered her sidearm and turned back to the camera.

"The governor earned himself a quick and painless death," she said flatly. "I can think of far worse, and I'm willing to do whatever needs to be done. Think on that before you decide if it's worth taking me on, Kintaro. You have until midday tomorrow to make your decision."

The image faded to black for a moment, then Ryan's image filled the screen as the message started over again. "This is Captain Ryan . . ."

"Shut it off," Sturm said flatly. The comm tech immediately moved to comply, and the screens went dark. Sturm turned away from them, away from the image of his father at the mercy of Ryan and her crew, of Governor Nordstrom's grisly execution. He placed one arm against the cool stone wall and leaned his forehead against it.

"Sturm, I'm sorry," Krenner said, coming over to put a hand on Sturm's shoulder.

Sturm raised his head and took a deep breath, fighting back tears of frustration and anger. He wanted more than anything to just reach through the viewscreen and throttle Susie Ryan with his bare hands. He wanted to strike out, to do *something*.

He turned toward Krenner and the others, his mouth a grim, set line, his eyes hard and cold.

"I'm going to the command base," he said.

"You're what?" several voices said in unison.

"I'm going to surrender to Ryan."

Krenner was the first to find his voice and speak.

"Sturm, you can't do that! That's just what Ryan wants!"

"Kren, if I don't do it, she'll kill my father!"

"For God's sake, think about it! Do you really think a pirate like Susie Ryan gives a damn about anyone's life but her own? Do you really think she won't just kill you *and* your father once she's got what she wants? She's already killed a lot of people to get at these 'Mechs. I don't think a few more are going to bother her one bit."

"That's why I've got to do something!" Sturm said. "I know she's serious. If I don't do what she wants, she'll kill my father. He and I don't see eye to eye on much of anything, but he's still my *father*, damn it! How can I just let him die?"

"Because you're in command," Krenner said evenly. "You have a responsibility to this unit and to the people in it. If you end up captured or killed, what happens to the rest of the Lancers, hmm?"

"What about my responsibility to my father?" Sturm asked. "You want me to just let him die?"

"No," Krenner said, "but you don't have a choice. I'm sorry, Sturm, but your father is just one man. You've got to think about all of the men and women in this unit, about all of the people in Niffelheim. What about them? What happens to them if Ryan gets her hands on these 'Mechs and decides not to leave any witnesses behind? Who's going to stop those pirates if they want to level the city and kill everyone in it?

"This is just what Ryan wants," Krenner continued. "She wants to end all this without a fight, so she can take the 'Mechs without having to damage them. She knows that if she captures you, our chances of being able to fight them go out the window. If you give up, she wins and gets what she wants without a fight."

"Well, thank you very much," Volker interjected from his place near the door of the room.

"Shut up, Volker!" Krenner threw over his shoulder. "I don't care how hot you think you are, you're not going to take on all of those pirates by yourself. We *need* you here, Sturm! Remember what I said, a MechWarrior has to choose his battles."

"Even if it means my father gets killed?"

"Yes, even then."

Sturm started to say something, then he stopped and looked Krenner in the eyes. His gaze slipped past the Master Sergeant over to Volker and Metz.

Then he let out a long, shuddering breath and all the fight seemed to go out of him.

"You're right," he said to Krenner. "You're right. There's nothing I can do about it, except make sure Susie Ryan pays for every life she takes."

"Maybe we can move things up," Laura offered. "Stage an attack on the command base before the time is up . . ." Krenner and Sturm both shook their heads simultaneously.

"No," Sturm said. "It wouldn't make much difference. If we attack the command base now, Ryan will probably kill my father or any other hostages out of pure spite. We've got to take on the Rebels on *our* terms. That's how I was able to get the better of them before, and it's what we need to do now. We've got to make them come to us when we're ready for them."

Krenner turned to Volker and Metz. "You heard the man, people, let's get back to it. Metz, you're due for cockpit training down in the 'Mech bay right now. Volker, I want to talk to you. Meet me down by the simulator pods."

Volker looked like he was about to say something, but then seemed to think better of it. He and Laura turned to leave, though Laura paused to direct a look of sympathy at Sturm before she followed Volker out. Krenner stayed behind and put a comforting hand on Sturm's shoulder.

"You gonna be all right?" he asked.

Sturm swallowed a bit and nodded. "Yeah, yeah, I'll be okay," he said. "I think I just need a little time alone. I'm going to my quarters, all right?"

Krenner nodded. "I'll take care of things. Just remember, we've got a briefing and training overview at 1900 hours."

"I'll be there," Sturm said. He clapped Krenner on the shoulder, then walked past him out of the room.

As he headed toward his temporary quarters, all Sturm could think about was Ryan's message and her threat, and the image of his father sitting in that chair, watching as Susie Ryan murdered Derek Nordstrom in cold blood. He thought too about what Krenner had said, that his first duty was to the Lancers and getting them all out of this situation.

I never asked for this, Sturm thought. *I never wanted to be in command, not this soon. All I wanted was to be a good MechWarrior.*

His quarters were small and dim, lit only by a small light fixture attached to the wall. He threw himself down on the bed and stared at the wall for a moment.

Then he felt the cool metal against his chest. His hand strayed to touch the fragment of his mother's BattleMech hanging from its leather thong around his neck. He thought about her and wished more than ever that she were still around. She would know how to lead the Lancers, how to make the tough decisions.

"What do I do, mom?" he asked the empty air in front of him. "It's one thing for me to die. I knew that could happen going into this. I could deal with dying to protect people, like you did, but I can't handle the idea of dad dying because of me. If Ryan killed him to get at me, I don't think I could ever forgive myself."

He laid there clutching the talisman and thinking for a long time before he made his decision.

Later at the training meeting, Sturm was completely composed and under control. Rumors about Susie Ryan's ultimatum had already spread through the rest of the unit, but Sturm felt remarkably calm and at peace with the situation. He and Krenner handled the evaluation of the trainee MechWarriors, with Sturm offering suggestions of areas for improvement and some unit tactics that could take advantage of the numerical superiority of the Lancers' Star of 'Mechs to the pirates' single lance. No mention was made of Ryan's threats. When Krenner asked Sturm if he wanted to talk about it, Sturm politely declined, saying there really wasn't anything else to say.

That night, after most of the Lancers were asleep, only a skeleton night shift remained on duty, mostly technicians working around the clock to ensure that the Clan BattleMechs were ready for action at a moment's notice, along with Laura Metz, putting in some extra hours in one of the training simulators. Sturm had to admire her dedication to what was probably a hopeless cause. He meant what he'd said about Metz showing a lot of promise as a MechWarrior. She seemed to grasp the basic operations very quickly and she was a lot farther along in her training after only a few days than a lot of apprentices were in months.

Sturm walked into the 'Mech bay carrying a plastic crate from one of the depot's storerooms.

One of the techs looked up from her work to greet him.

"Evening, sir, what are you doing out here at this hour?" Kayla Rossburg said. She stood up from where she was going over some feedback data on the performance of the *Peregrine*'s myomer muscles. Sturm knew Kayla in passing. She was a junior tech, but she knew her business. He shrugged a bit while carrying the heavy box.

"Couldn't sleep," he replied. "Too keyed up, you know? Thought I might check out the cockpit systems on Golden Boy." That was what Sturm had named his *Goshawk*. He hefted the plastic crate. "Got some extra survival gear to stow up there. After the last time, I want to make sure I've got enough of it." He smiled and Kayla returned the smile with a laugh.

"I hear you," she said.

"I won't be in the way," Sturm said. "You'll hardly even know I'm here."

"No problem," she said. "Go right ahead, sir. You know where everything is around here as much as anybody."

"Thanks," Sturm said. He walked past the techs and made his way over to the *Goshawk*, standing silently in its mechanical cradle. The minor damage it had taken in the raid on the command base was already repaired, along with some knocks the 'Mech had taken while Sturm was playing "ghost" with the pirate 'Mechs. He hadn't been able to fix them on his own, but the Lancer techs had made short work of it. The 'Mech was back in prime shape, with only some mismatched areas of paint, gray against bone white, to show it was ever damaged in the first place.

Sturm fixed a hook to the plastic crate and clambered up the chain ladder to the cockpit, trailing the rope attached to the crate. Once inside the cockpit he turned and hauled the the crate up behind him. He set it down on the command couch and opened it carefully, checking the contents again. This would be a bad time to find out that he'd forgotten something, but he wanted to make sure. Then the crate was stowed in the narrow space behind the seat and Sturm took his place at the controls. He pulled the cockpit canopy closed and unzipped his duty coveralls to reveal a coolant vest and a pair of shorts. He shucked out of the coveralls and stowed them with the crate.

Then he pulled Golden Boy's neurohelmet down from the web of cables where it rested and set it into place over the collar of his vest. The neural contacts were in place, and Sturm began to carefully power up the 'Mech's systems, one by one. He skipped over the normal safety checks. There simply wasn't time, and he knew he could trust the Lancer techs to have the 'Mech in perfect working order. He flicked his eyes over the displays one last time. Everything was ready to go.

Sturm hit a button on the command console and a deep rumbling sound filled the 'Mech bay. There was a humming and clunking of heavy machinery and a breath of frigid mountain air as the giant, concealed bay doors slowly began to open. Sturm saw several of the techs on the ground look up from their work in surprise as he gently pushed the control stick forward and the *Goshawk* stepped out of its niche and began moving toward the door.

Hurry up, he silently urged the door controllers as the doors slowly trundled open. He kept the *Goshawk* at a slow walk as he headed for the doors. By the time he got there they were open just wide enough for him to slip out into the darkness of the night. As soon as he was clear, Sturm sent the command to close the doors and they began cycling the other way. An indicator on his HUD showed an incoming transmission. Someone was trying to raise him on the commline. Sturm ignored it and kept the channel closed. He wasn't in the mood to offer any explanations. Soon he was moving out into the valley, and the doors shut behind him, cutting off the light from the 'Mech bay and plunging the valley into darkness, save for the dim light of the stars overhead.

Sturm had no trouble navigating through the valley. He'd done it several times before, and the *Goshawk*'s starlight sensors gave him more than enough illumination, even with its running lights off. Magnetic and thermal readings weren't very reliable, but he didn't need those to go by. In short order he hit the pass out of the mountains and began making his way toward the open tundra of Kore, toward the command base.

He paused as he reached the edge of the pass and glanced back toward the depot. It was completely hidden from sight by its natural and artificial camouflage, but Sturm knew where it was nonetheless.

I'm sorry, Kren, he thought, *I do have a duty to you and the Lancers, but duty to my father comes first.*

I've let him down enough times before this, but I'll be damned if I'm going to let him down now when he needs me most. I might not have been able to save my mom, but I can sure as hell try to save him. You can handle things without me. You've still got Volker. As long as Ryan has my father, I'm no use to you, anyway. I'm going to get him back on my own, or die trying.

22

The Koran Plains
Outside Niffelheim, Kore
22 April 3060

Golden Boy carried Sturm swiftly across the dark, frozen landscape of Kore. The 'Mech was moving at a good pace, around sixty kph, a brisk walk for the giant machine. Sturm didn't push the speed up too fast, since it would increase the 'Mech's heat signature and make it more likely for him to be noticed. As it was he had most of the *Goshawk*'s heat sinks operating in standby mode to reduce its heat output to the absolute minimum. He didn't want to be detected by any patrols or sensor sweeps the pirates might be sending out. That was making the inside of the cockpit unusually warm, and Sturm was already sweating profusely by the time he cleared the mountains. He wasn't sure if it was waste heat from the 'Mech or his own nervousness, however. What he was doing right now was foolish and dangerous. If Krenner knew. . . .

But Krenner doesn't know, Sturm thought. The drill sergeant would be furious with Sturm, but he didn't see that he had any choice. Susie Ryan was threatening to kill his father. Sturm wasn't going to let that happen. Not while he could do something about it. Even if that was exactly what Ryan wanted him to do.

He guided the 'Mech skillfully across the tundra using only the light from the stars and his 'Mech's own light-intensification sensors to help guide him. He'd crisscrossed the Koran plains in a 'Mech many times while training over the last few years and he knew them like the back of his hand. He knew how to avoid the various crevasses and pitfalls. He also knew how to make the most use of the terrain to cover his approach to the former command base of the Lancers.

Sturm angled Golden Boy on a wide arc around the command base, at the extreme range of the base's sensors. He knew, at this range, that the sensors were notoriously unreliable. They were always picking up weird magnetic and thermal readings from the local environment, to the point where the Lancer sensor techs usually ignored the strange "ghosts." Sturm wasn't certain the pirates would be quite so lax. But by now they were probably used to the existence of so many sensor ghosts. One more shouldn't be all that unusual.

As he approached, nature herself lent a hand. Sturm checked his long-range sensors and smiled grimly at what he saw. There was a storm front moving in from the north, he noticed. It was storm season, and sudden, fierce snow squalls were commonplace. The front would further help shield his approach, maybe even let him get a little closer than he'd originally planned. He checked the sensor readings again. The front should be here in just a few minutes, he thought.

Sure enough, the wind quickly picked up, scattering powdery snow before it. The sky darkened as heavy clouds blotted out the stars and large, fluffy flakes of snow began to fall. In a matter of minutes, the snowfall thickened to become a curtain of whiteness in front of the BattleMech. Sturm slowed Golden Boy's pace to better navigate through the blinding squall. His own sensors were limited in effectiveness, so he was sure the command base couldn't see very far either.

He brought the 'Mech to within a few kilometers of the base, closer than he would ordinarily have dared. He knew of a deep crevasse in the terrain, having encountered it several times on training runs. It was a favorite place for setting up ambushes on those training sessions. With great care, Sturm guided the *Ghoshawk* into the crevasse. The ten-meter-tall machine slowly hunkered down at Sturm's command, settling itself into the narrow space so that it was no longer visible from the ground-level.

Once the 'Mech was in place and Sturm was sure its position was stable, he powered down all of the *Goshawk*'s main systems. He double-checked the security systems, making sure they were set properly to his brainwave pattern. Anyone else who tried to use the 'Mech would get a serious jolt from the neurohelmet and be unable to operate the *Goshawk*. Then he disengaged the neurohelmet and stripped off his coolant vest.

Sturm reached around behind the command chair to where he'd stowed the small plastic crate. He pulled out a small towel and dried himself off as much as possible. Then he tossed the towel back into the crate and pulled out his coveralls, which he slipped back on as quickly as possible in the cramped confines of the 'Mech cockpit. Over the coveralls he strapped a belt holding a laser pistol in a side holster that tied down to his left leg. A commando knife went into the sheath in his boot-top. Then Sturm pulled out the cold-weather gear: parkalike jacket with a close-fitting hood, thermal-lined gloves, and a pair of tinted goggles to protect his face against the driving snow.

He cracked the 'Mech's cockpit canopy slightly, and a chilling blast of air blew inside, carrying a few small flakes of snow. The heat in the cockpit dissipated quickly, and Sturm struggled into the cold-weather gear. When he was ready, he pulled the small backpack from the crate and pushed the canopy open, standing up to slip the pack over his shoulders, letting it rest comfortably on his back. He moved his shoulders a bit to help distribute the weight evenly, as the wind howled up at the edge of the crevasse.

He stepped carefully out of the cockpit onto the hull of Golden Boy, pulling the cockpit shut. It closed and locked with a click. Sturm balanced carefully on the 'Mech's shoulder, the dull, pinging noises of the warm hull cooling in the freezing air barely audible above the sound of the wind. Using the maintenance handholds, he started to climb up the "hood" that protected the *Goshawk*'s head from behind. It currently rested almost flush against the side of the crevasse, enough for Sturm to nearly reach the edge.

At the top of the 'Mech's hood, Sturm took some climbing spikes from his pack and hammered them into the side of the crevasse. In fairly short order, he climbed the few meters to the top. He reslung his pack and started off toward the command base.

Normally, covering the two kilometers to the base would have been no problem. On Kore every MechWarrior was trained to handle outdoor excursions across the fierce terrain. However, the storm swirling across the surface of the frozen tundra was another matter. Visibility was extremely limited, and there was the possibility of becoming lost in the storm. Normal compasses didn't even work because of Kore's unusual magnetic field. But Sturm set the *Goshawk* to produce a regular signal on a particular radio frequency, allowing him to always know the distance and direction between him and the 'Mech. It increased slightly the chances that the 'Mech would be detected, but it also helped ensure that Sturm wouldn't wander off and freeze to death.

He walked through the storm toward the command base, keeping the signal from the *Goshawk* at his back. The snow limited visibility to only a few meters in any direction, and drifts quickly began to form along the ground, making the going harder as Sturm trudged along. It took some time to reach the outskirts of the command base. To Sturm, it seemed like forever, but in truth it was only about an hour.

Carefully, he circled the outer perimeter. He was in luck. The pirates hadn't bothered to repair the damage Sturm had inflicted on the perimeter fence when he liberated the other Lancers from the command base. He stepped over the crushed chain-link and posts buried in the snow and made his way toward the lights of the compound, barely visible through the white haze.

It was likely that Ryan was keeping his father somewhere on the command base, close at hand. Sturm knew the base well. It had been his home for the past several years. He was fairly sure where the pirates would keep prisoners, especially a single prisoner who was important to their commander. The pirates were smart enough to stay buttoned-down and inside in a storm like this, so there was nobody on guard-duty at the gate outside the base. The pirate BattleMechs were probably either safely inside themselves, or on patrol outside along the perimeter. Sturm didn't see any signs of them.

He began moving his way along the outskirts of the compound toward his goal. Along the way, he unlimbered his pack and reached inside for some things he would need if he was going to pull this off.

Reaching the main building wasn't a problem, nor was disabling the security scanner at the entrance. Sturm knew the right codes to override the scanner. The main codes had been changed, of course, but there was a set of emergency back-up codes in the system in case it was subverted by an outside agency. Apparently, the pirates hadn't found or disabled that sub-system yet. Sturm was inside in a matter of moments, with no one the wiser.

Once inside, he drew his laser pistol and held it at the ready as he made his way down the corridor toward the stairwell. He couldn't risk using the elevators and possibly getting trapped in one. Fortunately, it was only two levels down to reach the center's brig. No problem, Sturm told himself as he glanced down either side of the corridor. No one in sight.

He dashed across the corridor and down a short distance to the door, pushing it open, then flattening against it as the door swung shut. He was in the stairwell. Still no one in sight. It was strange that the pirates didn't have any guards stationed, but Sturm didn't really know the size of Ryan's force. From what the Lancers who'd witnessed the attack on Niffelheim reported, she had 'Mechs and infantry support personnel, but she might have them assigned elsewhere. Or perhaps she wasn't expecting any trouble this close to home. Or, maybe, this is a trap, Sturm thought. He'd considered that possibility several times, but it didn't change what he had to do.

He made his way quietly down the stairs to the sub-basement level of the building, where there was a small brig. It was only used to discipline the occasional member of the Lancers who got drunk and disorderly off-duty and needed a place to dry out and think about the follies of improper behavior. Sturm never had the misfortune of seeing the inside of it personally, but he knew that the cells were hardly maximum security. He was sure he could handle it.

At the bottom of the stairs, he tested the door and pushed it open gently. This door opened out into the main corridor that ran the length of the sub-basement level. The cells were on the far end, about ten meters away. With the door open just a crack, Sturm looked down the corridor and spied a single, bored-looking pirate on duty in front of the cells, leaning against the wall looking like he'd rather be anywhere else in the world. He had a holstered sidearm (a slug-thrower, Sturm figured) and was dressed in the somewhat mismatched fatigues worn by Ryan's Rebels.

No two ways about this, Sturm thought. He leveled his laser pistol at the pirate and took careful aim. The laser beam could be triggered in two different ways. The high-level setting fired a powerful coherent beam capable of burning through flesh, stone, and metal. The low-level setting fired a weak beam no more powerful than a laser-pointer or range-finder, but useful as a sight and a guide for the more powerful beam. A small ruby dot appeared on the pirate's left shoulder and started to track up to his head.

"What the . . . ?" The pirate turned and spotted the laser dot. Just as he started to move, Sturm fired. There was a crack of super-heated air, and a red beam of light speared the guard cleanly through the head. The man dropped to the floor instantly and silently, steam rising from the wound, which took off a large portion of his skull, but that cauterized itself almost instantly.

Sturm rushed down the corridor, ignoring the body of the guard lying on the floor. As he did, a familiar face appeared at the small barred window of one of the cells, the eyes widening in surprise as he spotted the dead guard and the dark-clad figure coming down the hall.

"Sturm!" Dr. Kintaro said in a loud whisper. "What are you . . . ?"

"No time to talk, father," Sturm said. "Step back from the door." The older Kintaro complied and Sturm aimed his laser at the door lock. He didn't have time to bother with keys or entry codes. Instead, the ruby beam melted cleanly through the locking mechanism and the bolt, allowing the door to swing out into the corridor.

Sturm reached out a hand toward his father. "C'mon, I'm getting you out of here. Let's go." Dr. Kintaro stepped out into the corridor with his son, staring in shock at the dead body of the pirate guard.

"Sturm, you shouldn't have come here," he said.

"I had to," Sturm said.

"No, you don't understand—" Dr. Kintaro was cut off by a sound from the far end of the corridor.

The door there swung open and a small group of pirates burst into the corridor, carrying assault rifles that they leveled at Sturm and his father.

"Freeze!" the lead pirate shouted. "Drop your weapon!" For a split-second Sturm contemplated firing at them, but there were three pirates, all armed with rifles. Even if he managed to somehow drop two of them before they could fire, the third could still fill the whole corridor with enough lead to finish both him and his father. He let the laser pistol drop to the floor with a clatter, and the pirates closed in.

"Stay close to me and do whatever I ask, father," Sturm said. "Please." Hidoshi Kintaro gave only the slightest nod of his head.

As the pirates closed in, another figure emerged from behind the door and walked calmly down the corridor. As she approached, she smiled and spoke loudly.

"So, this is the young MechWarrior who's been causing me so much trouble," Susie Ryan said. The pirate queen's good eye gleamed with triumph and she smiled broadly. "Well, Sturm Kintaro, it's a pleasure to meet you at last."

23

Shangri-la
Jotun Mountains, Kore
The Periphery
23 April 3060

*D*amn *that kid for being so stubborn, so loyal, so . . .
so like his mother,* Krenner thought. He was sitting
in the communications center of the Clan facility
Sturm had nicknamed "Shangri-la," scanning the
comm frequencies for any sign of a transmission
from Sturm or his 'Mech that would indicate what
he was up to. Krenner could guess where Sturm
would be going: to the command base to find his
father. He should have known Sturm would do
something like this, but he still hadn't seen it coming. He kept checking the comm-bands for any
word from Sturm, or any sign that he'd been captured by the enemy.

Krenner didn't like to think about it, but it was
a real likelihood that Sturm would be captured
and probably killed along with his father. He was
a good kid, a capable MechWarrior and even

smarter than his mother was, but he was still a young man alone against a gang of ruthless pirates. Krenner didn't rate Sturm's chances as that great, which meant deciding what must be done for the good of the unit.

He would probably have to take charge himself. He wasn't an officer, or a MechWarrior, just a ground-pounder, an infantryman. But he had the most experience, and he honestly didn't think Lon Volker could cut it in command. Volker was too wrapped up in himself, more worried about covering his own butt than looking out for the people under his command. The other trainees were too green to even see combat, much less take command. It didn't leave Krenner with a lot of choices. Even if he did take command, without Sturm, the unit was seriously underpowered. If only Sturm hadn't taken their best 'Mech with him.

The door to the comm center opened, and Krenner swiveled his chair around to glance back. Who else could be up at this hour, he wondered. He'd already sent the regular comm tech on duty to get some sleep while he took over and tried to get an indication of what was going on with Sturm. The relief shift wasn't due on for hours. Krenner thought there might be some news.

Lon Volker looked surprised to see Krenner sitting at the communications console. His startled look lasted only for a second before he regained his composure and shut the door behind him.

"Sarge," he said, "what are you doing here?"

Krenner grimaced. There was no point in keeping secrets. The news would be all over the base by morning anyway.

"Kintaro's gone," he said. "He took the *Goshawk* and went after his father. That broadcast of Ryan's really got to him. I'm hoping he might try to send a message, let us know if he's all right."

Volker's eyes widened. "Kintaro bugged out?" he said. "Huh. I always knew that kid didn't have what it took."

"Watch it, mister," Krenner said, his eyes narrowing dangerously. "Sturm Kintaro is a good MechWarrior, and a good man. He's been under more pressure in the last couple weeks than a MechWarrior twice his age should be. If he decided to place loyalty to his family above loyalty to his unit, I may not agree with him, but I can't fault him for wanting to save his father."

"Easy, Sarge," Volker said with a wave of his hand. "I know you like the kid, but, like you said, he was under a lot of pressure. Besides"—he shrugged his shoulders—"it's out of our hands now, right? We can't do anything for Kintaro, but we've got to figure out what's best for the unit, don't we?"

Krenner was a bit surprised by Volker's reaction. He'd been spoiling for a fight, but apparently Volker wasn't going to give it to him.

"Yeah," he agreed reluctantly. "I've been thinking about that while I've been sitting here, waiting for some word."

Volker stepped closer to the console and looked over Krenner's shoulder at the displays and readouts. "Have you tried raising him on any of the channels?" he asked.

"No," Krenner replied. "Can't do that. Any signals we send out strong enough to reach Sturm would also be strong enough to reach the command base. They could give away our position to the enemy, and Sturm still might not be able to receive us, or he might not be able to reply if he did. It's too much of a risk."

"But this set-up can send signals as far as the command base?" Volker asked.

"Easily. This system is at least as good as the one in the command center, maybe even better. But, like I said, any signal we send to the base is likely to give away our position to Ryan and her pirates and they'd be on us in a second. Besides, I've got nothing to say to that murdering bitch."

"Sarge," Volker began slowly, considering his words. "Look at the situation we're in. We're alone, out on the edge of the Periphery. We've got four 'Mechs and only one experienced pilot: me. Everyone else is greener than last week's rations. No matter how good the 'Mechs are, you can't get past that. We've got an enemy force with the same number of 'Mechs, but they outweigh us by at least a whole medium 'Mech, maybe even more if Kintaro got himself captured and they've got his 'Mech too. They've got experienced pilots, control of the city and the only spaceport on the planet. And even if the main company gets our signal, we're at least a few jumps away from help. It'll take them weeks to get here."

"If you've got a point, mister, start making it," Krenner said, although he was pretty sure he knew where this was going.

"I think we need to talk to Ryan," Volker said. "We need to consider surrendering." At Krenner's stormy look, Volker held up a hand. "Hear me out," he said. "We know Ryan isn't interested in this planet or any of us. All she wants is the 'Mechs and supplies from this depot. If she gets them, she'll probably boost offworld tomorrow and leave us alone. We can wait until reinforcements get here and there's nothing to worry about. She probably doesn't want to fight this out any more than we do. But if we force it, Ryan will plow right over all of us and take what she's after."

"And what about the Clans?" Krenner said. "Have you forgotten about them? If we give Ryan what she wants, she'll strip the whole place and take off. Then what happens when a bunch of angry Steel Vipers show up looking for their 'Mechs?"

"The Clans aren't going to bother coming back here," Volker said. "This place is too small and too far out. They've got other things to worry about. Even if they do come, if Ryan takes the 'Mechs, it's not our problem. We tell the Vipers where to find Ryan and they go after her. If we try and hold on to the 'Mechs, the Clans will be after us instead."

"Do you really think the Clanners are just going to leave us alone? Even if we don't have their 'Mechs?" Kenner asked. "And do you really think Susie Ryan is just going to vanish peacefully, leaving someone behind to tell the Clans, or the Storm Riders, or anyone else, just what happened here? Ryan has already killed a lot of good people to get at what she wants, Volker, and I don't doubt that she's willing to kill a lot more, either to get what she came for or to cover her own tracks. I've lost a lot of good people, a lot of good friends, because of the hardware in this place. I'll be damned if I'm going to let Susie Ryan walk away with what she's after without making her pay for it. If she wants these 'Mechs, the only way she'll get them is over my dead body!"

Volker stood and looked at Krenner for a long moment before his shoulders slumped and he shrugged.

"If that's the way you feel about it, Sarge. Are you sure?"

"I've never been more sure about anything. Negotiation is not an option."

"All right, then, we'll play it your way."

Krenner was surprised, albeit pleasantly, to see Volker so agreeable.

"Do you want to catch some sack-time?" Volker asked. "I could keep an eye on things here until the next shift."

Krenner shook his head. "No, thanks. I've got it. Couldn't sleep anyway. You go back and catch some more rest. We're gonna have a lot to do in the morning." He turned back to the console to search for any signs of a signal coming from the command base.

He heard a faint sound and his reflexes, honed by years of combat training, started to react, but too late. The shot from the flechette gun caught him full in the back, and sent him slumping over the console. Through the searing pain and the rapidly oncoming shock, Krenner heard footsteps behind him and then a firm hand pushed him off the console and out of the chair. He slid to the floor in a rapidly widening pool of his own blood and he heard a voice.

"Sorry you feel that way, Sarge. Over your dead body it is."

Then everything started to go black. The Master Sergeant's last thought was of Sturm and of Jenna and how sorry he was that he'd let them down.

24

Kore Lancers Command Base
Outside Niffelheim, Kore
The Periphery
23 April 3060

"So, you're Sturm Kintaro," Susie Ryan said, her good eye looking Sturm over from head to foot. "Strange, I expected you to be . . . bigger somehow."

Sturm gritted his teeth against Ryan's wicked smile. "Big enough to take down one of your 'Mechs," he said. "And plenty of your men."

Ryan's expression darkened instantly, like a cloud blocking the sun. "Yes, but here we are. I was pretty sure sympathy for your daddy's plight might bring you here, and it did. You should be proud of your father, Sturm. He tried to convince me it would never work, that you wouldn't come for him." Sturm glanced over at his father. *Is that what he really thinks of me*, he wondered. He knew his relationship with his father wasn't the best in the galaxy, but still, the idea that Hidoshi believed Sturm would let him die shocked him.

"Now that you're here," Ryan said, "we can have a little talk about where you've been and what you've been up to since my men left you for dead in the mountains."

"They shouldn't have assumed," Sturm said.

"That is easily corrected," Ryan replied, "unless you tell me what I want to know."

"You know I won't do that."

"Sturm," Ryan said, speaking in a friendly, conversational tone. "Do you understand how interrogation works? I mean *really* understand it? You can put on a brave front and be as defiant as you want, but the truth is, you *will* tell me what I want to know. If you don't, I will have your father tortured, then you. Assuming you can handle the sight of your father in that kind of pain, and I don't think you can, by the time I'm done you'll be begging to tell me everything. This isn't a threat, it's simply how things are. Now, why not spare yourself and, more importantly, your father, that kind of agony and simply tell me what I want to know? You've got to realize by now that you can't win."

Sturm glanced over at his father, then back at Susie Ryan. Her calm gaze didn't waver in the slightest. Sturm could tell she wasn't bluffing. She would gladly torture Hidoshi, him, and anyone else who could get her what she wanted. And Sturm didn't have many illusions about his ability to hold up under torture. Sooner or later, anyone could be broken. He didn't have much choice.

"Before I say anything, there's something you should know."

"Oh?" Ryan said, raising one eyebrow.

"Yes. You're right, there is a Clan 'Mech depot on this planet, and I did find it. But the place was rigged with an alarm system, and I tripped it when I found it. A hyperpulse generator sent out a signal into the Clan zone days ago. The Steel Vipers know someone has found their depot and they're probably on their way here right now. Besides that, we used the generator to send a signal for reinforcements. The rest of my company knows what's happening here and they're on their way."

The pirate queen's face scarcely changed while Sturm spoke. When he finished, she smiled poisonously.

"Well, then, all the more reason to hurry things along. It doesn't change my plans. All it tells me is that I need that information *now*, and the time for chitchat is over."

The comm unit Ryan wore at her belt chose that moment to signal for her attention. She raised the unit to her lips, never taking her one good eye off Sturm.

"Ryan, go," she said.

"Captain, we're getting a signal from the mountains, the one you told us to look out for."

"Can you get a lock on it?"

"Yes, sir, we've already got it. Coordinates show it to be near the mountain valley where we took out the *Thorn*."

"Good work," she said. "Get the men to their 'Mechs and outfit as many overland vehicles as possible. We're leaving for the site immediately. I'll be there shortly. Ryan out."

As she slipped the comm unit back into her belt, Ryan smiled triumphantly at Sturm.

"Well, it seems we won't be needing to have that conversation right now," she said. "My original idea has worked out after all. I'm glad not everyone on this backwater planet is as stubborn and short-sighted as you and your little band. That signal told us the exact location of the Clan depot you've been using. Very soon, we'll take it by surprise, and those five 'Mechs and other equipment will be mine. All your defiance and fighting have been for nothing."

Ryan drew the sidearm from her belt, a slim laser pistol, and slid the barrel under Sturm's chin. He did his best not to flinch at the touch of the cool metal. Ryan gently tipped his head back a bit with a slight pressure to his throat.

"Technically," she said softly, "you're of no further use to me. I could simply kill you right here and now. Lucky for you, I'm feeling in a generous mood. I might also need you to provide some details about the depot and the 'Mechs once I've captured them. So you get to live. For now." The laser pistol withdrew, and Sturm fought down the urge to shake his head and clear away the memory of its touch. Ryan jerked her head toward the pirates accompanying her.

"Lock them up," she said. "We can continue this little chat once we're back with my new 'Mechs."

"Yessir!" the pirates responded, hustling around to push Sturm and his father forward with their rifles. Ryan stepped aside and opened the door to one of the other cells. Sturm and his father stepped inside, and the door shut behind them with a clang.

"See you soon," Ryan said with a smile, and she exited the brig with a laugh that echoed in the confined corridor. One of the pirates remained outside the cell on guard.

Sturm stood near the door and listened until he heard the footsteps fade away into the distance, then he checked his wrist chronometer.

"Sturm, I'm sorry," Dr. Kintaro began. "You shouldn't have come back for me."

"I had to, father. I couldn't just leave you to die."

"You should have," Hidoshi said gravely. "Your people are more important. Your mother taught me that."

Sturm realized that his father was echoing Krenner's words earlier. "Then maybe I'm not all that much like mom, after all," he said. "I couldn't just leave you behind when there was a chance of doing something."

"But it didn't gain you anything," Hidoshi said. "Now your unit needs you and you can't help them."

"I wouldn't give up yet," Sturm said. "This isn't over. I may take after mom a lot, but I picked up a couple of things from my father, too," he smiled.

"Eh?" Hidoshi said, giving his son a quizzical look.

"Smarts," Sturm replied quietly. He checked his chronometer again as it ticked off the seconds. Not much longer. He hoped it was long enough.

"Wait for it. It'll be a few more minutes. I just hope that gives us enough time."

"Sturm . . ." Hidoshi began, "thank you for coming back for me. I haven't always approved of the choices you've made, but I want you to know I've always been proud of you."

Sturm smiled and touched his father's arm. "Thanks," he said. "That means a lot to me. We've got a few more minutes, so here's what we need to do . . ."

The minutes ticked by with agonizing slowness, but Sturm hoped it was enough time for the pirate 'Mechs to begin heading for Shangri-la. Time enough to put some distance between them and the command base. He watched as his chronometer ticked off the remaining few seconds as he crouched close to the cell door. Five seconds, four, three, two, one. . . .

"Now," Sturm whispered.

The explosions rocked the command base with a rapid series of dull, booming noises, audible even in the sub-basement level of the building where Sturm and his father were imprisoned. The building shook and the lights immediately went out, plunging the room into near-total darkness. Emergency lighting in the hallway kicked in within seconds of the blackout, but Sturm was already moving by then.

The smaller sidearm concealed in his boot-top was enough to blow open the lock on the cell door. Sturm kicked it outward with enough force to slam into the pirate guard who stood, stunned, outside of the room, trying to get his bearings in the darkness and noise. The door hit him with a clang and sent the pirate stumbling backward. Sturm leapt out of the cell and punched the man hard in the face. He went down in a heap.

Sturm grabbed the rifle off the unconscious guard's body and handed the smaller sidearm to his father. Hidoshi took the gun like it was a poisonous snake, then firmed up his nerve and held it more firmly. Sturm looked over at his father, his face barely visible in the dim emergency lighting, as alarm klaxons sounded distantly across the compound.

"Let's go," Sturm said, then he headed for the stairs, with his father close behind.

The command base was in chaos. The explosive charges Sturm had planted on his way into the base destroyed the main generator shed and set off blasts at several other points along the perimeter of the base, including the outer fence. Armed pirates were running in all directions, looking for signs of intruders or of the possibility of an attack. At the moment it was clear that nobody knew what was going on, and no one had any real control over the situation. That would make things a bit easier.

"All right," Sturm said, as he and Hidoshi crouched near the top of the stairwell. "We make a run for the vehicle bay and take the first transportation out of here. I'll clear a path for us as best I can. If anyone gets in your way, shoot him. Don't stop for anything, no matter what, okay?"

Hidoshi nodded. "I understand."

"Let's do it, then." Sturm pushed the door open and burst out just as an armed pirate came running down the corridor. Sturm put a burst from his rifle into the man, who went down in a smear of blood on the tile floor. Sturm and his father started running without even looking back.

The compound was pure mayhem, with men rushing in all directions and several fires burning in some of the outer buildings. Sturm and his father hit the ferrocrete at a run and headed directly for the vehicle bay.

"Hey!" someone shouted from nearby. Sturm fired a burst from his rifle in that direction. Whether he'd hit his target or just forced the man to keep his head down, he didn't have time to tell. Still, the shout and the gunfire caught the attention of other pirates, and several began heading in their direction.

"Keep going!" Sturm shouted. He turned and fired a spray of bullets that sparked off the ferrocrete and the buildings, sending their pursuers scattering for cover. As Sturm ran, somebody returned fire, and a line of richochets snapped at his heels. He bolted for the vehicle bay.

The side door was open, and Hidoshi stood just inside. On the floor lay a pirate, rolling around and clutching a bloody wound in his side. Hidoshi stood in stunned fascination at the sight as another pirate came in through the open main doors.

"Dad!" Sturm yelled in warning. He came through the door and fired at the pirate, dropping him before he could shoot. Hidoshi Kintaro snapped out of his distraction and turned to his son.

"Thanks," he said.

"That's two you owe me," Sturm said with a grin.

The younger Kintaro picked out a snowmobile and started pulling it out of its niche in the bay.

"Give me a hand with this," he said to his father. Together they wrestled the small vehicle out into the open. As Sturm moved to throw one leg over the saddle, Hidoshi saw another pirate come around the corner of the open door. Without thinking he raised his gun and fired. The shot missed, but the ricochet sent the pirate back for cover. Sturm looked up in surprise.

"Thanks," he said. He fired off a burst from his rifle to force the pirate to keep his head down.

"One you owe *me*," Hidoshi replied dryly.

Sturm unslung his rifle and passed it back to his father. "Cover us. We're getting out of here."

Hidoshi took the gun as Sturm kicked the engine of the small vehicle roaring to life. Hidoshi clambered onto the back, one hand on the gun, the other holding on for dear life.

Sturm opened up the throttle and the snowmobile shot forward on its treads, skidding across the ferrocrete. As they shot out of the bay, the pirate near the door tried to take his shot, but Hidoshi fired the rifle in his direction. The kick from it nearly knocked him off the snowmobile, but he managed to hang on. At least one of the shots caught the pirate, who went spinning back into the wall, where he slumped down and did not move.

The snowmobile crossed the few meters of ferrocrete and shot out onto the snow-covered tundra, kicking up a spray of icy powder and picking up speed as it headed for the gap in the fence. More of the pirates had noticed the escape attempt and ran toward the edge of the ferrocrete. Chattering gunfire kicked up tiny explosions of snow around the speeding vehicle as Sturm wove back and forth in an evasive pattern.

"Hang on and keep low!" he shouted back, over the wind whipping past. Hidoshi did his best to comply. The rifle was of no use to him at the moment. On the back of the speeding and swerving snowmobile there was no way he could even aim it. The vehicle shot out through the gap in the fence and sped across the snow as the gunfire started to die away behind them.

"Woo-hoo!" Sturm whooped as they roared across the snow.

"Don't celebrate yet, son!" Hidoshi shouted. "Look!"

Sturm glanced over his shoulder. Some of the pirates were already in pursuit.

25

Shangri-la
Jotun Mountains, Kore
The Periphery
23 April 3060

Alarm klaxons sounded throughout the Clan 'Mech depot. Awakened from a fitful sleep, Laura ran down the corridor, pulling on her coolant vest over a thin T-shirt. She'd taken to sleeping in her training "uniform," exhausted by the grueling training schedule set up by Sergeant Krenner and Kintaro. As she headed down toward the 'Mech bay, she spotted Volker in the hall and called out to him.

"Lon! What the hell is going on?"

"The pirates," he shouted. "Their 'Mechs are heading this way. It's only minutes before they get here. We need to get down to the 'Mechs and get them outside."

Laura was stunned by the news. It couldn't have come at a worse time. "The pirates?" she said. "But how? How did they find us?"

"It must have been Kintaro," Volker aid. "He's gone missing, along with his 'Mech. As near as we can tell, he headed for the command base. He must have been captured by the pirates. Or else he decided to surrender to them to try and save his father."

"Surrender? Do you really think he'd do something like that?"

Volker shrugged. "I don't know. All I know is that Kintaro is gone and Krenner's disappeared, too—"

"Krenner's gone?" Laura had seen the look on Sturm's face after Ryan broadcast her threat to kill Dr. Kintaro if Sturm didn't surrender. Still, she was surprised he'd taken off on his own. But not Sergeant Krenner. He'd never abandon his post, especially not at a time like this.

"Are you sure?" she asked Volker, who seemed to be taking the whole thing with amazing calm. "Are you sure Krenner's gone?"

"I can't find him anywhere on base," Volker said, "and he doesn't answer any pages. Nobody knows what happened to him. Maybe he decided to go after Kintaro. All I know is that with him and Kintaro gone, I'm in charge now. We need to go get our 'Mechs right now, MechWarrior!" Volker's voice took on a commanding tone he'd never used with Laura before. Of course, Laura was never a MechWarrior under his command before, entrusted to help protect the lives of the remaining Lancers from the threat of pirate BattleMechs. Laura snapped to attention and nodded gravely, then turned and started for the 'Mech bay at a run. Volker followed closely behind her.

When they reached the bay, Clancy and Flannery were already getting their 'Mechs—a *Peregrine* and a *Vixen*—ready. Techs swarmed around the two remaining Clan 'Mechs in the bay, Volker's *Hellhound* and Laura's *Vixen*, the twin of Flannery's.

"Status!" Volker shouted to one of the senior techs. The man looked up from checking a reading on one of the display screens.

"They're all ready to go, sir," he responded. "Fully loaded. Still no word from Sergeant Krenner or—"

"That's all right," Volker said. "We'll handle it. Mount up!" he called to the other MechWarriors, and headed for the *Hellhound*.

Laura ran over to Lady Fox and began climbing up the chain ladder to the cockpit. From there she climbed into the command couch and pulled the neurohelmet down from the tangle of wires where it rested, setting it in place over the padded collar of her coolant vest and quickly checking the fastenings. It gave her a chance to ignore just how nervous she felt. She was taking the *Vixen* out of the 'Mech bay for the very first time. Until now the only battles she'd fought in it were simulations. She'd never even trained in the cockpit of an actual 'Mech beyond familiarizing herself with the controls and systems and having her brain wave patterns encoded to the neurohelmet.

Now, she and the others were on their way to fight a group of ruthless pirates who outclassed and outgunned them. She was terrified and she wished that Sergeant Krenner was around or, more importantly, Sturm Kintaro. Somehow, having either of them here would make her feel more like they had a real chance of winning. She wondered briefly what must be happening to them, wherever they might be. Then she ran through the final checks to get Lady Fox going. According to the chatter over the commline, the pirate 'Mechs were closing in, and they had to get out there.

At the same time, not far from the former command base of the Kore Lancers, Sturm Kintaro was swerving his snowmobile from side to side in an effort to avoid the machine gun fire coming from the pirate hovercraft pursuing them. It was a Winterhawk, much like the hovercraft the Lancers stole in their escape from the command base, armed with a machine gun turret and a small missile rack. Sturm was grateful the pirates hadn't tried firing any missiles at him and his father, at least, not yet.

"They're gaining, Sturm!" Hidoshi Kintaro shouted from the back of the fast-moving snowmobile. Sturm glanced back. His father was right. The Winterhawk was closing in on them. It was definitely faster than his smaller vehicle, and the lead they'd gained in their escape from the command base was rapidly closing.

Sturm swerved again to avoid another chattering burst of machine gun fire, which kicked up small explosions from the snow-covered ground.

"Hang on!" Sturm yelled back to his father as he gunned the engine as fast as it could go and angled the snowmobile toward their destination. They shot over a bump in the terrain, momentarily airborne before slamming back down onto the snow. They were almost there. Sturm just needed to keep things going, stay ahead just a little longer.

A dull whoosh sounded behind them and Sturm's blood ran cold. He kicked the snowmobile into a turn to get them out of the way as fast as possible.

"Dad! Keep your head down!" he shouted. The pair of missiles arced in, but the unguided munitions were way off target. Still, the force of the explosion when the missiles struck the frozen ground sent ice, snow, and dirt showering into the air. The shock waves nearly knocked the snowmobile over, but Sturm managed to keep it upright and roared past the small blast crater and toward the crevasse. He hoped the smoke and debris from the exploding warheads would hide them for a few precious seconds from the view of the hovercraft's gunner.

As they neared the crevasse, Sturm skidded the snowmobile to a halt, mere meters away from the edge.

"Let's go!" he said, and he and Hidoshi made a run for the edge. They disappeared over it as the hovercraft came barreling through the swirling smoke of the missile blast. Its turbofans whined as the vehicle slowed, approaching the crevasse and the abandoned snowmobile. Weapons turrets slowly tracked the area, but there were no signs of the escapees. Slowly, the hovercraft closed in on the rent in the terrain, sensors active, weapon systems at the ready.

Suddenly, a gleaming white form came rocketing out of the crevasse on plumes of fire. The

Goshawk vaulted more than a dozen meters up into the air, arcing over the Winterhawk and coming to land a short distance behind the hovercraft. The Winterhawk started to move to the side as the *Goshawk* touched down and leveled its right arm at the vehicle.

A blast of hellish green light flared from the pulse laser, sending bolts of energy pounding into the small hovercraft. The Winterhawk's armor vaporized instantly under the force of the blast, and the laser pulses penetrated into the interior of the vehicle. Some of the crew tried to escape at the last second, but they were too late. The laserfire touched off the remaining few missiles in the hovercraft's ammo bins, and the Winterhawk exploded in a black and orange fireball, boiling up to the leaden skies of Kore.

Inside the cockpit of Golden Boy, Sturm grinned behind the faceplate of his neurohelmet. Dr. Kintaro clutched the back of the command chair, where he was wedged into the narrow space behind the pilot's seat. Sturm started to strip off his outer garments. The jump and firing the large pulse laser was already spiking the heat in the cockpit. He turned slightly, trying to look over his shoulder, but the bulk of the neurohelmet made it difficult.

"I wish I could drop you off somewhere safe," he said to his father, "but I've got to get back to the depot. Ryan's people are probably almost there by now, and there's nowhere around here I can let you off. I need to . . ."

Dr. Kintaro laid a hand on his son's shoulder. "Say no more. I understand your duty, son. I'll be all right here with you. You go and do what you have to do. Don't worry about me."

Sturm paused for a moment, then nodded.

"All right," he said. "Hang on tight, we're going to have to move fast." He pushed the control stick forward, and the fifty-five-ton BattleMech began running across the open tundra of Kore toward the mountains. Sturm only hoped they weren't too late to stop a slaughter.

The Lancer 'Mechs exited Shangri-la through the cliffside doorway, out into the snow-covered valley of the Jotun Mountains. The valley was very defensible, with only one pass leading into it that the pirate 'Mechs could fit through.

That gives us some sort of chance, Laura thought as she guided the *Vixen* through the deep snow and rocky terrain. She'd learned how to handle Kore's terrain on the simulators, but it was still slow going. She didn't want her 'Mech to slip and fall. Flannery and Clancy seemed to be having similar difficulties, but Volker's *Hellhound* was moving briskly. He would probably be the first to arrive near the pass.

"Lancer One to all units," came Volker's voice crackling over the commline. "Deploy around the pass. I'll take point. We need to keep them from making it into the valley."

Laura keyed her own commline. "Lancer Four to One," she said. "What about setting up an ambush up in the higher elevations above the pass? It would give us the element of surprise."

"No," Volker replied. "It would take too long for you to get up there, and it looks like you're having trouble enough with the terrain as it is. We don't need to lose a 'Mech by having somebody fall on the enemy. Stick to the lower elevations."

"But if we stay down here, we'll be overpowered by the—"

"That's an *order*, MechWarrior," Volker broke in harshly.

"Yes, sir," Laura said. Maybe Volker was right. The higher elevations were rocky and steep, covered with snow. They would probably be difficult to climb, especially for an inexperienced MechWarrior. But she still thought they were relying too heavily on the protection of the narrow pass. They might be able to hold the pass against the pirate 'Mechs from the ground, but if Ryan's Rebels managed to get through the pass into the valley, the Lancers would be fighting on the ground against a superior enemy force. It made sense to try and take any tactical advantage they could. Still, Volker was the more experienced MechWarrior and he *was* in command.

Volker continued as if he hadn't been interrupted. "Lancer Two, take up position on the northern side of the pass. Three and Four, stay off to the southern side. Keep out of sight for now. We don't want to give ourselves away to the pirates. I'll cover the pass and draw their fire, then we can close in on them."

The other three MechWarriors responded affirmatively and moved to obey Volker's orders. Laura kept her sensors running full sweeps of the surrounding terrain for any signs of the enemy. As expected, the heavy magnetic and thermal interference made any readings highly suspect. Still, she thought there were indications of some approaching 'Mechs.

"Lancer Four to Lancer One," she said. "I've got readings on four unknowns that seem to be moving into the area. Repeat, I think I've acquired the hostiles."

"Don't think, Four. Know for sure," Volker barked. "I don't show anything. Double-check your readings."

Laura frowned. She was almost *sure* she'd read the sensor information correctly. She started to check the readings. It was possible the interference was causing some kind of sensor ghosting, but the ghost-images moved fairly quickly, and the magnetic and thermal readings seemed to match.

"One, I'm getting similar readings on this side," Clancy said from her *Peregrine*. "Do you want me to move to—"

"Negative, Two," Volker cut in. "Stick to the plan and hold your position."

"Sir, I think they're coming through the pass!" Laura called to Volker. Was there something wrong with the *Hellbound*'s sensors? Some other kind of interference? How could Volker not be getting the same readings as the rest of—

"C&C to Lancers! C&C to Lancers!" a voice broke in over the commline. "We just found Sergeant Krenner! He's dead! Somebody shot him and put his body into a storage locker! Repeat—"

Suddenly, the *Hellbound* turned and raised its right arm. A blast of emerald light lanced out from its heavy pulse laser, slamming into the torso of the *Peregrine*. The smaller 'Mech stumbled back, armor seared and blackened along its chest as several other 'Mechs poured through the opening in the pass.

"What the hell . . . ?" Laura started to say. She reached for the controls of Lady Fox just as a voice crackled over the commline. A voice she recognized from the broadcast earlier from Niffelheim.

"This is Captain Ryan to the Kore Lancers. You are outnumbered and outgunned. Surrender your 'Mechs and stand down and you will not be harmed. If you resist, we'll take those 'Mechs over your dead bodies. It's your choice. Your commander has already wisely made his."

"Sorry," Volker's voice came over the comm, "but I got a better offer. I'm not planning on dying on this iceball. I suggest you wise up and do the same. Krenner's dead and Kintaro's finished. Give up now and nobody has to get hurt."

Laura checked the heads-up display inside her cockpit. Clancy's *Peregrine* was damaged, although not seriously. Her and Flannery's *Vixen*s were intact. Arrayed against them were four Clan 'Mechs that all equaled or outweighed them, along with Volker's old *Panther*. Taken together, the Clan 'Mechs outmassed the Lancers by fifty tons. The *Fenris* and the *Panther* blocked the pass, while the *Puma*, Volker's *Hellhound*, and *Ryan's Mad Cat* were moving into the central part of the valley. They stood between the Lancers and the only way out.

They were trapped.

26

Jotun Mountains
Kore
The Periphery
23 April 3060

"Volker, you son of a bitch . . ." Laura began. She couldn't believe it. Sure, Volker could be a little selfish sometimes, but to betray the Lancers to One-Eye Ryan and her band of pirates? The confused mass of feelings she had toward him instantly resolved themselves into a singular one of anger and betrayal.

"Sorry, Laurie," Volker said over the comm. "It's every man for himself out here. I want off this rock and a chance at some action. I know a lost cause when I see one and I'm not interested in being a martyr. I want to pilot a 'Mech, and Ryan's going to give me the chance to do it. This 'Mech is mine, and I plan to hold on to it."

"Your time is up, Lancers," Ryan broke in. "I've made you a generous offer: surrender, and none of you will be harmed. We'll collect our 'Mechs and equipment from the Clan depot and we'll leave. If you refuse, we'll kill you and *then* take what we came here for. It's a simple decision. Now, *stand down.*"

Laura hesitated only for a heartbeat. What Ryan was saying was true: the offer was exceptionally reasonable. None of the newly christened Mech-Warriors had any real experience. They hadn't been piloting 'Mechs long enough to feel the sting of becoming dispossessed after only a few days. Giving in to Ryan's demands seemed like the easiest way to settle this whole mess without anyone getting hurt.

Assuming you trust Susie Ryan, the Pirate Queen herself, to actually keep her word, Laura told herself. She thought about everything Ryan had done to the people of Kore, and to the Lancers, since arriving on-planet. She also thought about Volker and his betrayal. Could she simply allow them all to get away with it? To kill so many good people and then just walk away with the prize they'd come for?

She opened up a channel to the other two Lancer 'Mechs. She knew everyone would be listening in, but at this point, she didn't much care.

"Clancy, Flannery, do what you need to do," she said. Then, "As far as I'm concerned, Ryan, here's your answer: if you want my 'Mech, you're going to have to take it from me. And Volker, I'll see you in hell!" She leveled the *Vixen*'s pulse laser at Volker's *Hellhound* and mashed down on the firing button. A burst of blazing green light seared out, slicing along the other 'Mech's left arm, slagging cerametallic armor as it went.

The shot broke the silence in the valley, and the BattleMechs of both sides moved into action. Laura checked the positions of the other 'Mechs on her HUD, trying to figure out who to go after first. She wanted more than anything to hit Volker, and hit him hard, to make him pay for what he'd done to her and the rest of the company. But she did her best to control her emotions. She remembered what Krenner had told her, that a warrior needed to stay calm and level-headed. It was Susie Ryan who was the biggest threat. If she could disable or destroy Ryan's *Mad Cat*, the others might very well surrender or at least back off and give the Lancers some breathing room.

The commline crackled. "We're with you, Laura!" came Clancy's voice as her *Peregrine* moved forward. Flannery's *Vixen* was also moving, heading for the enemy *Panther*. Laura was glad they were siding with her, but she only hoped she wasn't leading them to their deaths.

"Go to the secondary frequency and let's do it!" she said. Volker knew all of the Lancers' comm frequencies. It wouldn't be long before he was able to tap into their communications again, so she intended to take advantage of the few seconds they had.

She got *Lady Fox* moving to evade a laser blast from Volker's *Hellhound* and sent a new scramble code to the other 'Mechs. "Reset communications as soon as you're able!" she said. It was going to be tough to coordinate the attack without effective communications, but Laura wasn't sure the pirates were going to give them any kind of a break. The enemy 'Mechs were moving in on the Lancers, but for the most part they were holding their fire. A couple of shots were fired after Laura's *Vixen* nailed the *Hellhound*, but the pirates had otherwise ceased fire.

What are they waiting for, Laura wondered. *Why don't they start shooting?* Then she realized why not. They wanted the 'Mechs. That was the whole reason Ryan's Rebels had come to Kore in the first place. If they used their heavy weapons against the Lancer 'Mechs, they would very likely cripple or even total them. Ryan had probably ordered her people to try and take the 'Mechs with as little damage as possible. She knew the Lancers were trapped in the mountain valley with no real means of escape. The *Vixen*s were fast, but not jump-capable. Though the *Peregrine* had jump jets, it was no match for the pirate 'Mechs, and it would take several jumps to clear the mountains and make it to open ground.

"They're probably going for hand-to-hand and close-range pinpoint attacks," Laura transmitted to the others. "Let 'em have it with all you've got! Maybe we can slow them down!"

"Roger that!" came Tom Flannery's voice. The *Panther* moved in on his 'Mech. It outweighed the *Vixen* by a few tons, but overall, the Clan 'Mech was better armed and armored. Plus, the *Panther* relied heavily on its arm-mounted PPC, which gave Flannery a slight advantage. He fired his torso-mounted medium lasers at the oncoming 'Mech, beams slashing into armor and sending up thick clouds of superheated steam in the frigid air. The *Panther* responded with a volley of short-range missiles, several of which connected with the *Vixen*'s torso in small explosions.

Clancy's *Peregrine* faced down the *Fenris* and the *Puma*. The *Puma* was in the same weight class, but was armed with long-range PPCs, intended for fire-support. Not close-in fighting. The *Fenris* was a heavier 'Mech, but it also relied on a PPC as its main weapon. For its weight, the *Peregrine* was well-armed, with a large pulse laser in its torso and paired medium pulse lasers on either side. Ton for ton, the *Peregrine* was a tough 'Mech, but it was still facing two 'Mechs of equal or greater weight-class.

Neither pirate 'Mech fired on the *Peregrine*, moving in for hand-to-hand combat. Clancy fired her 'Mech's lasers at the *Fenris*, slashing across the enemy 'Mech's leg and torso, vaporizing armor and leaving blackened scars along the 'Mech's hull. As the enemy BattleMechs rushed in, the *Peregrine* triggered its jump jets and soared into the air like its namesake on pillars of fire.

Good move, Laura thought. Clancy's opponents didn't have jump-capability, so the *Peregrine* had the advantage in maneuverability. Laura caught the landing on her HUD. It wasn't the most graceful, with Clancy struggling to keep her multi-ton machine upright when she landed on the mountain slope. She wasn't going to be able to pull off too many jumps like that without falling flat on her face.

Laura had to concentrate on Volker's *Hellhound*, which was closing in on her. For a brief moment, she hoped he wouldn't have to go through with this, that when it came down to Volker fighting his former friends, he would back down. But the *Hellhound* kept right on coming, and fired its paired short-range missile launchers in her direction. Volker apparently cared less about Susie Ryan's orders than he did about coming out on top.

Fortunately, the Lady Fox was one of the fastest 'Mechs on the battlefield. Laura kept moving like she'd learned to do in the simulators, and the missiles went wide of their mark. She spun and fired her arm-mounted laser, shooting a blazing pulse of coherent light into the *Hellhound*'s shoulder flange, sending up gouts of steam and droplets of melting armor.

Laura checked the HUD again and saw that Ryan's *Mad Cat* was standing near the pass into the valley, but the fearsome 'Mech was taking no other action. What is she waiting for, Laura wondered. Ryan apparently preferred not to risk her own neck. Instead, the *Mad Cat* would make sure none of the Lancer 'Mechs were able to make it out of the valley, keeping them bottled up long enough for the pirates to deal with them.

Laura banked the *Vixen* to evade a blast from the *Hellhound*'s large laser. The beam melted and exploded rocks along the walls of the valley. Loose snow and debris cascaded downward. Laura kept her 'Mech moving to avoid the mini-avalanche. *Looks like I've got more to worry about than the 'Mechs,* she thought. *Got to watch out for the terrain, too.*

She countered by firing all three of her 'Mech's lasers at the *Hellhound*. The emerald beams cut across the distance between them. The medium lasers cut into the *Hellhound's* torso, but the large laser missed as Volker shot his 'Mech into a leap, jump jets firing. He returned a laser blast that caught Lady Fox in the left arm. Warning indicators lit up on the damage display. The armor on her 'Mech's arm was slagged. Another hit in that location might do some serious damage.

The *Fenris* and the *Panther* were closing in on Clancy's *Peregrine*, clambering up the mountain slope to reach it. Clancy was taking advantage of the situation to fire down on them with her lasers, doing some additional damage to both 'Mechs, but not enough to stop them. She readied her 'Mech for another jump, but before she could take off, the *Fenris* reached her and struck out with its right fist.

The jump jets fired, but the *Peregrine* jumped off-balance. It soared over the heads of the two pirate 'Mechs, then down toward the valley floor. Laura caught a glance in her HUD as Clancy fought to control the jumping 'Mech, but it tumbled to the side and crashed down into the valley and was now lying on one side. The pirate 'Mechs turned and began skittering down the slope toward her.

C'mon, Clancy, get up, get up! Laura shouted in her mind. There was nothing she could do to help. She wasn't close enough, and she still had Volker on her tail. She tried firing a laser pulse across the path of the oncoming 'Mechs, hoping to buy Clancy a moment to right herself.

Meanwhile, Flannery's *Vixen* was locked in a struggle with the *Panther*. The pirate 'Mech closed the distance between them and threw a savage punch at the *Vixen*. It clanged against the 'Mech's shoulder armor, denting and crumpling heavy armor plates. Flannery responded by firing his 'Mech's torso lasers directly into the *Panther*. Armor hissed and vaporized under the touch of the beams, but the *Panther*'s torso armor was heavier than the *Vixen*'s. It withstood the attack.

The Lady Fox's sensors screamed a warning as several SRMs arced in toward her. Laura tried to get out of the way, but it was too late. The missiles struck in the *Vixen*'s left arm, where the armor had been slagged away by the *Hellhound*'s laser. The blast shook the cockpit, and the damage indicators whooped a warning. The *Vixen*'s entire left-arm assembly was blown clean off by the blast. It lay, smoking, on the rocks nearby. Volker's *Hellhound* was heading toward her, obviously intending to follow up on the devastating attack. Laura did her best to ignore the damage and kept her 'Mech moving. Speed was about the only advantage she had over Volker's larger and more heavily armed machine. But her flight was taking them further and further away from the main battle. Laura could quickly find herself cut off with no way of getting help from the others.

They're trying to split us up, she thought. She looked for a way to get back toward Clancy or Flannery, but there was none that didn't involve passing dangerously close to the *Hellhound*. Laura knew that if she got within close-combat range of the larger 'Mech she was as good as finished. Volker clearly had no mercy when it came to saving his own tail. She didn't doubt that he would kill her. Or anyone else who got in his way, at this point.

Clancy's *Peregrine* was getting to its feet, but the other two pirate 'Mechs were closing in. The *Puma* leveled its PPC at Clancy's 'Mech and fired, followed by the *Fenris* launching a pair of short-range missiles. The PPC bolt struck like man-made lightning, boiling and melting armor along the *Peregrine*'s leg, while the pair of missiles slammed into the 'Mech's torso.

"Keep moving, Clancy!" Laura called over the comm.

"I've got failure of one of my jump jets!" came the reply. "Gonna try, but they've got me boxed in!"

The Lancers were taking a pounding. They'd done some damage to the pirate 'Mechs, but even if they managed to finish them, there was still Ryan's *Mad Cat* to deal with, and it could probably destroy the Lancers' lighter 'Mechs by itself. They were going to need more than just good tactics to get out of this one.

They were going to need a miracle.

27

Jotun Mountains
Kore
The Periphery
23 April 3060

Sturm pushed the *Goshawk* to near top-speed to reach Giant's Pass. He guided the huge machine across the icy surface of Kore's plains skillfully, reaching the pass in record time. The snow-covered terrain was churned to icy mud by the passage of other BattleMechs. It was clear that Ryan's Rebels had already arrived. Sturm only hoped he wasn't too late. In the narrow space behind Sturm's command chair, Dr. Kintaro crouched, holding on for dear life.

"Sorry, Dad," Sturm said. "It doesn't look like I'm going to be able to let you off for this. I've got to get to the rest of the Lancers as soon as possible. I wanted to keep you out of all this—"

"Sturm, we live in a universe that's at war," his father broke in. "I learned that a long time ago. I thought moving out here, to the edge of known space, would get us away from all of the fighting. But your mother's death showed me that wasn't going to happen. I was the one who wanted to keep *you* safe from all of this. You do what you must, and don't worry about me. I'll hold on and stay out of your way. You're a warrior. You have responsibilities. I understand."

Sturm smiled inside his neurohelmet. Maybe his father really did understand. "Thanks," he said. Then he started moving into the pass. Golden Boy's sensors were at maximum, carefully searching the area for signs of the enemy, for the possibility of an ambush. If the pirates had already taken out the others, Sturm would have to run, but he wasn't sure where. The only other option was surrender, and he didn't like that one at all.

As he came near the opening of the pass into the valley below, he saw the Lancers locked in combat with Ryan's Rebels. The pirate 'Mechs outnumbered the Lancers nearly two to one, but Susie Ryan's *Mad Cat* stood near the entrance of the pass, guarding the way out, while her other 'Mechs took on the Lancers. Sturm could see Clancy's *Peregrine* being double-teamed by two of the pirate 'Mechs, while a *Vixen*—either Flannery or Metz—was fighting Volker's old *Panther*, recovered and repaired by the pirates. Of the other *Vixen* or Volker's *Hellhound*, he saw no sign. Where were they? Could the pirates have already taken then down?

Although he wanted to go to the aid of his fellow Lancers, Sturm knew that Susie Ryan's 'Mech was the main threat. She blocked access to the valley and, at the moment, she had her back to him. The interference in the mountains seemed to be shielding his 'Mech from Ryan's sensors, but it was only a matter of moments before her visual scanning picked him up.

Sturm sized up the situation in an instant and made his decision. He moved the *Goshawk* out into the open near the *Mad Cat*. It took only a moment for Golden Boy's targeting computer to get a lock. The golden cross hairs aligned along the *Mad Cat's* exposed rear quarter. Sturm saw the giant Clan 'Mech start to move, swiveling its torso toward him. She'd seen him! But at that moment, he mashed down hard on the firing buttons and let loose with everything he had.

Missiles roared away, trailing smoke, while four emerald lances of light stabbed out from his 'Mech's arm and torso. The lasers scored, melting armor along the *Mad Cat's* rear, then the missiles impacted and sent fragments and droplets of molten ferro-fibrous armor and twisted metal flying. Sturm glanced up at his HUD; he'd done some serious damage to the *Mad Cat's* back, penetrating the armor into the 'Mech's internal structure. Ryan was turning her 'Mech toward Sturm quickly, bringing all its massive firepower to bear. Sturm recalled facing off with a *Mad Cat* in his last training session with Sergeant Krenner. That seemed like an eternity ago. He knew the kind of capabilities the 'Mech had. He needed to get out of the way, *fast*.

"Hang on, Dad!" Sturm said, then triggered the *Goshawk's* jump jets, just as Ryan opened fire on him. The 'Mech rocketed up into the air, up, up, and over the *Mad Cat*. Sturm fought the controls to twist the *Goshawk* in the air and land facing his opponent on the other side. The *Goshawk* hit the slope of the valley, metal feet digging into the snow, dirt, and rock, and finding purchase there. The *Mad Cat*, having turned toward where Sturm had been a moment before, had exposed its left flank. Sturm locked on to it and fired.

Lasers sliced through the thin rear armor and cut into the 'Mech's internal structure and systems. Droplets of molten armor froze almost instantly in the chill air. Sturm checked his HUD and whooped, "YES!" The display showed a heat buildup in the *Mad Cat*. One of his shots must have scored some damage to the fusion reactor or its coolant systems. Ryan's 'Mech was running hot, which would limit her options a bit. The more weapons she fired, the more waste heat would build up inside her 'Mech.

Sturm keyed open his commline to the other 'Mechs. "Okay, Lancers, it's time to show these pirates how we do things here on Kore!" he said.

"Kintaro!" came Tom Flannery's voice. "Man, are we glad to see you! Volker's turned on us. He's working with Ryan! He's got Metz pinned down over there. She needs some help!"

"Roger that," Sturm said grimly. *Volker! That lying sack of*—Sturm could hardly believe it. Yet Ryan could only have gotten the signal from someone inside Shangri-la, and it was no secret Volker wasn't too happy with Sturm being in command of the Lancers. Volker was arrogant and boastful, but Sturm had never imagined he'd turn against his own people.

He checked his visual scanners and spotted

Volker's *Hellhound* right where Flannery said it was, further down the valley. Another *Vixen*, Metz's *Lady Fox*, was trying to hold him off, but she was no match for the heavier 'Mech, or the more experienced pilot.

"Flannery," Sturm said over the comm, "I'm going to help Metz and try to keep Ryan busy. What's your status?"

Flannery's *Vixen* was locked in combat with the pirate *Panther*. Both 'Mechs had taken some hits, but the *Panther* seemed to be getting the worst of it. "I can handle it," Flannery said. "Go!"

Sturm didn't stop to question, but pushed the stick forward and sent the *Goshawk* running down the slope toward the battle going on further down the valley. He glanced up at the HUD and saw the *Mad Cat* recovering its bearings and turning toward him again.

"Hang on!" he yelled and triggered the 'Mech's jump jets again. The *Goshawk* rocketed up in a graceful arc as the *Mad Cat* fired again. A swarm of missiles arced in, trailing white smoke. Several caught the *Goshawk* in the leg as it jumped. The blast shook the 'Mech. Sturm fought the stick to keep Golden Boy on course as the impact threatened to send the 'Mech spinning out of control. The damage display showed some armor blown off the one leg, but his main systems were still intact.

Sturm brought the *Goshawk* in for a somewhat rougher landing than he would have liked, but he managed to keep the 'Mech upright. He hit the ground and started to run again toward the melee between the *Hellhound* and the *Vixen*. By this point, both of those 'Mechs had spotted him. The *Hellhound* was turning slightly toward the oncoming *Goshawk*, raising its right arm-mounted laser.

Sturm zigzagged his 'Mech into an evasive move as Volker fired at him. The hellish green pulse of the laser missed the *Goshawk* only by meters, sending up a shower of small rocks and super-heated steam from the slope where it hit. Sturm responded by firing his own laser at the *Hellhound*, scoring a hit along the 'Mech's already scarred torso, melting off ferro-fibrous armor. Metz wasn't wasting the opportunity Sturm's appearance provided, and she also opened fire on the *Hellhound*. Her large laser seared into the *Hellhound*'s torso, sending armor fragments flying.

Checking the HUD, Sturm could see the *Mad Cat* making its way down into the valley toward them. The heavier 'Mech was much faster than it looked, even though it lacked jump capabilities. It would be on them in a hurry, then Sturm and Metz would be facing off against two tough opponents instead of just one.

Just then, Laura Metz's voice crackled over the comm. "Glad you could make it to the party," she said. Then the line crackled again and another voice broke in.

"Yeah," Volker said, "glad you could make it, kid. I'd hate for you to miss this."

"Why'd you do it, Volker?" Sturm asked. "Why betray your own people? Do you have so little honor?"

"Honor?" Volker sneered. "Honor's no good to me if I'm dead. Wise up, kid. You and your little play soldiers are done. It's not too late to end this.

Give up the 'Mechs and we'll be out of here. Don't be stupid. Don't make me kill you."

"Not even on your best day, Volker."

"Really?" Volker said. Sturm could almost hear his smug grin over the comm. "You mean like I handled big, bad Sergeant Krenner?"

"What?"

"Krenner's dead, Sturm. He's not coming to help you this time. There's nobody backing you up. Give it up."

"No!" Sturm shouted. It was a lie! It had to be! He turned the *Goshawk*'s weapons on Volker's 'Mech. "You bastard!" he screamed, mashing down on the firing buttons. Blazing green pulses of laser light shot out, along with the hammer of heavy machine gun fire. With Volker's 'Mech already moving, only one of the medium lasers hit, scoring some of the armor along the *Hellhound*'s arm. Sturm started to turn, tracking Volker's movements. He was going to get that son of a bitch if it was the last thing he—

"Sturm! Behind us!" his father shouted. Sturm had just started to check his HUD when heavy laser fire impacted Golden Boy from behind. Damn! In his anger, he'd forgotten about the *Mad Cat*! Volker was deliberately goading him! Damage indicators lit up like a Christmas tree, showing heavy damage to the 'Mech's rear armor and internal structure. The thin rear armor was practically vaporized by the beams, which had penetrated to damage some of the 'Mech's myomer muscles and internal skeletal system. The damage was pretty bad, but nothing vital was crippled. Still, another hit like that and Golden Boy was done for.

Sturm turned toward the incoming *Mad Cat* as it rushed down the slope at him, scattering loose rock and sending snow flying. With a momentary glance of regret toward Volker's *Hellhound*, Sturm triggered his jump jets again and leapt up the slope, away from the *Mad Cat*.

The heat in the cockpit was climbing dangerously. He'd been firing his weapons and overusing the jump jets. Sturm and his father were both drenched in sweat, and Sturm was worried about his father's ability to take the heat. He wasn't wearing a coolant vest like Sturm was.

He swept the valley with his sensors, pinpointing the other 'Mechs. Metz was heading toward his position, moving away from Volker as the *Mad Cat* closed in. Sturm saw that Flannery had managed to disable the *Panther*, which was lying on the ground with its head smashed and smoking. He was already helping Clancy against the other two pirate 'Mechs, making it more of a fair fight. They might have a chance, if they could seriously damage or take out one of the other pirate 'Mechs, particularly the *Mad Cat*.

"This heat's going to cook us first," Sturm muttered to himself as he checked the heat monitors. He needed to let some of it bleed off before he tried anything else clever.

"Heat! Of course!" came his father's voice from the back of the cockpit. Sturm was worried that the heat might be getting to him. "Sturm! I have an idea!"

"This isn't really the best time—" Sturm started

to say. Both the *Mad Cat* and the *Hellhound* were readying to fire on them.

"I think I know a way we can beat them!" his father said. Sturm kept Golden Boy moving to evade the incoming missiles and laser fire. He seemed to be drawing their fire, allowing Metz to put some distance between herself and the other 'Mechs. Her *Vixen* was banged up, but didn't look critically damaged.

"Okay, I'm listening," Sturm said.

"This whole region is volcanically active," Dr. Kintaro began. "It's filled with pockets of—"

"The point, Dad! Get to the point!" Sturm nearly screamed. This wasn't the time for another one of his father's science lectures.

"The magma!" Kintaro said. "There are pockets of molten rock under these mountains. You were mapping them out in the surveys! If you focus enough heat on the right spot—"

Sturm would have slapped his head if it weren't encased in the neurohelmet. The idea was so crazy it might just work. He opened a comm channel to the *Vixen*.

"Metz, we need to focus all the firepower we've got on a particular spot! I'll target it, and you follow my lead, understand?"

There was only a momentary pause before she replied. "Roger that."

"Do what you can to keep them busy," Sturm told her. Then he started to sweep the *Goshawk*'s sensors along the desolate slopes of the mountains. The magnetic interference made it difficult to detect and identify metallic masses with any certainly, so Sturm relied on the 'Mech's thermal imaging. He ignored the heat spikes of the BattleMechs and the near-misses that left hot craters and scars on the terrain, looking for more subtle but no less present heat signatures.

"There!" Dr. Kintaro said, pointing over Sturm's shoulder. "Along there!" Sturm looked at the sensor reading. It could be a buried magma pocket. He was willing to trust his father's knowledge of the subject. He focused Golden Boy's targeting computer on that spot and locked on. Just then, a wall of missiles screamed in from the *Mad Cat*. It was too late to get out of the way without losing the target lock.

"Hang on!" Sturm yelled just before the missiles impacted. The force of the multiple explosions shook the *Goshawk*, blasting away torso armor and causing the sensors to shriek reports of damage. Most of the 'Mech's torso armor vanished in the blast. The safety harness and padding of the command couch protected Sturm from the worst of the shaking, but his father . . .

"Dad, are you okay?" Sturm called out. "Dad?" There was no response.

Sturm craned his neck to try and look behind him. All he could make out was the form of his father, slumped behind the command chair, unmoving.

"Dad!" he yelled. There was no movement, no answer. There was no way for Sturm to help his father, assuming he wasn't beyond help already.

He spun back toward the fight. The Lady Fox fired a laser pulse that struck the damaged leg of Volker's *Hellhound*. From the way the 'Mech now limped, the blast had clearly crippled it. The *Mad*

Cat was preparing to fire again. Sturm confirmed the target lock and gripped the firing controls.

"Okay," he said, tears of anger mixing with the sweat and grime on his face, "you want to fight? Let's turn up the heat." He mashed down on the firing button and triggered all of the *Ghoshawk*'s lasers. The emerald beams stabbed out at the rock face where he aimed. A few seconds later, Metz's *Vixen* joined him and concentrated even more heat on the same spot.

The dark igneous rock softened and ran like butter under the touch of the laser beams. A faint tremor rippled through the ground. Small rocks tumbled down the cliffside as the snow around the area superheated and roared into a thick cloud of steam. The heat in the area spiked on Sturm's sensor readings. Then the remaining stone of the cliff exploded outward in a gout of glowing, molten rock that poured into the valley like a geyser.

Susie Ryan must have figured out what the Lancers were doing at the last moment. Her *Mad Cat* tried to run, heading toward the higher ground, but it was an instant too late. Volker's *Hellhound* tried to move, too, but it was hampered by its crippled leg, and the same hit must have also destroyed the jump jets there. The molten stone poured down into the valley. It spattered and sprayed both 'Mechs, melting and hissing on their armor and exposed surfaces. Ryan's 'Mech was fast, and less damaged, but the tremendous heat of the magma and the *Mad Cat*'s exertion built up. Sturm watched as one of the *Mad Cat*'s shoulder-mounted missile pods exploded. The detonation almost knocked the monster 'Mech over, but the

Mad Cat kept fighting its way toward the higher ground.

Volker wasn't so lucky. The *Hellhound* was swamped by the flowing magma. It slipped and the molten rock started to cover the 'Mech. Sturm momentarily felt pity. It wasn't a good way for anyone to die. But when he thought about how Volker had killed Krenner in cold blood, he hardened his heart toward his former comrade. Volker deserved whatever he got. Sturm was surprised when he saw the *Hellhound* keep moving. It all but crawled up out of the flow of molten rock, then dropped onto the solid ground, like a drowning man pulling himself out of a river.

The *Mad Cat* cleared the magma and moved another few dozen meters up the slope before coming to a stop. Its armor was blackened, scored, and melted in several places. Sturm's sensors showed that the missile pod explosion had done critical damage to the *Mad Cat*'s internal structures. Sturm trained all of Golden Boy's weapons down toward it, fixing a lock with his targeting computer before opening a channel.

"Better part of valor," he said, "is knowing when to cut your losses. Do you want to walk away from this, Captain Ryan, or do I open fire?"

28

DropShip **Tammuz**
Outbound from Kore
The Periphery
24 April 3060

In the darkness of space, the *Union* Class DropShip *Tammuz* burned its way toward the JumpShip keeping station at the system's nadir jump point, millions of kilometers below the star's southern pole. Outside the ship, the small gray-white orb of Kore slowly receded into the background, becoming just another bright star in the endless night sky.

Inside the DropShip, Susie Ryan stood, alone for a moment with her thoughts. The faint hum of machinery filled the small cabin, and the thrumming of the ship's massive engines was familiar and strangely soothing. Ryan's own injuries had been minor, but she'd lost a number of her men on Kore, along with two good 'Mech pilots, to say nothing of the prize she'd been forced to leave behind. The whole operation was a debacle, and Ryan was glad to be leaving Kore behind and heading back to her own domain. The 'Mechs she'd brought to Kore were all badly in need of repair, and she didn't doubt her enemies had been busy during her absence. This was a temporary moment of weakness for her, and she was mentally working out ways to make sure no one could use it against her.

A knock sounded on the door, jarring her out of her ruminations.

"Come," she said. A member of her crew poked his head inside the door. Once he was sure his captain wasn't going to take it off at the shoulders, the rest of him followed. Captain Ryan had not been in a good mood since the Rebels left Kore.

"Cap'n," he said, "we just got word from the JumpShip. They're ready to jump out as soon as we get there."

"Good," Ryan said. "I want to be away from this godforsaken system as soon as possible."

The man nodded and began to withdraw, then hesitated on the threshold. Ryan glanced over with her good eye.

"What is it?" she asked.

"Ah, nothing, Cap'n," the man stammered, afraid he'd made a fatal mistake. "It's just that, well, why'd you bother bringing him along?"

With a nod of his chin, the pirate indicated an object taking up a fair amount of space in the small cabin. It was a life support capsule, just over two meters long and made of transpex, banded with gleaming metal. The capsule maintained a high oxygen environment perfectly balanced for the patient within, allowing him to withstand the stresses of space travel back to the Pirate King-doms. Monitors glowed and beeped, reporting his condition, and the machinery hummed and hissed as it assisted his breathing and maintained his vital functions. Most of his skin was covered in protective wrappings; the small amount that could be seen was an angry red.

Ryan looked over at the capsule silently for a moment, then glanced back at the fearful crewman.

"We had to salvage something from this disas-ter," she said quietly. "I've got my reasons." The crewman knew better than to press his luck any further and quickly withdrew, the door closing silently behind him.

Susie Ryan studied the unconscious form of Lon Volker, cradled inside the life-support cocoon. He'd been severely burned inside his 'Mech and almost didn't survive. The boy, Kintaro, had been surprised when Ryan asked to take him with her. She'd been almost as surprised when he agreed. It was going to cost some hefty C-bills to keep Volker alive and get him proper treatment once they reached Star's End. In fact, there was no guarantee he'd even survive the trip. Still, if he did . . .

Ryan smiled quietly to herself. If Volker did sur-vive—and she would spare nothing to make sure he did—she wouldn't come away empty-handed from the expedition to Kore. She would mold Lon Volker into what she needed: a living weapon that hated Sturm Kintaro more than anything else in the universe. A weapon she only needed to prime and point in the right direction. Kintaro would pay for the damage he'd done to her plans in good time.

She patted the clear plastic casing one last time and settled down on the wall-bench nearby to spin out the rest of her plans.

29

Kore Lancers Command Center
Outside Niffelheim
Kore
The Periphery
2 May 3060

"Kintaro? The colonel wants to speak with you."

Sturm stood immediately, nervously straightening the bottom of his uniform tunic when the colonel's aide spoke. He'd been waiting outside the commanding officer's door for what seemed like hours. He wiped damp palms against his trousers and squared his shoulders before going inside. He was more nervous now than he'd been facing all of Susie Ryan's 'Mechs at Giant's Pass. Still, it wasn't every day the commander of the Storm Riders company came out to Kore.

Sturm stepped into the small office and looked across the desk at the man who'd occupied it for the past few days. Colonel Gerald Quinn had served in the Lyran military before becoming commander of a mercenary unit. Though well past forty, he still had the fit, trim build and military bearing of a much younger man. The pale blond of his hair hid the few traces of silver, and the lines around his eyes and mouth merely gave him a more formidable presence. He wore a crisp uniform in the dark blue of the Storm Riders, and looked like he'd be much more comfortable in the cockpit of a BattleMech than sitting behind a desk.

"Come in, Mr. Kintaro." Colonel Quinn spoke in a light tone that still carried an air of command. Sturm stepped into the room and moved to stand at attention in front of the desk.

"At ease," Quinn said. Sturm relaxed his stance slightly, clasping his hands behind his back.

"How are your 'Ghosts' doing?" the colonel asked.

Sturm allowed himself a bit of a smile. The Storm Riders had taken to calling Sturm's rag-tag group of trainee MechWarriors "the Winter Ghosts," after the legend Sturm used against the pirates. He was quite proud of the moniker.

"They're fine, sir. In fact, we're ready to return to duty."

Sturm was glad the rest of his MechWarriors had survived the battle of Giant's Pass with only minor injuries. Once Susie Ryan agreed to a cease-fire, the Lancers had allowed the surviving 'Mechs from Ryan's Rebels to withdraw from the valley and limp back to the command base. The next day, the pirates boarded their DropShip and boosted off, leaving the command center back in the hands of the remaining Lancers. They'd won.

It was only a few days later when they received word that the DropShip *Osiris*, carrying Storm

Rider reinforcements, was inbound for Kore. They were surprised to discover that Colonel Quinn, commander of the entire Storm Riders company, was on board, along with a full company of BattleMechs and support personnel. With their help, the Storm Riders quickly had the command center operational again, and the damage from the pirate raid was being repaired. The company also had personnel combing through the Clan depot, gathering all the information and material that could be shipped off-planet.

Sturm and his people had little to do with it, however. They were almost immediately placed on temporary medical leave while they recovered and provided the command staff with complete reports about the depot and the attack by Ryan's Rebels. Now all the reports had been filed, everyone was recovering fine, and Sturm found himself standing in Colonel Quinn's office.

"And how is your father doing?" the colonel asked.

"Quite well, sir," Sturm replied. "He's out of the infirmary and back to work. The medics say his injuries weren't that serious, just heat exhaustion and a mild concussion."

"He's pretty tough," the colonel observed. Sturm smiled a bit.

"Yes, sir, he is that. We couldn't have beaten Ryan's Rebels without him."

"Yes, I read that in your report," the colonel said. "Tell me, do you think your father will be able to manage here without you?"

"Sir?" Sturm asked, puzzled.

Colonel Quinn smiled, the first time Sturm had seen him do that.

"You can still write to him, of course. HPG communiqués still get out here from the Inner Sphere."

"The Inner . . ." Sturm began, then realized he was starting to sound like an idiot.

"I know talent when I see it," Quinn said. "Effective immediately, I'm transferring you and your Winter Ghosts off Kore to our home base for some additional training. When you're ready, you and your people will be assigned out in the field. The Storm Riders have a lot of work to do apart from baby-sitting corporate mining colonies, Kintaro. Assuming, of course, that you're agreeable?"

"I . . . of course, I mean . . . yes, sir!" Sturm couldn't help but grin, and Colonel Quinn returned the smile in equal measure.

"You did good work here, Kintaro. That's why I'm promoting you to lieutenant in command of the Winter Ghosts lance. After a few months of training back home, you'll be ready for field duty. Go and get your people together and tell them to report for duty. Then you can oversee getting those 'Mechs loaded onto the DropShip. You sure as hell earned them."

The colonel picked up a computer pad from his desk and handed it to Sturm.

"The HPG relay at the Clan depot picked this up yesterday."

Sturm took the pad. On the screen, written in glowing letters was a short message. It said, "ENJOY WHAT YOU HAVE STOLEN. WE AWAIT THE DAY WHEN YOU MEET US ON

THE FIELD OF HONOR, BANDITS." It was signed with the seal of Clan Steel Viper.

"They're not coming?" Sturm asked.

"It doesn't seem so," the colonel said, retrieving the datapad. "Apparently the Steel Vipers have bigger fish to fry than one isolated 'Mech depot out here. Still, they're obviously none too happy. That's why I want to make sure you want to keep those Clan 'Mechs. They're distinctive, and they'll make you a target for any Clan warriors you run across."

"Like you said, sir, we earned those 'Mechs, both with the people we lost retaking Kore and the people who died defending it this time. I aim to keep them. But I'm concerned about Kore. What happens after we leave? What's to stop the Clans from coming back here?"

"I've already assigned a new lance to garrison duty here," the colonel said, "plus some additional support vehicles and personnel. Alfin still wants to study the technology in that Clan hideaway you found, but they've agreed to cede the 'Mechs and most of the equipment over to us, considering the valiant efforts of members of the Kore Lancers in protecting their interests. Kore will be very well looked after, and I doubt that the Clans are going to bother to return. They must know by now that there's not much point in fighting over this particular hunk of rock. Any other questions?"

"No, sir." Sturm said. "Thank you, sir."

"All right, then. Dismissed." Sturm saluted, then turned and walked toward the door.

"And Lieutenant?" Quinn said. Sturm stopped

with his hand on the latch and turned back toward the colonel.

"Sir?"

"Well done."

Sturm stepped out of the office to find Metz, Clancy, and Flannery waiting for him. He saw the concerned looks on the faces of the people he'd come to consider comrades in arms. When he told them the news, a loud whoop went up outside the office, and the new members of the Winter Ghosts headed off to meet their future.

About the Author

Ghost of Winter is Stephen Kenson's first novel set in the BattleTech® universe. He is already familiar to fans of the Shadowrun® series as the author of the novels *Technobabel* and *Crossroads*, also published by Roc Books. Steve lives in Milford, New Hampshire, and readers and fans of BattleTech® and Shadowrun® can reach him via E-mail at talonmail@aol.com.

Inner Sphere Designations for Clan 'Mechs

Clan Name	Inner Sphere Name
Adder	Puma
Bane	Kraken
Black Python	Viper
Conjurer	Hellhound
Dire Wolf	Daishi
Executioner	Gladiator
Fire Moth	Dasher
Gargoyle	Man O'War
Glass Spider	Galahad
Hellbringer	Loki
Horned Owl	Peregrine
Howler	Baboon
Ice Ferret	Fenris
Incubus	Vixen
Kit Fox	Uller
Mad Dog	Vulture

Mist Lynx	Koshi
Huntsman	Nobori-nin
Nova	Black Hawk
Stone Rhino	Behemoth
Stormcrow	Ryoken
Summoner	Thor
Timber Wolf	Mad Cat
Vapor Eagle	Goshawk
Viper	Dragonfly
Warhawk	Masakari

Goshawk

Mad Cat

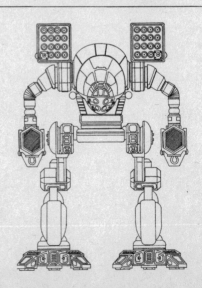

Hellhound

Puma

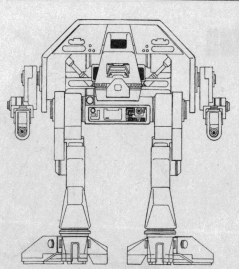

Uller

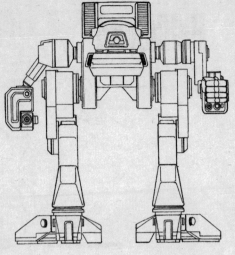

Vixen

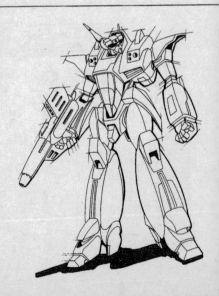

Union-C Class DropShip

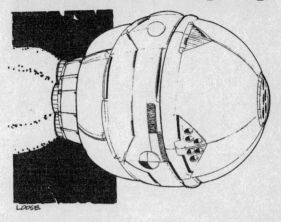

Merchant Class JumpShip

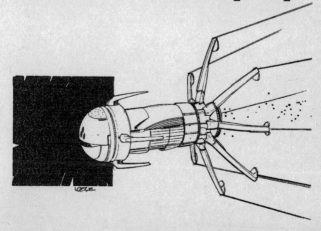

Excerpt from the
next exciting MechWarrior:
Roar of Honor

On sale in October

Prologue

Minsk Mountains
Strana Mechty
Kerensky Cluster, Clan Space
14 February 3059

Outside the cave a horizontal wall of snow driven at cutting speed blurred her field of vision. Star Captain Angela Bekker pulled her parka tighter as the icy fingers of the chill wind reached into her. The small fire at the mouth of the cave offered some comfort, but not much. Not after what she had been through.

Farther back into the cave lay Sprange, still moaning from the mauling he had taken in the ghost bear attack of two days ago. He and Angela had been part of a group of forty-eight Ghost Bear warriors braving the dangers of the Minsk Mountains in their Clan's annual Clawing rite. Only the highest-ranking unClawed warriors in each of the Clusters—the rough equal of regiments—were eligible. Once into the mountains the group had broken up into smaller hunting parties of some ten warriors each.

It was a solemn rite, Ghost Bear warriors climbing into the frozen regions of Strana Mechty to hunt the mighty creature for which their Clan was named. Armed with nothing more than long spears, only the bravest and strongest could ever hope to defeat a ghost bear in single combat. Half the hunting parties never returned at all, though at least one warrior usually did succeed in killing a bear.

Angela Bekker's team, however, did not have much luck. Just before the storm, they had split up in hopes of covering a wider area. Though each carried survival gear and even a defensive laser pistol, only the spear could be used in the actual hunt. They also carried rations, but those had been used up several long and grueling days ago. Now the storm had turned this from a ritual hunt into a test of survival.

Angela and Sprange had been blinded by a blizzard almost as fierce as this one when a ghost bear, hidden under a mound of the snow, had suddenly risen up and attacked. It had bitten and mauled Sprange before he'd had a chance to react, his spear lost forever in a powdery white drift. He would have died had Angela not wounded and driven off the huge beast. She had saved Sprange's life and they both knew it.

Angela drew in a long lungful of air through her nose and felt her nostrils freeze with a bitter sting. Glancing over at the crumpled form of Sprange, she thought back on all the years they had known each other. Created from the same batch of genetic material, the two had been together since birth. They had spent the whole of their young lives growing up together in a sibko, enduring the harsh training that would forge them as Clan warriors.

"You should go down the mountain," he moaned. His broken ribs and right shoulder seemed to make even breathing difficult and painful.

"Be quiet," she commanded, but without harshness. "We are Ghost Bears. We are sibkin. I will not waste a perfectly good warrior to save myself."

"You have always been the stronger," Sprange said, shifting position slightly. "You earned your bloodname and rank in just a few short years. I am not your equal and we both know that. You should save yourself." There was respect in his voice. Clan warriors prized a bloodname above all else. The right to bear a surname, each one descended from one of the founders of the Clans, had to be won on a field of combat. Only the finest warriors could compete for a bloodname. Only the best ever won one.

And only the cream of those ever slayed a ghost bear in the Clawing, Angela thought.

She had won her bloodname piloting an old Warhawk OmniMech. BattleMechs and OmniMechs were the pinnacle of military technology and had dominated battlefields for the last three centuries. Standing nearly three stories tall and roughly humanoid in shape, a heavily armored 'Mech could move at incredible speed. It also carried the firepower of a tank platoon—a startling array of missiles, lasers, and other implements of death and destruction.

Another gust of wind buffeted the last flickers of their small fire, which began to smoke as it died. There was little left to burn. Now, with the day starting, they did not have much time if they were ever going to do what they came for. There was no loss of honor in failing to kill a ghost bear during a Clawing, but Angela Bekker was not one given to surrendering an ideal. Trying to flush out one of the mighty creatures seemed impossible. The ghost bear was notorious for the way it hid itself in the massive snow drifts, patiently waiting for its prey to come to it. There had to be another way to end this ordeal. Otherwise she and Sprange would die here in the cold.

Her mind played over everything she knew about the legendary ghost bears as she fought back another wave of shivers. They were hunters; powerful, white-furred creatures that stood over five meters when they rose to strike. The cold did not bother them. They ruled these pitiless mountains, where they managed not only to survive but to thrive. It was said they could smell blood for kilometers and would hunt their prey by smell alone.

Then the idea came to her. It was a dark thought, one that would ask great sacrifice on her part. Honor was at stake, and for Angela Bekker little else mattered. From her earliest days in the Prowling Bear sibko, she had been steeped in the idea. Sacrifice was expected from a warrior for the sake of glory or victory, and she resolved to win the honor of slaying a ghost bear. Silently, with great care, she wedged the shaft of her spear into the earthen floor, then braced it securely against a large rock protruding from the ground. The sharpened tip pointed toward the opening of the cave.

"What are you doing, Angela?" Sprange asked weakly.

She did not look at him, too busy testing the shaft of the spear to be sure it would hold against any weight brought against it. "I am going to kill a ghost bear," she said finally.

"Is one coming?" There was no fear in Sprange's voice. He sounded almost relieved. He would not survive another encounter with one and had resigned himself to death. It was the way of the warrior, and for a warrior to die during the perilous Clawing ritual did not bring shame.

She looked back at him. "One will," she said, drawing her utility knife. The blade shimmered in the dying light of the fire, and she stood silently looking at it for a moment. She then stepped just to edge of the cave opening, her feet crunching on the snow.

With one sweeping move of the blade in her left hand, she severed the fourth and fifth fingers of her right.

Angela screamed, but it was more the fierce howling of an animal than the sound of pain. Blood sprayed in the air and against the cave wall. She felt a warm rush suffuse her body, then she doubled over in agony. The knife slipped from her fingers, and almost instantly was buried in the snow piling up at the cave entrance. Angela drew her small laser pistol and fired at the cut place on her hand. A wisp of smoke brought the smell of burning flesh as she cauterized the wound. She wailed again, less loudly this time, but now it was in pain.

With her good hand, Angela picked up the two severed fingers and tossed them out into the snow. She half-staggered to the back of the cave where she had braced her spear. Her breathing was rapid, and left clouds of steam in the air as she fought back the agony in her hand.

"It is only a matter of time now," she said, standing to her full height as if to tower over her own pain. Her blood would be the bait.

"We will both die here," Sprange said.

She looked at him and smiled. "There is no fate more fitting for two Ghost Bears, quiaff?"

For the first time since he had been mauled, Sprange smiled. "Aff."

The minutes passed slowly, then suddenly the cave entrance darkened as a shape loomed before it. Angela lowered her stance slightly, breath still ragged, heart pounding through every part of her body.

The great ghost bear lumbered into the cave, its bulk just barely able to fit. It was oddly silent as it came, as ghostly as its name. It was enormous, and its white fur looked silvery by the firelight, especially around its neck, a sign of its age. The bear spotted its prey at the rear of the cave and seemed to explode with a roar that shook the very rock walls around them.

Angela did not flinch. She focused on the eyes of the ghost bear, staring deep into its soul. For the creature to have lived so long, it was indeed one of the greatest of its kind. It stared back at her, not like an animal but like a fellow warrior taking the measure of his foe. It took a step forward, then seemed to coil back slightly. She knew what it was doing. The great ghost bear was preparing to spring.

Angela lowered herself slightly and reached out to where she'd rigged up her spear. The ghost bear did not hesitate. It leapt with a speed and agility that seemed impossible for a creature of its size. It came right for her, its eyes still locked with her own. It was as if this most magnificent of beasts was leaping at her very soul.

In that instant she angled the point of the spear directly at the leaping bear, keeping the base of the shaft still anchored against the rock. The ghost bear, caught in mid-flight, impaled itself on the spear, which drove straight through its body and out its back. Time seemed to slow, and the cave and Angela's awareness of the moment became a blur. Sounds in the cave were muffled, a dull roar in her mind. She did not remember rolling, but somehow came up beside the great creature as it lay dead between her and Sprange. The ghost bear's huge teeth had ripped her light blue parka as it fell.

The end was so sudden, so stunning, that she hardly knew how to respond. First, she had to make sure the bear was indeed dead, and prodded it with her foot. The beast gurgled slightly, a death rattle that would haunt her dreams for years to come. Dizzy either from her loss of blood or the exertion, she looked over at her comrade. Sprange stared at the beast that had nearly killed them, his mouth agape, his eyes wide. He turned to her slowly.

"I do not believe it," he said.

Angela nodded. "The ghost bear is a hunter that knows the wisdom of waiting for its prey to come to him. I have only done what it teaches."

"What have you done to yourself, though?"

Angela looked at the charred flesh where her two fingers had been. "I did what was necessary. I am, after all, a Ghost Bear warrior."

She got up and retrieved her knife. "Now we do what we must—we survive."

Two days later they were found by a patrol, Angela garbed in the hide of the great ghost bear she had slain, Sprange being pulled behind her on a makeshift skid.